THROUGH HER EYES

KATE SOROKAS

A WILD QUEENDOM

Cover design by Ana Grigoriu-Voicu

ISBN 979-8-9937104-0-2 (paperback)

ISBN 979-8-9937104-1-9 (ebook)

Published by A Wild Queendom, 2026

Cleveland, Ohio

First Edition

For Lindsay, Maya, and Sara—for raising me into the mother I am today.
For mothering my soul when I needed it most.
To Paul, Paulie, and Milo—we did it.
Teamwork makes the dream work.

AUTHOR'S NOTE

Dear Reader,

I'm so happy you are here! As you turn or swipe the pages of *Through Her Eyes*, know that you are making my dream come true of becoming an author and putting this tale of motherhood and magic in your hands. But here are a few warnings that might give away plot points. For those who don't like surprises... stop reading here if you don't want to know more!

My motherhood journey was hard in ways I never expected and some of those experiences are inspiration for what Maggie experiences. If you see yourself in any of those moments, I am giving you a giant hug from afar.

If you have experienced postpartum anxiety, depression, psychosis and/or Dysphoric-Milk Ejection Reflect (D-MER), you are not alone. Talk to your friends, partner, doctor, or whoever you can to remind yourself that you are loved and worthy of support and help to feel like your best self.

Finally, this book contains a situation with abortion as a choice to enter (or not) into motherhood. One of the characters in this book chooses abortion, as do one in four women in their lifetime in the United States. Two chapters focus on this choice and experience. If you choose to skip those chapters, you will still be able to keep up with the plot.

Much love,

Kate

PART I

CHAPTER ONE

As soon as I see the advertisement for the fire ceremony posted outside an ancient ruin, I know I'm fated to be there on our last day in Ireland.

"We could stay in Kildare for one more night, Caden!" I squeal as I grab his arm in excitement. Caden sighs loudly as his practicality to stick to our plan presses against my desire to pivot. But the magic of the Irish faeries must be affecting him because he rebooks our hotels right in front of the flyer. I open the registration for the event and sign up for the last spot available—my spot.

"Babe, remember how my oracle card this morning was for the Celtic fire goddess from Ireland? She knew I was destined to be here!" I'm delighted as the feel of the universe's magic unfolds around me once more.

"Well, Maggie, it looks like you've got a fire blessing to attend." Caden gives a low laugh because even he is impressed by what he would call a major coincidence. He likes to think he's too grounded to buy into my "woo-woo" beliefs, but I know he's seen too many major coincidences to dismiss my daily ritual of oracle cards and astrological readings.

He's even talked about looking forward to our future children howling at the full moon like their mama. One day.

STANDING in the circle of women, swaying with the rhythm of the chant softly rising and falling around me, wind swirls, lifting leaves and dirt from the ground to rise and move around the corners of the ancient church we've taken over for the afternoon. The bright flame of the white candle in the middle of the sacred fire temple ruins flickers and threatens to cease dramatically but does not go out.

In the corner of my eye, I see Caden covertly lift his phone to take my picture as my turn to move into the center of the ring of women gets closer. My smile comes fast and quick, lifting the corners of my mouth and brightening my eyes like I have a secret trying to burst from my lips… or like I am about to receive a blessing from a Celtic priestess on a fated afternoon around the flame from a fire that has been burning for centuries. St. Brigid's flame, or Brigid the Celtic fire goddess' flame, depending on who you ask.

My mom's voice whispers in my ear, "Your Irish eyes are smiling." My forever tell for when I'm up to something. And while I swear I can feel her presence behind me in the circle, her own green eyes smiling, my heart tightens knowing she can't be here to witness this moment that already feels monumental, life-changing, even though it's barely started.

Taking pictures and video is very frowned upon but Caden can't help himself. He's patiently walked alongside me as I've made the pilgrimage that brought us here, across thousands of miles, home to Irish roots, back home to myself. He has to document the moment we didn't know we've been waiting for, pushing for, for months.

Pure Irish fairy magic has lured me here to this circle of women humming softly along with the Celtic words of the chant growing louder and louder in the worn-down stone walls. The sacred feminine circle of support I've craved for years surrounding me as I make promises to myself, to my past and future self, to the maiden-version of myself standing here in crumbling stones of a sacred site pulsing with ancient energy.

My face settles into a softer smile and tears well as I lock eyes with the priestess who has organized this sacred experience. A fire ceremony to receive blessings from sacred Celtic goddesses. Goddesses of rivers, mountains, the sky, and flame from long ago still being invoked, loved today, as Ireland pours her heart into healing and connection.

I startle when she invokes Brigid, Celtic goddess of fire, healing, poetry, and Spring. Hearing her name in this circle after attributing my presence here to her gives me a full body chill. I send a quiet thank you to the goddess and turn my attention back to the priestess.

She motions me forward, and I cry openly as she grasps my hands. "Do I have your permission to bless your spirit?"

I nod and her bold voice once again fills the ruins. The flame of her handheld candle moves around my body, tracing a pattern I can't translate.

Her words burn away my fears, my worries, all the hurt holding me back from expanding into this next chapter of life I so desperately crave. I open my heart to give up the broken pieces to be made whole, to call in the wisdom and strength of the women around me—the women who have come before me for generations.

Truth hardens inside of me, calcifying the choice I came here to make, feeling like a boulder pressured into a precious gem in my chest. Hope alchemized into a dream that I am ready to receive, to embody.

Smoke fills my nose, acridly burning my eyes as tears well. I begin to pray, to send up blessings to the Celtic goddesses we are here to honor. To request their support in the next season of my life's journey. To weave love all around me and to give me the strength to do what was not done for me. To love in a way I was not loved, to protect in a way I was not protected.

The wind gathers speed, blowing my curls around my face like a halo, as if in answer to my prayers. Pure light fills my womb, building in my chest, my heart. My face warms as the glowing light seems to flow through the top of my head and into the sky, out of my fingertips and back into the priestess who is gripping my hands once again.

My eyes blink in surprise when the priestess tugs on my hands and pulls me into a hug. A warm motherly hug you can sink into and know everything will be okay. Her own Irish eyes smiling, she whispers into my ear, squeezes me one more time, and then sends me back to my place in the circle.

Later, Caden and I gather our belongings and start the short walk back to our hotel. He pulls out his phone to show me some photos of the ceremony.

"What did she say to you right here?" I look over and see him holding out a photo of me gathered in the priestess' arms, her mouth near my ear. "You were the only one I saw her whisper to during the ceremony."

I turn to him, placing one hand over my heart and my other over his own.

"The goddess Brigid offers you a piece of her heart to fuel your own in what is yet to come. Never forget you are the flame."

Caden and I return to the hotel and lock eyes as we step into the unexpectedly rowdy crowd filling the small lobby bar, music pouring from somewhere inside. I start to ask if he wants to get one final beer on our last night in Ireland when he presses the room key in my hand.

"I'll meet you upstairs in a few minutes," he murmurs into my ear as his hand runs down my back, over my hip, and lands on the curve of my ass. His intentions for tonight are clear and welcome as fingers curl into the gauzy layers of my most goddess-like dress.

Caden swiftly kisses me and disappears into the crowd around the bar.

My reflection in the mirrored walls of the elevator feels dull and faded, just like Caden's photos of the fire ceremony. I swear light beams must have been flowing through my fingertips, from the crown of my head, fueled by my inner soul fire burning bright

The smell of smoke and fire drifts into the hotel room with me as I freshen up, making the decision that we came to Ireland to consider. The magic of the fire blessing sealed my fate as the light burned away my fear and strengthened my resolve to break my family's legacy of trauma.

The door opens and Caden smoothly walks inside holding a glass of champagne and a Guiness. He holds out the flute to me, love shining in his eyes, in his soft smile.

"Maggie, I..."

"Caden, we..."

I take the champagne as we both try to talk at the same time, stumbling over our words and laughter. Caden sets his pint down and wraps his arms around me. I take a big swig of champagne and feel the words burst out of me.

"Let's do it, Caden. Let's make a baby. I'm ready."

"Me too, Maggie, me too. You've just made me the happiest man in Ireland."

Laughing in his arms, I tell him about the clarity that flooded me in the circle of women. "My life is so different as an adult than my childhood, than my mom's when she had me. We get to create our own family, our own legacy of love."

Tears well in Caden's eyes as he kisses me deeply and walks me backward to the bed. I tip up the champagne flute, finishing the sparkly liquid, then thank the magic of the Irish fairies for divining the fire ceremony that burned away the last bits of my fear of motherhood, of failing at motherhood, just as Caden starts to pull up the hem of my gauzy goddess dress.

CHAPTER TWO

10 months later...

C aden stands next to the bed, handing me nursing supplies ranging from soft cotton burp cloths to ice water as I request them.

He's desperate to find the magical combination of ice pack and snack that will quell my crying.

Alma slips into the bedroom just as a fresh round of tears bursts from my eyes. My quiet sobs are barely audible over the cheeky, British-accented jokes about doughballs on the baking show playing on the small TV we installed on the wall for my postpartum recovery.

The air is thick with tension and exhaustion as wave after wave of despair racks my body, my heart breaking with each letdown. I was so convinced I could do this, that I could be a good mother, but the deep waves of grief that overtake me each time Jillian nurses convince me it's a lie. That I've already failed her. That I will never be happy again. That I made a mistake becoming a mother.

That my sweet daughter whose soft brown hair I can't stop from rubbing against my cheek and skin I constantly press my nose to will never be happy with me as her mother.

The emotional pain rolling up my spine and pulling me under each time I nurse is turning into an insidious poison, slowing eroding the confidence I've built up since the fire ceremony. I thought I had healed enough to love, to mother, my baby. My days-old baby who is now both the love of my life and whose hunger I fear more than anything.

Just like she has since the first day we met at work, Alma reads the room and quickly calculates that she has walked in on my and Caden's first argument as new parents while days-old Jillian nurses away on my breast.

"Why can't you stop crying, baby? This is supposed to be *happy*. Our first memories of Jillian at home are going to be of you crying." Caden gently pleads in a soft voice as he runs his hands down the sides of his face and turns to the window.

Fresh tears form in my eyes. I whisper my response to avoid disturbing Jillian, to be able to speak around the sobs choking my every breath.

"I want my mom, Caden. I don't know how to describe it any other way. I just did this massive thing, squeezing out a baby, tearing open my soul, and I want to be *held*."

Caden steps back over to the bed and sits down on the edge, holding my free hand and whispering how much he loves me, how much he loves Jillian, into my ear. Our shared confusion and overwhelm keeps this moment from boiling over, but the tension is thick.

Neither of us expected the sadness that would consume me after I gave birth to Jillian, how hard the change in hormones would hit. How each letdown with Jillian feels like I am reliving my life's tragedies over and over again.

Alma gracefully maneuvers a sleep-deprived Caden to the guest bedroom so he can shower and nap after being up with us all night. Then, Alma climbs into bed with me, holding me while sobs shake loose from my chest, my shoulders wrenching back and forth, rubbing my back when the tears force gasping breaths.

Throughout it all, I hold Jillian gently, protecting her from the emotional shitshow ravaging my body and mind.

In this moment, Alma may not be my mom, but she is my chosen sister, and her love is enough. Steady in the storm of my emotions, she supports me as I recenter myself, the evidence of my pain in the blotchy skin of my face and runny nose.

A breeze moves through the room, ruffling Alma's hair and drying the tears on my cheeks. I breathe deeply and whisper my biggest fear.

"Alma, I don't think I'm okay. I don't think I'm going to be a good mom. Promise me that if I start to do anything… concerning… that you'll talk to Caden."

Alma shushes me and wraps an arm around me and the now sleeping Jillian. "I've got you, Mags. You're going to be an amazing mom. You're already in protective mama bear mode right now."

"But, Alm, I'm so sad, so distraught, especially when Jillian first starts nursing. It's like I'm going to drown in despair and never be happy again. I don't know how much more of this I can suffer through and still be able to come back to myself."

"What happened to the lovey-dovey hormone that you push out when you give birth and nurse? Didn't you say you felt like you saw stars when you first laid eyes on Jillian? This sounds like the opposite of that."

"This feels like the opposite. Why does my heart feel like it's being torn open each time I breastfeed? Maybe it's a sign that I'm a terrible mom. That I wasn't supposed to do this."

Alma lets out a big sigh and grabs my phone. "Let's call the midwife, Maggie. Maybe she can help. This can't be typical. You would have read about it in your new mom research. Or at least it would have popped up in a breastfeeding reel at some point."

Alma and I are so close that our algorithms have synced and now hers is *also* full of midwife and doula content on childbirth and breastfeeding. And because she's determined to be Jillian's favorite person, she has been watching and forwarding them to me constantly since I told her I was pregnant after Caden and I returned from Ireland.

I reluctantly swipe open my phone and call the midwife, uncomfortable with both asking for help and admitting this is hard. But I'm more determined to be the type of mom who can admit when something isn't working and seek out support than I am to continue to pretend I'm okay so I let the phone ring through my discomfort.

I explain why I'm calling, Alma's hand making soothing circles on my back, and the midwife immediately reassures me that she has an inkling on what might be going on. Her calm, confident tone slowing down my tumultuous brain, her orderly and thoughtful words spinning chaos into facts. Facts I can latch on to in the wild waves of emotion interrupting my new motherhood bliss.

"Dysphoric Milk Ejection Reflex, D-MER for short, means that each letdown is like being on a roller coaster of sadness and shame," she explains over the speaker phone. "Your hormones shift with each let down and, for some women, that cause waves of negative emotions."

Alma squeezes my hand as the tension leaves my shoulders. I didn't realize how much I was dreading the midwife not having an answer, an explanation, until she was offering this lifeline.

"Oh my gosh, yes! I've been describing it more like drowning than a roller coaster though. It's hard to see through the sadness until it fades away."

"One of my patients described her experience like being on a roller coaster, but she never knew if the drop was going to be more kiddie ride or Millennium Force. You are so newly postpartum. If this is D-MER, then the effects may be stronger until your hormones level out a bit."

The midwife coaches me on breathing and visualization techniques that might be helpful and promises to have more information when she comes for her home visit the next day.

But it's her parting words that almost bring tears to my eyes *again*. "Remember, no matter how strong the sadness may feel, a D-MER diagnosis doesn't mean you're a bad mom—or even sad. You are an amazing mom for being vulnerable enough to say something doesn't feel right and to ask for help."

The flames on the candles across the room flicker as we end the call. Alma gives me a hug and pulls Jillian from my arms. "Now that we have some potential answers, why don't you do your thing and research the heck out of D-MER?"

"Thanks, Alma. Thank you for believing me when I said something was wrong."

She gives me a one-arm hug, and we settle in for the new version of girls' night. Me, Alma, and Jillian snuggled in bed watching shows and giggling over silly social media posts.

At some point during the night, Alma and Caden trade places, and I wake up with Jillian snuggly swaddled in her basinet next to the bed, and Caden's hand wrapped around mine as he sleeps deeply.

I curl into his side, knowing from the pressure in my breasts that Jillian will be ready to nurse soon.

And instead of being consumed by the deep fear that overtook me yesterday at this sensation, I breathe deeply and remind myself of what the midwife explained to me on the phone yesterday with Alma.

"Above all, trust that you are a good mother."

CHAPTER THREE

Four months later...

Blood puddles around my feet. A whooshing sound fills my ears as police lights flash red and white, creating odd shadows on the brick walls of the bar and buildings in the alleyway. Off the dumpster. The open back doors of an ambulance. Bouncing off the bumpers of police cars.

I wake in a panic—pajamas drenched, heart racing under the lace edging of my camisole. The soft comfort of my pillows doesn't soothe the throbbing ache in the base of my skull like usual. I blink to clear the flashing lights from my eyes.

Clawing at my blankets, I push them down around my waist as I sit up and look around my bedroom, barely recognizing the space, my heart slamming against the confines of my ribcage.

Waves of heat prickle down my body, from my neck to my arms, my fingertips, and back up as cold sweat breaks across my forehead. My stomach tightens into a ball of sour fear churning with anxiety and panic, zinging down my spine and activating my nervous system like lightning flashing in the sky. Fuzzy fragments of dreams hang in the air around my head.

I whisper into the dark quiet, "I'm home. I'm safe." Grounding myself in the silky soft sheets wrapped around my legs, I begin my breathing techniques usually reserved to soften the emotional waves of my letdowns to slow my pulse.

Clumsy and dissociated, I grasp for a firmer hold on reality, working to distinguish the physical sensations of my dream from how I feel now, fighting to be fully awake in my bed. I exhale slowly, intentionally through my mouth, visualizing the panic, the fear, of the dream being blown away from me.

What the hell was that? What type of dream makes me feel so full of panic and fear, frozen in place in my bed?

The kind of dream that you're too scared to think about because what if it was real? The kind of nightmare that prevents you from trying to go back to sleep because what if you fall right back into it? If you open your eyes again, are you awake or in the unknown reality created by your mind?

My hand unconsciously sweeps across the flat sheets and unrumpled pillows of Caden's tidy side of the bed, finding it empty. He's not here. Again. Craving his warm steadiness right now, I reach for his pillow and pull it into my body. I bury my face into the soft cotton, breathing deeply. The smell of his woodsy body wash on the pillows instantly calms my nervous system as if signaling that his practical calm will make everything okay, even from afar. It's not quite the same as his strong arms holding me close, but it has the desired effect and calms my body, completely grounding me back into reality, now wide awake in the dark.

Our daughter's soft cries echo from her crib across the room. I'm used to waking up on my own, since Caden's job keeps him away more than home. I pick up Jillian and settle into his side of the bed, avoiding the cold damp of the sheets on my side.

A sigh loosens from my chest.

Jillian must have pulled me from the flashing lights, pooling blood, and desperate confusion… at 2:30 a.m.

This may be the first time I'm grateful for her nighttime wake-ups.

I clumsily fumble around the nightstand for my phone in the

dark, plugged in as always on Caden's side because I've once again misplaced my own charger.

Holding her and feeling her tiny mouth latch on as she snugs in and tucks her hand under my breast, I breathe in and out deeply. I repeat like a mantra with every rise and fall of my chest under Jillian, "I'm safe. My daughter is safe." And then I begin to box breathe to loosen the tight hold on my neck and shoulders as I wait to see if my letdown will wreck me with despair or just make me a little sad.

Nighttime is tricky for new moms. Everything from emotions to shadows always feels bigger in the dark, especially heightened by my D-MER. I exhale as the hormonal roller coaster this diagnosis causes with each letdown turns out to be mild tonight. Just a soft wave of nostalgia-laden grief drifting through my heart as Jillian continues to nurse, unaware of the impact her suckles have on my nervous system.

My fingers drift to the small fine-line tattoo on my neck, just behind my ear, as I take deep breaths and hold my daughter close. Having a touchpoint tattooed on my body to breathe with settles my anxiety, centers me in the dark.

Thanks, drunk college Maggie, for getting a St. Brigid's cross tattooed on Halloween while waiting for parties to start.

Not quite the drunk college story it sounds like, I had planned on getting this particular tattoo since the week my mom died, to match her own cross, but had to borrow a little liquid courage on Halloween to finally walk into the shop.

The artist, who turned out to be pagan, told me the cross represents a goddess who protected and empowered the powerless in Ireland centuries ago.

Caden and I were both surprised to see the same tattoo at the fire ceremony in Kildare last year. The priestess who led the ceremony also shared the story of St. Brigid and her roots in the legend of the Celtic goddess, Brigid, that night around the fire. A touchpoint across memories and generations.

The energy in the room shifts once more as I breathe. Each

exhale softening the dark edges of shadows as the moon seems to glow brighter, visible through the fluttering curtains on the window.

Picking up my phone and scrolling, I heart photos from Alma's night out, which ended forty-five minutes ago according to the time stamp. Looks like the invitation to "just a lowkey karaoke happy hour" turned into a late night out with a hottie. Oh, to be twenty-eight and able to go out until 2:00 a.m. on a weekday and still shine at work the next morning. We are overachieving eldest daughters at our core.

How did I get so lucky to have her pick me as a friend?

A picture of Alma and me at my baby shower hangs on the wall, near a large St. Brigid's cross made of rushes gifted to us when Caden and I married. Alma's one of those women who lights up a room with her confidence and ability to connect with anyone. While she's always dancing and starting conversation with strangers, I'm more lowkey drinks in the kitchen and deep talk about moon phases and trauma responses. Alma comes prepared with the best playlist for every occasion, and I always have an oracle card deck in my bag. My quiet depths connected with her sparkling butterfly nature at work a few years ago on her first day in the office, and we became inseparable. Our yin and yang aspects balancing us out into stronger versions of ourselves both individually and together.

Caden once commented that Alma and I have the type of female friendship that people make reels and memes about on social media—and it's true. Women who witness all your layers and love you because—not despite—them. Women who raise your babies like their own and mother you when you need it too. Women you are equally happy doing a grocery run with or dancing champagne-tipsy under the stars, moving between laughing and crying with every shared joke and story. Who leave treats (and sometimes drugs) on your doorstep and tell hard truths with soft words.

Of girlfriends who will follow you to the depths of Hell and hold your hand while you spiral and walk out at your side when you're ready. They won't leave you there or drag you out before it's time. The depth and intimacy of our friendship has woven into my DNA, wrapped around my nervous system and healed the fractures I couldn't heal myself.

While Caden's black-and-white personality provides the structure and consistency I crave, he struggles to understand the magic Alma and I experience in the world. He once joked that he was worried I would leave him for Alma, maybe even a little jealous of our connection. I just laughed and kissed him silly.

He doesn't like to talk about spirituality that often and rarely sober. When I show him what I'm focusing on manifesting each moon cycle, he tries to listen politely, but I can tell he's screaming on the inside. And I get it. I smile and nod when he talks about the latest in hunting gear too.

A shiver runs down my back as I see a breeze move through the room, ruffling Jillian's curls. I pull the Irish wool blanket, a keepsake from our trip, around us and sweep my gaze around the room.

Is the window open?

I reach over to grab another blanket from the foot of the bed. Maybe it's excessive, but the abundance of cozy blankets and luxurious pillows makes me feel special and held at the end of the long days of motherhood and, quite frankly, womanhood.

My bed is a symbol of abundance, wealth, to me. The opposite of the flat, scrappy pillows and blankets covered with scratchy pilling, good enough to keep using when you're poor, but not enough to be comfortable or even warm on the cold winter nights. How many times had I folded and fluffed and shoved my pillows into a comfortable shape to stay up late reading as a child? Now I simply buy as many pillows as I need to feel good. If my mom could see me now, she might think I'm a yuppie, but she'd be proud that I can afford comfort over just getting by.

My laptop—and half-written novel—sits on the desk in the corner with its dead battery. My professional research on supporting children with hard childhoods through community systems (or village building as I call it) is fulfilling, but not an outlet for the creativity bubbling beneath the surface, pushing against my skin to be released, waiting for me to reconnect with my former self. My dreams. The woman I spent thirty-six years growing up and into before I spent six hours in labor becoming a mother. Somehow, my transition from woman, or maiden, to mother has never felt fully complete. The threads from *before* always tugging me back through rose-tinted nostalgia worsened by the D-MER's effect on my emotions.

Before my daughter stole my heart and motherhood stole my life.

"Everything feels worse in the dark," I whisper out loud just to remind myself. I consider calling Alma to pull me out of this potential anxiety spiral, but I break the evening's spell when my eyes fall back on the wall of framed photos, specifically one of my mom smiling, pregnant with me, hung next to one of me pregnant with Jillian. My mom smiles and laughs in the photo on the wall, hand on her giant belly—three generations of women cocooned inside each other. Always connected through our wombs.

I pick up my phone to scroll away my rising grief of missing my mom. It's simply too much as my body is still wound up and confused from the fear in my dream and hormones. My pain cuts most deeply at night since Jillian was born, when the shadows make the edges of the loving memories of my childhood fade a little to reveal the emotional neglect hidden underneath...

Maybe the emotions from nursing are amplifying my fear in the dream... turning them more into a nightmare.

What the DUCK was that? Autocorrect has changed my fucks to ducks for so long now that I've basically adopted this new four-letter word as my swear word of choice. Probably better for Jillian in the long run. A toddler running around muttering "duckkk" under her breath when she drops something is less embarrassing than a toddler whispering "fuckkk" under her breath like I used to pre-autocorrect.

Focus. The dream. Blood. Flashing lights. A screaming woman.

Jillian's tiny mouth quivers into a quick suckle as she dreams. Do I risk laying her down in her crib or stay put for the rest of the night? Her sixth sense of being moved from arms to her bassinet is like a siren going off that I can't stand to hear right now. I can barely handle myself. The anguish in the dream melding with my grief in the darkness is leaving my sanity balanced on the thinnest edge.

Emotions are bigger in the dark. In the night.

I breathe deeply, the cool night air expanding my ribcage and belly while I ground myself in the present moment, feeling the soft, woven threads of the carpet under my toes, smelling the bouquet of flowers I impulse-purchased at the café yesterday, seeing the moonlight dance across the wall, hearing Jillian's soft swallows, tasting… my sour nighttime breath. I sip from my giant hospital water bottle as I gather the energy to lay Jillian down in her crib.

I quietly pad across the room to the crib as a text notification from Alma lights up the screen in the dark.

ALMA

Bring me a coffee tomorrow, Mags? Pretty please?! Ya girl's gonna be tired.

I heart her message and tuck my phone away. Alma's favorite cinnamon vanilla syrup is next to the espresso machine just for her and her late-night coffee requests. It takes a village, right? And someone needs to caffeinate the best friend of the village.

My exhausted body is being pulled back to sleep, heavy eyes closing on their own as my chest and shoulders tense with the unconscious knowing that I am headed right back to that alley of flashing lights.

CHAPTER FOUR

"Take another little piece of my heart now, baby. Break it. Break another little piece of my heart now, darling…" I sing and dance along with Janis Joplin as she plays on the jukebox at 2:00 a.m. in the neighborhood bar.

Soon, last call will shut down the music for the night, and those awful bright lights will flip on and shove me back to reality, but I'm not ready to give up all the glory and joy of dancing and singing tonight. No one seems to care if a seventeen-year-old is holding a beer or not. Everyone here is simply trying to let go of their own problems, not pick up new ones.

Janis sings me into a magical, musical universe where I can be anyone and anything, arms waving above my head as my hips sway back and forth. Her power flows through my veins.

I can't wait to get far, far away from all the fear, shame, and meanness that make up my every day here.

Bolstered by my plans and the hits on the joint I shared with my brother earlier, I dance and groove as I dream of my new life waiting on the other side of graduation. Even he doubted my plan while the joint moved back and forth between our fingers, smoke circles breaking in the air around us. "Don't you think I wanna leave, too? Nothing's as simple as it seems."

The future that shined bright a few moments earlier, playing out like a movie *projected across Irish flags layered on the wood-paneled walls of this small-town bar, dimmed a little with the memory of his words. Why does it seem impossible to graduate, get a job in the city, and simply exist without all this poverty and fear pressing me down? What does it mean if my own brother doesn't think I can do it?*

I know in my soul I gotta get out of this town. My life, all this work I'm doing to leave, will mean something. I know it. So, I move out of the arms of a guy who graduated with my brother to dance alone. I don't want promises of love —or an unplanned baby—to tie me down here like I've seen with too many of the girls ahead of me.

I dance my way over to the bar, looking for my brother. Leaning against the scarred wooden bar top, I gaze over the crowd. An arm snakes around my back, resting on the bar, and a hand wraps around my shoulder, thumb caressing my bare, freckled skin. The guy I was dancing with followed me to the bar and leans in, speaking directly into my ear to be heard over the music.

"Wanna take off?"

I shake my head no and lean in to shout in his ear. "I've got school tomorrow. I've gotta get home."

Shrugging like it's no big deal, he turns to the bar to order one more beer before last call. "You graduate soon, yeah?"

I nod.

"Stickin' around or still got that big plan of yours to take off to the city?"

Craig must be telling his friends about my "big ideas" if this guy knows I'm leaving. I hold up a peace sign. "I'm outta here, man. I can't live in this town no more. No jobs, and everyone is down and out. I got big dreams. I'm headed to the city the first chance I get."

Lifting his cold beer to me in a cheers, he mouths "good luck" and takes a swig. The fact that he's not dismissing my dreams is kind of hot, but I can't go down that road, mistaking lust for love. One night isn't worth it.

I shiver while my lower belly tightens with a longing to be touched, kissed, but mostly to be seen, to be special to someone, anyone. I push away from the bar top before I give into this longing and dance through the crowd, pushing my way to the bathroom. Groans fill the room as the ceiling lights flip on and the jukebox stops mid-song.

The flickering fluorescent lighting in the bathroom keeps time as I finish the chorus to the last song without the music. I might be a tiny bit glad my brother convinced me to sneak out of the house with him to go to the bar tonight. Between school and work, I don't have a lot of time for fun. But Craig was right—one night out dancing wouldn't hurt. I'm sweaty, carefree, and just stoned enough to be hopeful about tomorrow instead of considering it with the usual heavy weight of dread in my chest.

"You know you got it if it makes you feel good," I sing to the mirror in the dirty bathroom, confident I've got it all figured out. "I've just gotta get through the next year, and I'm on my way out of here."

CHAPTER FIVE

*Hips and shoulders swaying,, I close my eyes and throw my head back,
belting out song lyrics in front of the bathroom mirror. Pounding on the
door interrupts my last note—*

"Already?" I groggily whisper as my alarm plays a quiet, jaunty tune, nothing like the pounding echoing in my ears. I blindly reach for my phone, feeling like I'm the one with the hangover headache instead of Alma.

A glance tells me girls' night is tonight. Talking to another adult when Caden's gone is life-giving, especially when Alma spills the tea and helps me clean my pump parts during our weekly girl dinner.

"How can I resist my tiny best friend?" she croons at Jillian while playing peekaboo and spilling all the details of her latest Bumble date. With no family around to lean on, Jillian and I both live for these dinners with Alma. Her mere presence helps regulate my nervous system and keeps the loneliness of solo newborn parenting at bay.

Caden's practicality and meticulous planning may have helped us plan out Jillian's birth for exactly six weeks after I graduated with my doctorate, but we didn't anticipate that his work travel would be harder in new ways given that I was used to being alone pre-Jillian. We navigated diapers, baby gear, and brunch with a newborn like champs, but some of the hardest parts of parenting have been completely unexpected.

I'm so lonely. Days on end alone with a newborn wreak havoc on my nervous system, but in the way of a slow drip, drip, drip of water ruining a foundation rather than a tsunami wave like sleepless nights.

The constant monotony is a special type of torture for my overstimulated brain. I'm not meant to mother alone. No one is. And I hate feeling like a failure at this. At being *bad* at motherhood. I've never been *bad* at anything before. This sinking feeling of failure is just as new to me as diaper rash and nipple blebs.

Humming along with the fragment of my dream, lingering across my mind like cobwebs, while I get dressed, I remember that my mom used to play this song from her Janis Joplin cassette in the car when she drove my friends to the mall. We would belt out "break another little piece of my heart now, baby" before searching for cute boys to flirt with while we slurped on iced raspberry mochas and tucked perfume samples in our pockets for the next Monday at school.

Usually, sad memories float to the surface from my disassociated childhood since I've given birth. Uncovering a heartwarming one feels like a gift. A core memory to fuel my inner flame with love and worthiness.

I quickly type the memory into the Notes app on my phone so I can celebrate this small win during my next therapy appointment. I started seeing my therapist again after being flooded with new, and not so sweet, memories of my childhood during postpartum.

It's during those appointments that I can wonder out loud what it would feel like for my mom to pop over so I can shower without worrying that Jillian will cry. For her to whisper, "It's supposed to be hard. You're doing great," while I unload my frustrations and fears and sadness that motherhood feels like too much, like I'm failing constantly.

That I can whisper that I wait to put on my makeup until I'm in the office parking lot because I cry on the way to work.

About my overwhelm from the number on the daycare bills and paychecks being too close together to warrant my stress.

The forced numbness that stops me from too closely examining my grief and fear and pain so my façade doesn't crack.

Therapy is my hour to fall apart and then put myself back together so I don't shatter on the days between appointments.

Being a motherless mother means I pay a trained professional to hold space for me to nurture myself, to mother myself. Choosing motherhood gave me the chance to overcome my own grief about my childhood and my therapist is a vital space holder in my village so I can continue to be my best self.

Alma, Caden, and my mother-in-law all try to support me. But the "you chose this, and you can do this" vibe to their pep talks is a bit like snacking on stale popcorn. Underwhelming and kind of sad you went there in the first place. Not exactly the village I need right now.

"What type of village *do* you need?" Caden and Alma's identical exasperated voices echo in my thoughts, trying so hard to understand, to meet the needs I can't quite articulate. Words slip through my fingers—allude me always—but the way I want my village to feel is so real. Tender touch, warm hugs, consistent support so my nervous system can relax knowing that I will be taken care of so I can be present during the hardest moments of motherhood, trusting that rest is coming. Checking in on *me* and not just the baby. I've got the baby covered… but need a little help covering *me*.

And because Alma and Caden want to be so much more than what society expects of fathers, of friends, they translate my descriptions of what a village *feels* like in my mind to our reality. And, thus, the origin of Wednesday girls' night. Right in the middle of Caden's travel weeks to keep me sane, well-fed, and rolling in clean pump parts.

The fact that they organized it all without me having to ask, to plan, after that village conversation was a gift in and of itself. We are all figuring out what it means to be a family, a village, together. Because, in a way, we all chose this. Chose each other. A chosen family.

Jillian wakes, and I scoop her up to nurse one more time while I scroll on my phone. I "like" and "haha" random morning texts from friends and coworkers. Venmo money for a birthday celebration at work. Voice-text Alma to make sure she got out of bed this morning. Respond to meeting requests that I'm 99% sure could have been an email from my boss, Jack, who is invested in pre-pandemic office culture.

Jillian coos and wiggles in delight as I tickle her and sing while I quickly curl my hair. A light breeze floats through the bathroom, barely noticeable except for my shiny, still warm curls moving in the gentle air. I pick up my phone to text Caden that we need to check the window seals but immediately get distracted by the ringing of my "out-the-door alarm" trilling in the background.

Shit, I'm going to be late if I don't leave in exactly three minutes.

One final glance in the mirror, and memories of my dream flood back to me. The song. The Janis song I'm humming was in my dream, and suddenly, I don't feel like I'm here anymore...

CHAPTER SIX

Transfixed, I lock eyes with myself in the bathroom mirror as I sing, dabbing at sweat and smeared mascara. The combination of dancing and beer has given me a wild, powerful glow. The girl— no, woman —looking back at me has no doubt she will conquer her dreams and leave this town behind.

"WHERE THE HELL ARE YOU?!"

I flinch and freeze, the pounding on the bathroom door kickstarting that too familiar hot acid through my gut, a sure sign something bad is happening. I'm not at home where my dad could snap at one of us and the whole night or even week would be ruined. My mom hadn't thrown away our dinner because of a smart-ass comment made by my brother—he was at the bar with me. Dancing and drinking and flirting with girls from the "good" side of the tracks.

My eyes scan the hallway as I walk back to the bar, sweat breaking across my brow as my stomach tightens again. Where is my brother? We need to head home now or else I won't make it to school tomorrow.

My name floats above the shouts and flirting, teasing voices of stragglers reluctant to leave, slowly dragging their feet to the door, trying to find someone to leave with maybe. Lights are flashing around the room through the windows, disorientating me as I try to see who is shouting my name. It doesn't sound like my name now but more a primal roar from somewhere deep in the bar.

Where the hell is Craig?! Who is yelling?

A hand wraps around my wrist as someone grabs my arm and yanks me to the door.

"What the hell?! Leave me alone!" I yell, pulling my arm away and pushing through the crowd back to the bar. To where Craig was last.

I know too many people here in that vague way of older neighborhood kids and people from church in a small town for someone to try and grab me and get away with it. Putting space and a person or two between us, I spin around to confront whoever grabbed my arm. Rage drains out of me as fear rises. Not just in my belly this time but all the way up to my lungs, heart, shoulders, and head. The one-two punch of the fear of knowing something has gone terribly wrong and the panic of not knowing what.

My cousin Ronnie reaches for me again and grasps my arm tightly in his hand, white-faced with wide eyes, pulling me to the exit. "Where have you been, Bean?!? I've been searching for you."

Immediately embarrassed by hearing my childhood nickname tossed around in such a grownup space as a bar, I shove his arm away and viciously whisper, "The bathroom, you psycho. Let me go!" and belligerently push at the strong arm pulling me away from the bar, away from the fun and safety of the night.

Ronnie gets pissed as I pull in the opposite direction of the door and finally, exasperated, turns around and says, "Stop fucking around. It's Craig. He's outside. It's bad, Bean, it's real bad."

Angry red skin pulses under the tight hold of Ronnie's hand on my arm as he again pulls me across the bar, not caring who I bump into as he drags me to the door. I bump shoulders with the guy I was dancing with earlier, almost knocking the beer from his hand.

"Hey! Watch it!" he shouts as he turns around, our eyes locking as he looks from my face to Ronnie's hand on my arm. "You okay?" he yells over the din of voices.

I nod in the fluorescent lights and wave him off, already knowing I will never be okay again, even without knowing what is waiting for me outside.

With one more pull, Ronnie maneuvers me through the bottleneck of people at the door and into the white and red flashing lights in the night.

My heart drops into my stomach at what I see, and I almost throw up right on the shoes of a police officer at the entrance to the alley.

CHAPTER SEVEN

My stomach tightens in fear as the Budweiser I drank just minutes ago threatens to make its way back up my throat and coat the ground at my feet. Red and white lights flash across my face, hurting my eyes where tears are already threatening to fall. I don't think I'll ever be okay again.

I blink rapidly as my phone alarm trills again on the bathroom counter, sounding the warning that I should be in the car *right now.* I shake off the strangest sense of déjà vu, my stomach rolling with nausea, the light changing from flashing white and red to the bright bathroom lights I get ready under every day. My grip on the curling wand loosens and the smell of singed hair burns my nose.

Whoops. One minute longer and I would be down a curl along with a little of my sanity.

Jillian shakes her wooden teether and kicks her legs froggy style in her bouncer. Her delighted squeals break the last of the trance that held me captive to the mirror. Duck. I must have gotten sucked right back into that dream, and now a hot mixture of panic and fear courses through my veins again. I snooze the alarm and shake my shoulders and head to clear out the adrenaline and cortisol amping me up.

I… what? Spaced out? Time traveled? For at least a few minutes. How did I lose touch with reality for that long? My balance feels off-kilter, like I stepped back from another reality and back into this one. I almost feel like I could wipe stardust off my dress.

Guilt piles on the fear still creating waves of nausea in my belly as I realize that I completely disassociated from Jillian while my eyes were locked in the mirror in another time and place, leaving us both vulnerable. My heart squeezes, aching in its pain to wish this away and terrified that it can't. But I've got to push the pain aside, down, along with the guilt, and I vow to do better for Jillian.

But how can I fix this if I don't know what's happening?

Forcing that ominous thought back to the deep pit of my fear where it belongs, I fly through the last few steps of our morning routine, the checklist on the fridge under a magnet of newborn Jillian. Things keep slipping out of my sweaty, shaking hands. Important things. Like my coffee mug.

"Ugh, shake it off, Mags." I put on my Spotify day list, aptly titled "Awkward Middle School Dance 90s Style," and the songs are perfect to dance and sing these bad vibes out on the way to work.

I'm backing out of the driveway bopping to the Spice Girls ("I'll tell you what I want, what I really, really want…" *Coffee. Subsidized childcare.*) when I realize I forgot Alma's coffee. I run back in, hoping that a few more minutes when I'm already late won't matter, and glance in the mirror one more time, reassuring myself I won't get sucked away again. I'm in control today.

AFTER A LONG MORNING in meetings that most definitely could have been emails, I put my head down and quickly walk to the small break room I use to pump breastmilk three times a day. Once the little machine is whirring in the background, the dream that won't quit from this morning comes to mind. How vivid it was. How I never remember my dreams, but clips of this one keep popping up throughout the day and distracting me as I work.

What happened outside the bar? Why were the people in the dream scared?

I fire off a few quick responses in the company Slack channel and RSVP yes to an upcoming work happy hour. I quickly scroll through some articles a colleague sent me on the impact of maternal health on childhood with a suggestion of looking for links to my research on community support.

These will be perfect to help organizations get more funding for supporting moms. It's almost like kids and moms could both benefit from a village. What a novel idea.

Jack has already commented on my RSVP to the happy hour with a thumbs up. My absence from the last few have been "noted," and Jack, with his low self-esteem and control issues, has let me know that he will feel "personally let down" if I don't show up to the next gathering at the local cantina for free queso and half-price margaritas—no matter that the happy hours go long after my childcare for the day ends.

Jillian's daycare is twenty-five minutes away from work, so no, I can't just pop over in rush hour traffic and pick up Baby J and bring her back to hang as Alma so optimistically offered when I shared the bullshit lowkey pressure being put on me to show up at the next event. Even if, according to Alma, "everyone loves a baby in a bar!" Caden promised to be here next week so I can show my face stress-free and try to piece back together my slowly unraveling professional identity.

A massive sigh loosens my chest while tears sting the back of my eyes, threatening to fall again. Life would be simpler if I could be all in on motherhood. I signed up to be a working professional mom balancing it all with an amazing co-parent by my side. The feminist dream I was raised to believe in. Instead, I'm drowning in the constant effort of it all. Loving and mothering Jillian isn't hard. It's that alongside *everything else*.

I yearn to be present for this dream come true unfolding in front of me.

Instead, I'm over here sweaty and smelling a little bit like milk 24/7 while I chase my dream of building community settings that support youth, and maybe mothers too, based on these new research articles. Of communities that catch kids who are falling through the cracks and just need a few supportive grown-ups in their lives to say, "I've got you. I'm here when you need me. All that hiding you do of what's going on at home? I see it, and you're stronger for it, and you're not alone."

My life is what it is today because of the web of community support woven around me early on. Invisible threads holding me up when I didn't know my world was crashing down around me on the daily. Even when my mom died and I landed in a school a state away from my whole life, my new biology teacher cornered me after class. While I was still trying to figure out why people in Ohio had Southern accents after moving from Chicago suburbs, she had been piecing together the details of how I'd unexpectedly popped up in her classroom. She pulled me aside one day after class and told me that she had heard how I ended up here.

"If you ever need anything, and I mean *anything*, all you have to do is show up in my doorway and I'll help you, you understand? You need someone in your corner, and I'm telling you that person is me. I'm making you my business until you graduate."

She and I both cried when I hugged her hard on stage for my high school graduation two years later. I'd defied all the odds and made it. She'd made sure I made it.

Blinking rapidly, I let that memory fade and wrap up my "commitment to the organization" on Slack. I set my phone down and let the dream fill my mind again. I freeze-frame moments to more closely examine each one, trying to tease out why I woke with tears on my face and sore shoulders from tension in my sleep.

An old conversation with my friend Maya comes to mind. That one time when I went to a nude beach for the first time with her. She asked me if I had ever had any experience with my own past lives... as one does naked in the sand.

We let the sun and waves coax us into a blissful, relaxed state over a ceviche lunch as Maya described her belief in timeline hopping and past lives. How everything is already in our grasp because it already exists for us in a different timeline of our lives. We just have to grab it.

My forehead furrows in concentration as I bite my bottom lip, the familiar tension in my neck creeping up. I jump as my phone trills an incoming call, all thoughts of Maya and the beach forgotten.

LATER THAT WEEK, it's Jillian's bedtime. I try not to breathe as I quietly ease the door shut and wait in that tense pause between two worlds—mother and woman—to see if I can escape downstairs. A deep sigh of relief slips out as I quietly walk downstairs to Netflix and scroll until my own bedtime.

I nod off during the second episode with a half-typed text glowing on the phone in my lap, but I'm pulled back from sleep when the TV suddenly goes quiet and Netflix asks me the ominous question of "Are you still watching?"

Accepting that, no, I am in fact no longer watching, I turn the TV off and head upstairs to bed. My phone is lighting up with notifications. Emails about a nonprofit board I was asked to serve on but probably can't manage in this new season of life. The dreaded company Slack channel. A flurry of texts in Caden's family group chat because he shared a social media memory of when I graduated with an 8-month pregnant belly.

I traded my PhD hood and gown for nursing bras and pacifiers real quick after graduation 6 months ago.

What a different kind of hard… Finishing a dissertation with my deadline literally looming in my lap. My bump growing with each completed chapter—along with my confidence that I would gracefully transition into motherhood.

Alma texts, and the notification pulls me out of my anxiety spiral of questioning if I will ever work and mother without feeling like I'm drowning.

ALMA

You still good for yoga after work tomorrow?

Shit. I forgot. Again.

I start to type out my "no" but can't make myself press send. She had suggested our favorite yin yoga class after I confided in her about how little sleep I was getting between nighttime wake-ups and the dream repeating over and over. Alma was confident that I could meditate my way to answers and rest after I showed her my outline of the dream and theories on if this could be a past life of mine.

She laughed when I told her that Caden was still reeling from me trying to explain my theory that I could be timeline jumping to him on videochat. But he was proud I talked to my therapist about postpartum psychosis. Just in case.

Tears fill my eyes as overwhelm consumes me. Sometimes, this life feels like death by a million cuts. Decisions around diapers and first foods and sleeping arrangements. Boundaries with family and the futile efforts of finding a babysitter. Guilt about both wanting to be away from your kid *and* that you're away from your kid.

The hormones, emotionally charged nursing sessions, and dreams are an unnecessary layer on top of the normal hard of parenting.

I absolutely thought Jillian was going to fit in the neat boxes I carved out for her in my Outlook calendar, just like everything else in my life. Instead, I'm completely unmoored by motherhood, still trying to get my feet under me. The Maggie in my graduation photos would be horrified by this new version of herself if we met for coffee today. This was not our plan.

These are the moments when I wonder if postpartum is this hard for everyone. I can't quite tell, even when my therapist reminds me that yes, parenting is hard for *everyone*. Social media shows happy, shiny moms balancing babies on one hip and sourdough on the other. The mothers around me seem tired, sometimes dull with acceptance of this version of motherhood, but not shiny wet from actively drowning. Maybe if I stop fighting, stop wanting more from this season of life, I will float back to the surface and find contentment.

Climbing into bed, I'm vaguely aware of feeling surprised as the dream pulls me in again as soon as I fall asleep.

CHAPTER EIGHT

Ronnie pulls me toward the exit as my stomach churns, heart races, and brain scrambles to figure out what is going on. Dread's slowing my feet like my shoes are made of cinderblocks.

We weave through people holding bottles of Bud and little glasses of whisky, drinking their last sips as slowly as possible, ignoring the bartender as he shouts for folks to start heading home.

We get closer to the heavy metal door, propped open to allow the flow of customers out and the flashing lights of the police car in, and I notice a shift in the people around us. Now, instead of looking at the bartender to see if he's serious that they should go home, they're looking at us. Sad, pitying glances tossed our way as we move urgently—well, at least Ronnie is moving urgently—to and out the door.

"What the hell is going on?"

Ronnie responds by jerking me outside into the night.

Fucccck. Eyes wide, I'm frozen to the spot just outside the bar door as sirens wail and lights flash around me.

"What is going on, Ronnie?! Where's Craig?!"

But Ronnie isn't looking at me. He's looking at the entrance to the alley next to the bar. Why won't he answer me? I search the faces lit up by the flash of police lights for my brother. My eyes settle on a pack of men—boys, really—who *look unkempt and sweaty. All of them are breathing hard while one holds his nose, and another has a small trickle of blood running down his face.*

"Figures," I spit out at Ronnie. "Fucking figures Craig would get in a fight. Where is he?"

Half-made plans to run back home before I'm found here are flying through my head as my heart flips between panic at being caught by the police or my dad —because, which is scarier?—and worry for Craig.

And then Ronnie puts his arm around my waist and walks me past the group of guys talking to the police. Where did all that blood on them come from?? … and around the corner of the bar. More blood. This makes sense. This must have been where the fight started. All good fights start behind the bar…

Someone is collapsed on the ground with a crowd of police officers surrounding them in the alley… My eyes land on the pair of red-stained white Keds. My brother's white Keds.

And then I do throw up that Budweiser, stomach heaving as it empties itself of all that fun and freedom right onto the pavement.

CHAPTER NINE

Sweaty and wrapped up in my sheets, I wake with tears streaming down my cheeks. I can't tell who's crying… the woman in my dream or me or the baby. Maybe all of us. My last thought before I flew into consciousness was "Nooooooo!" as my heart dropped into my stomach, and I curled into a ball as if to protect myself from whatever was coming.

What is happening to me? Maybe I am actually losing it a little bit…"

Caden and Alma both promise I'm not losing it. Stress, hormones, lack of sleep—they each have a list of reasons why I don't need to worry about these dreams, reassuring me that they are just dreams. That they will fade away on their own.

I made them each separately promise that if I start acting odd, concerning, anything out of whatever my new normal is, they would call me out. I almost don't trust my mind. Bit by bit, I don't seem to have control over myself anymore.

Apparently, I'm not the only one waking up panicked. Jillian's crying as if she has seen a ghost and, not only did it scare her, but it made her hungry. This baby needs a boob, and she needs it *now*.

I uncurl my tightly wound body and scoop her up, wet tracks of tears shining in the soft glow of the tap light we installed by the bed for nighttime nursing. Desperate, hungry hands grab at my chest with soft, ineffective fingers tangling in the cloth of my sweat-soaked shirt.

Hungry noises whisper in the dark as Jillian gets her first few drops of milk, followed by the moist sounds of her lips sucking as she settles in. After a minute of tiny, frenzied breaths to get the milk flowing how she likes it, her body relaxes just as mine tenses, and she tucks her hand under my breast, settling in for a late-night snack.

I breathe deeply as my letdown brings along a dopamine drop that feels like despair and shame. Twin flames, burning me from the inside out. I fight the urge to run away, to escape.

"This is a reaction to a dopamine drop, not a real emotion. This is a condition, not a judgment. You are a good mom."

I breathe deeply and repeat this reminder to myself as the emotions move through my body in one of my worst letdowns in weeks. After a few minutes, the heat of shame, the urge to flee, fade away as my oxytocin and dopamine level out.

Jillian rarely wakes panicked. Could she sense my tension? I consciously work to unclench my hands from fists as I release the panic with deep breaths.

As I slowly drift into this land between conscious and unconscious realms, confusion and frustration cloud my mind, making my rest fitful and frustrating.

And as quickly as one breath in and out, I'm back in the dream, looking through the eyes of a scared teenager as she slowly falls to her knees in shock.

Fear, despair, panic, and nausea are all churning in my body—in her body—but, in this moment, shock has overtaken all other emotions and keeps them tamped down, as if her mind knows there's no time for any of that nonsense. Not in this bedroom or that alley.

CHAPTER TEN

T hose red Keds. No, those white Keds stained red with blood. A whooshing sound fills my ears, echoing all around me. I'm vaguely aware of police lights flashing red and white. Creating odd shadows on the brick walls of the bar and buildings in the alleyway. Off the dumpster. The open back doors of an ambulance. Shining off the bumpers of police cars.

The medics and police officers move like ghosts around me with a sense of mechanical urgency. Their arms gesture and wave and put up police tape. Two squad members with gloved hands open black bags and pull out gauze and towels and a needle filled with a clear liquid. Lights flash off a pool of blood on the ground. The mouths of everyone around me are moving in the lights, but all I can hear is whooshing.

Whoosh. Whoosh. Whoosh.

Are they talking? I can't make out what they're saying over my own heartbeat and fear.

Whoosh, whoosh, whoosh goes my heart in rhythm with the flashing lights. The roar of blood pulsing through my ears, drowning out the reality trying desperately to sink in.

A police officer rises from where he was squatting next to the Keds and turns to speak to Ronnie, who is still tightly grasping my arm. Is Ronnie holding me up? In place? Both? He's nodding and rubbing his free hand down his face to *wipe away tears. I wonder if he doesn't want anyone to see him crying or if he simply wants to wipe away this moment, this awful reality.*

Like most men in my family, I've only seen Ronnie cry when his baby was born and his mother died.

Why isn't he home with that baby now instead of holding me hostage in front of these Keds?

I can't look away from the feet in front of me. From the blood-stained Keds. Avoiding the bloody and sad reality above those shoes.

Suddenly, I feel like I'm floating above them all, looking down from above… as if in a dream. Watching this horror show spill out in the alley to the front of the bar. I'm vaguely aware of the police officer still talking. Of faces turning to me. Of Ronnie's hand firmly pulling on my arm. His other hand reaching around to hold my shoulder. Me shaking my head "no" when he tries to grab me. Then, Ronnie shakes me gently, as if trying to wake me up. Shock and disassociation are protecting me from this nightmare right now, and I don't want to leave this dream to come back down to earth.

My name is shouted as my body jerks with a harder shake. Ronnie's face appears directly in front of mine, eyes sad and desperate.

He blocks my view of the red and white Keds as he asks, "Are you okay? You need to be okay, Bean. This is not okay. Craig is not okay."

He shakes me one more time. Harder. My body snaps back and forth. He snaps me out of the shock. Out of my last few precious moments of denial before my whole life trajectory changes.

As if woken up suddenly, my eyes widen and start urgently scanning the alley, trying frantically to piece together what the hell happened to my brother. The whooshing stops, and in its place, whispers. So many people leaving, turning to stare and whisper as they walk past. The story will be all over town tomorrow… in offices, the grocery store check-out line, the gas pump.

A brawl outside the bar on the wrong side of town, and blood everywhere. "But did you see his head?!" will be whispered across desks and over lunches.

But for me, it's the exact moment in time when my and Craig's lives are divided forever by a before and after.

CHAPTER ELEVEN

The idea of a *before* and *after* lingers in my mind, and the smell of iron fills my nose as I slowly wake up—almost as if the bloody alley is on the other side of my dark room. Before and after.

A glance at my phone shows me only a few minutes have passed. *But what was that?*

Jillian is blissfully asleep. Moving to lay her down, I tread quietly in the summer night, listening to the sounds of animals and insects outside my window, and letting the last few moments of my dream roll through my mind.

The woman in the dream is stuck in that liminal space between before and after. Knowing what was will never be again but having no idea what is coming. It's a precious, rare space—like childbirth. The ultimate liminal space between worlds, between realms.

No one told me about the before and after of motherhood—of what I would shed in that liminal space and what I would gain. Or maybe they try. But they do it in the way of "just wait" and "you'll see." How not fucking helpful is that? I lost infinitely more than my free time and energy and sleep when I became a mom.

A memory of a conversation with Alma a few weeks after I gave birth comes to my mind. How she both couldn't understand that I was grieving my "before" and was equally frustrated about my lack of patience with her and her twenty-something, single lady antics that I used to pee myself laughing over at post-work mocktails just a few weeks earlier.

Becoming a mom knocked my world off its axis. The transition from maiden to mother is more like the phoenix burning and rising from the ashes versus flowers blooming in spring. The shock of the stark difference between the before and after. How it feels like nothing I did before motherhood matters to others and how the identity I spent my pre-baby years cultivating is consumed by this tiny person I created and pushed into the world. People used to ooh and aah over my ability to work full time, volunteer, run half-marathons, and go to graduate school.

Now they all think I should be happy. Satisfied.

Why is my own pain over losing those parts of myself to motherhood triggering them?

I miss that version of myself too. Satisfied feels a lot like settling.

Alma can't understand how I'm drowning in this before and after, this transition, of motherhood. A middle of the night race to the hospital. Deep, guttural moans filling the hallway, making heads turn. I waddled into the emergency room. Hurtling down hallways and up elevators in a wheelchair as I wailed in the late stages of contractions and through transition. Water breaking at the nurses' station. Caden's calling his mom and Alma on speakerphone with the news that "it's time!" from the delivery room while my moans broke me apart in the background. And finally, after twenty minutes of pushing, my liminal space ended, and my precious baby girl was born.

So much gained, but also a loss, isn't there? A loss of self. Of myself as a woman. Of a life I spent years creating and dreaming up simply vanished. I've grown into a bigger and wilder life as a mom but had no inkling how much of myself I would lose as I gained this new tiny human—and identity.

I struggled to explain my frustrations and unexpected overwhelm to Alma while Jillian wailed on my chest, to tell her that I was feeling lost and incompetent in this new version of my life, while she tried to comfort me with the usual new mom platitudes of "you've got this" and then distract me with her recent dating app chats—which I used to love to dissect with her pre-baby. Another loss. Eventually, my snapping at her got to be too much, and she left with promises to stop by again soon and text me later.

Ugh.

I sigh loudly and pick up my phone to text her. I send the first funny reel in my feed with a quick "pump + lunch?" text, already smiling thinking of her jokes about "my udders" and firsthand scoop of the *hot goss* from around the office.

A quiet gust of wind blows around the room, swaying the open curtain panels and rustling plant leaves. I've started leaving the window open a few inches at night to blame the unexpected breezes on. My mind is racing to explain away the unknown source of wind. It seemed easier to open a window than continue to wonder about spirits moving around the room.

Sometimes I feel like the girl from the dream might be here with me, feel her dread and fear shadow my joy and love, always waiting right on the edges of my happiness to pull me down, pull me into her realm.

How do you "just let it go?" I've tried putting these dreams in a bubble and blowing them away like Caden suggested, but it's not working. Fear and grief are consuming me in the dark of the night, whispering sad, lonely thoughts into my mind about being a failure, wasting my potential, and more.

A FEW HOURS LATER, I wake with no memories of dreaming but lowkey desperate to find out what happens next. Needing to know is distracting me during every step of my morning routine. Do I get to find out what happened to this woman and her brother? How does this end? I'm desperately waiting for the season finale of a show I never meant to start watching.

THE DAY FLIES by on autopilot, and I finally end up where I was longing for at bedtime: in the alley behind a bar.

CHAPTER TWELVE

A hand waves and fingers snap in my face, pulling my gaze from my brother on the ground to the police officer.

"Ma'am? I have a few questions for you. Do you know this person?"

I stare blankly at the officer for a beat too long. My silence fills the air under the chaos around us, and he shifts uncomfortably.

The officer gestures to my brother as the medic removes the gauze covering his face.

"No," I whisper as my brain scrambles to make sense of what I'm seeing. My brother, but... but not my brother. Dark hair shiny with blood. His face... His face. HIS FACE. Part of it is puffy and bruised. His eyes are swollen shut. The other part is just... just... missing. Missing?! No. That's not right. His face is there. Skin. Lips. Swollen and bloody but still the same lips all of us have. His nose. But there's something happening above his eye. It's dark and bloody and damp-looking. But not like his hair. More like flesh. Like deep, wet darkness.

No. No. No. What's going on? Where is all this blood coming from? Why is his head smashed in?

Oh, no.

Oh. No.

A police officer's gloved hand lifts a brick and places it in a brown paper bag, dark red blood already drying on its hard surface.

Information tumbles together in my brain like the locks in a safe. The young men, rumpled and sweaty, clothes askew, who look like they just got into a fight outside the door. The brick. My brother laying on the ground with blood pooled around him.

Fear and rage sharpen my focus on the boys who did this to my brother as they stand in a circle around a different police officer, spitting out "yes, sir" and "no, sir" and gesturing from the door of the bar to the alley.

But Craig's not moving.

One medic works to slow his bleeding while others lift his body onto a stretcher, his arm hanging off the edge. Flashing lights and loud sirens slowly fade as the ambulance departs.

My stomach is knotted, and fire races up and down my arms and legs as I fight off the urge to run away. To run to safety.

"Is he... Is Craig... " The word "dead" is stuck on my tongue like the stutter of the little boy I babysit sometimes. Hanging there between me, Ronnie, and the man in the police uniform.

"He's alive," says the police officer. "He's alive but in serious condition."

"He's going to be okay, right?" asks Ronnie.

"It was a bad fight, but he's in good hands now. Nothin' more you can do right now." The police officer sounds bored, disengaged, as if he's used to repeating this non-answer at each crime scene. "But I still have a few questions for you two."

Nothing more we can do?! What did we even do?! What did Craig do?

With the lights and sirens of the ambulance gone, a heavy quiet takes over the dark night, and exhaustion settles in.

"There was a bad fight?" I interrupt whatever the officer was saying to Ronnie.

Nodding, the officer continues to direct his attention to Ronnie. "How do you know the victim? What happened inside the bar? Did you see the fight start?"

Ronnie and the officer's words fuel the flames of my red-hot rage, overcoming the grief and fear. Rage is the easiest emotion to grab a hold of in this alley, and I let the fire consume me. I'm distantly aware of Ronnie and the officer talking as I turn toward the group in front of the bar who just carelessly ruined a man's face. His future. Over what?!

An officer hands back IDs that are then slid into wallets and pockets while he says, "You're free to go home, but the police will be in touch."

Home. These fuckers are free to go home. HOME?! How the fuck are they free to go home when my brother is missing half of his head and flying in the back of an ambulance to the hospital as fast as the driver can swerve down these pot-holed streets?

Who knows if Craig will come home? Will ever be okay again? My mind seems to know that I can't possibly handle this trainwreck of thoughts and sends hot anger pulsing down my arms and legs.

A few of them look bashful and sorry. I'm angry. Furious. And yet, I can't do a single thing. I'm powerless. And being powerless is more overwhelming than fear.

CHAPTER THIRTEEN

Stretching as I wake, the warm release pulling on my muscles down my back drains away the heavy emotions left from my dream, like powerlessness and rage have no place in this cozy bedroom on this side of consciousness.

Already excited for Caden to get home tonight, I debate how to tell him that the dream continues on. That I'm sucked in and need to know what happens next. Maybe I'll sit on the counter with a glass of wine and tell him how I'm officially sucked in, full Dr. Maggie mode on this dream, charting out the story and diving into articles on past lives (my favorite theory on what's happening). He will nod and be grateful we aren't talking about timeline jumping while he tackles bottle-washing duty.

Bottle duty is his penance for traveling during the week and my favorite way for him to reconnect with me. I'm happy to let him worship me between my knees if he still feels guilty later... *his* favorite way to reconnect when he gets home.

With that image burning away all memories of my dream, I run downstairs and grab my first cup of coffee before Baby J is up for the day.

LATE THAT NIGHT, I crawl right back into bed while texting with
Caden about his delayed flight. He will be home after I'm asleep.
I'm not even mad because I'm ready for the dream tonight. For
some reason, the hard part feels over. What could be worse than
watching your brother almost bleed out from a head injury after a
bar fight? The powerlessness and rage of the girl swarmed my body
the night before—but we must be nearing the end of this story.
Right?

Hmm… story. Is it a story?

It's surprisingly realistic for a dream. No crazy time travels. No
wild twists and turns like a magical talking animal that make you
know, "Oh, I'm obviously dreaming." It's quite the opposite. This
dream feels wildly real. As if I'm living in the moment with this girl
—*as* this girl? This is my number one data point for why I think I'm
revisiting a past life. How else can I explain knowing the names and
so many details of this girl's life?

*Well, let's see what happens on tonight's episode of me slowly losing my
mind.*

Questions whirl in my mind as my eyes close and breathing
deepens, settling into sleep in the warm summer breeze, vaguely
aware of my hair being pushed off my forehead by the wind.

A hand softly wraps around mine and pulls me gently into a
deep sleep, back to the dream.

CHAPTER FOURTEEN

I move through the living room full of people and TV trays covered with plates of half-eaten casseroles, following the pull of an invisible hand gently guiding me forward. The ceiling fan spins and makes the lights flash like in the alley of the dream. Every time I try to let go, the room fades, and the hand's grip tightens and holds me in place, as if whatever, or whoever, brought me here, wants me to stay. To see. To witness. We pause near a woman talking softly into the mouthpiece of a phone. An old-school rotary with a cord phone.

"Yes, Craig's home, thank god, but it's not really him. It's... it's like his shadow came home and moved into his room." She pauses and then, "She's... okay. I don't think she took it well, but she loves her brother and wants him to get better. She feels guilty for what happened and feels like she has to now."

Nurses crowd the room and bring with them bandages and file folders of notes. Neighbors and friends carrying casseroles are given quiet updates on how Craig's doing, how much his sister is giving up by dropping out of school to help her mom care for him. A shiny new TV is visible through the doorway used most by the nurses.

The words before and after keep splitting conversations in two. Before Craig got hurt in a fight and after. Before he snuck his sister out to the bar... and after.

My mind spins as I watch nurses move supplies and people efficiently *around the room, and I catch a glimpse of a teen girl walking out of what must be Craig's room, tears rolling down her cheeks, bloody bandages in her hand.*

"Did you learn how to change his bandages?" says an older, tired-looking woman from across the room.

"Yes, Mom. I almost threw up when they uncovered the stitches and then called the hole in his head an 'indentation,' but I learned how to change them. You probably should too. I won't be around all the time. I've gotta work and get my GED stuff started."

Her mom simply grunts in response and waves a hand as she turns back to her conversation, ignoring the wrenching shoulders of her daughter as she walks away. The hand tenses in mine.

A pair of simple words that split our worlds in two are screaming in my mind.

Before. After.

Simple on their own. But never in reality. This is the same girl who was in the bar with big dreams to go to the city after school! What is she doing here? Why is her family okay with her settling?

The answer to my questions floats across the room as one neighbor gossips to another. "He's going to need round-the-clock care for months. The dad is too drunk to be counted on and the mom too selfish to not punish her. She blames her for him being out and getting in that fight. Doesn't seem fair to me to ruin her life, though."

I want to grab on to the daughter and hug her, to turn her around and yell for her mom to get up and take care of her son. But even as my arms move to the girl to wrap her in a motherly hug, my hands float through her, and I remember it's a dream.

Instead, I follow her to the kitchen where she's arguing with a woman in loud whispers while washing dishes at the kitchen sink. The woman has the same brown hair, but with more weariness etched across her forehead, her temples… An older sister, maybe?

The hand stills me in place as the girl says, "And now I'm just another poor girl with no high school degree since I dropped out of school to help with Craig. I get that he's hurt. Like his world is ruined, but why does mine have to be too? It's not fair!"

The sister keeps handing wet plates from the sink to the girl from my dream to dry and stack while she nods and makes soft noises of agreement.

"So, what? Now I work at the drive-in selling movie tickets at night and watching babies and washing clothes during the day? For what? So I can give Mom my money to hoard garage sale trinkets and lottery tickets instead of pay bills? Does she even think of the fact that with each scratch off she burns through, she's eating up a little bit of my soul?"

A wretched sob breaks, and the older sister turns on the tap again to cover the soft, angry cries muffled under the kitchen towel moments ago being used to dry dishes. Then, the girl suddenly pushes the towel into her mouth and screams while she bends over herself, fists squeezing and pulling the towel while she bites down hard. She falls to her knees, muffled sobs racking her body. Even her rage is made small and kept hidden in this house that has no space for her or her dreams. Tears for this girl stream down my face as the hand lets go and the kitchen fades away...

CHAPTER FIFTEEN

I wake up with a tear-streaked face and a light-filled, empty bedroom. Caden has Jillian downstairs for a morning bottle.

So, he *was* listening during our video chat before his flight home—him propped up on the windowsill over the kitchen sink while I prepped bottles for the next day. Listening with raised eyebrows and lips pressed together in a firm line while I babbled about how I almost fell asleep sitting in traffic earlier this week. Concern and guilt had filled his eyes in equal measure while I reassured him, both of us, that these dreams (flashbacks?) would end soon.

He has me already looking forward to jumping back into bed with him later tonight. I've missed his body and, from the other looks I was getting during our video chat when I changed into my pajamas, I know he's missed mine too. Smart man to set up his advantage by helping me get some rest now. Great sex. Extra sleep. And is that hot coffee on the nightstand? Yes, please. To *all* of it.

Andddd I'm going to let him have an extra cup of coffee before I fill him in on how I was pulled into a dream last night by an invisible spirit… ghost?

I ponder that thought while I use the extra time this morning to take an everything shower and coax my eyebrows back into an arch. I send a selfie of my perfectly winged eyeliner to Alma, my ultimate hype girl. She's always proud when I "effort" these days and preens over my hair when it's not in a ponytail or, worse, mom bun. Usually, her responses are immediate and enthusiastic at this hour when she's mid-scroll before getting out of bed, but it's oddly quiet. Huh.

Zipping up my dress, I distract myself by humming another Joplin song that's come up on my playlist lately: "Freedom's just another word for nothin' left to lose."

Is that how the girl in the dream feels? She lost control over her life—adult responsibilities laid at her feet. What else did she have to lose at that point? Would she ever feel free?

I usually tell Alma the latest scoop on the dreams at work, but theorizing on the mental state of the girl in the dream might be too much. Admitting how much these dreams are messing with my head feels dangerous.

How can I tell her—or Caden—this dream has taken over my life? They think sleep deprivation is the reason that I'm a mess, not that unwanted emotions and memories are flooding my reality.

How am I having such powerful flashbacks to a dream?

Why am I seeing this girl's tragedy play out in my dreams and then popping up in my days at the most random times? And why do I see each moment through her eyes? Like I'm reliving her worst nightmare repeatedly with her. *As* her.

Searching in my closet for my slides, I don't hear Caden come into the room. I stand up and back into his chest, immediately pulled into him and wrapped in strong arms. A surprised shriek escapes as his hands slip into mine and instantly bring me back to the hand guiding me in my dream. He lets out a low laugh in my ear and holds me close.

"Do you feel free?"

He freezes, and I immediately know it was the wrong thing to say.

On a long exhale, Caden takes a step back and turns me around.

"Do you?" he asks.

His raised eyebrows and tight smile tell me all I need to know about how these next few minutes are going to go.

"Yes and no... Like yes, of course, in the sense that we have everything we need and all the privilege that comes with that. Healthcare, savings account..."

He waves his hand, signaling for me to get to the point. He's much more interested in the "no" than me breaking down how our racial and economic privilege gives us freedom.

"And I'm trapped. Stuck. Like life is moving too fast on repeat day after day. I miss feeling free."

Caden puts his hands on my face, brushing away the tears that have started to form.

"Babe, do you really want to mess up your makeup right before you leave for work?"

Ugh, no, absolutely not.

And he knows I'm vain enough to pull myself together. I don't want to ruin my look. Wiping the side of my thumb under my eyelashes, I breathe deeply and compress all that longing back to where it belongs, under my ribs in my chest, building pressure until it blows me wide open one day. Just not today. This has been a defining part of my motherhood journey. Ripping open my soul and then being shushed to calm down, much like a newborn.

What if this had been part of the birth course we took? Like heads up, people are going to call and text and drop by to see how you're doing in the first few weeks, but they only want the "shiny, happy mom" answer. "We are *so* happy. The baby is doing great. We don't need a thing!"

Caden is familiar with my speech on society only wanting happy answers from moms. That deeply uncomfortable conversation where he asked me to stop posting my honest experience about motherhood on social media sits between us now, tainting what was one of the first mornings where I've felt like "me" in months with past hurts and a bit of shame for both of us.

"I'm not saying you don't want or deserve all of that, babe. You do. I'm just saying that you need to have some perspective, too. It's not that hard compared to other moms out there."

And there it is... the shame bomb dropped between us. Again. Caden, along with most of his family and our mutual followers on social media according to him, feels like I've gotten too whiny about how deeply shockingly hard motherhood has been for me. The lack of community and support and moms in my life devastates me regularly. Alma has hinted that my excessive complaining gives her doubts that I even like Jillian sometimes.

"Don't disassociate on me now, babe. I'm not trying to gaslight you and say this isn't hard. I can see that brain of yours blowing up this argument to me hating on how hard motherhood is for you. Shaming you. I already told you I shouldn't have said that everyone is talking about you. I'm trying so hard to figure all of this out *with* you, to be your partner in creating a parenthood experience that feels fulfilling for both of us. I'm telling you now that I understand this is hard *and* it's not forever."

Why is it that, because other mothers survived this shitty experience of motherhood, I'm expected to *and* not complain about it? I'm supposed to save myself while drowning—and pull others up from the water too. I showed him the DMs I got about the series of posts that had "everyone we know" questioning if I was okay. Mom friends sent messages of support, proclaiming "same" over the overwhelm of losing my identity after becoming a mom, thanking me for being real about the duality that is motherhood.

Caden shifts to take my hand, but I turn away from him and back to the closet, hands clenched at my sides as I blindly stare at the rainbow of pencil skirts and nursing tanks.

"And on top of my existential crisis around motherhood, these dreams are ruining my sleep. Messing with my work. At least we knew what was happening with the D-MER, figured out how to make it manageable. I can't figure this out, Caden. I can't research my way out of this."

And there it is, the miserable truth of this dream laid between us.

"I'm not okay, Caden. I'm just not okay." My voice cracks as the tears threaten again.

"Maggie, you're not going mad. These dreams aren't making you crazy. If anything, your obsession with the dreams are the problem."

I open my mouth to interrupt and he goes on, "I know it's been hard, baby, not enough sleep or time… or freedom, I guess. But it will get better, easier, once you start sleeping more, yeah? Maybe you can let go of your need to figure these dreams out. Just let them be dreams and nothing more."

I shrug as he pulls me to his chest and squeezes me tight.

"Not everything is a sign from the universe, Mags. Sometimes life is just hard. But you're not alone. You'll never be alone again."

I breathe in the woodsy smell of him and pause, not wanting to waste the precious days we have together between his work trips locked in the same shame-inducing fight over and over again.

He releases me and picks up my empty coffee cup, swirling it around his finger. "Want a refill?"

I give him a saucy wink. "Yes, please." I push him backward to the bed.

His eyebrows raise. "Oh, you won't mess up your makeup for the struggles of mothers everywhere, but you will for this?" he asks, gesturing up and down his body, smirking.

I laugh and give him a hard push onto the bed.

A text pings my phone loudly enough for me to jump. Alma sent an adorable selfie of her making a whoops face while biting her lip and looking at the ceiling with a very sleeping, seemingly very sexy dark-haired man in the background… His back is to the camera, but a bare shoulder and arm are in the frame. She follows this up with a stream of emojis ranging from fire to eggplant. Alma may go out a lot but rarely brings anyone home.

Sighing, I do my best friend duty and respond back with the double exclamation point on the picture.

ME

Trade you coffee for details?

I need to put my best friend hat on today and be here for all the salacious details on this unexpected hookup, but I want to scream. In envy. In frustration. In the guttural roar of all women trying to survive this world.

Jillian starts to wail as Caden glances at my phone. He groans while standing up and closing the window as the wind gusting in blows a pile of sticky notes on the ground. "Hmpph. I guess I'll go make Alma her usual coffee, too."

CHAPTER SIXTEEN

My legs are frozen in this dirty, too small room, light filtering in jagged lines through broken blinds. Eyes locked with a scared man holding a gun in his hand on the bed. He moves to put the barrel of the gun into his mouth.

I wake suddenly, gasping hard as I fly up, and my hands careen into my steering wheel.

"What the hell?"

My eyes open, wide and searching, as I remember I went to take a quick nap in my car between meetings. The windows fogged up from my warm breath, and now my heartbeat pounds in my ears in the suddenly too-small hybrid vehicle.

Rolling down the windows and raising my seatback, I let the cool fall air blow into the car. The gunshot reverberates in my ears.

My pounding heart moves too-hot blood through my body, pulsing up and down my arms and legs. The instinct to run away from this gunshot, from this car, is hard to resist but I hold tight to the steering wheel, familiar waves of cold sweat rolling down my body and hot fear clenching in my stomach.

So much for just letting the dreams be dreams and nothing more.

Panting and fumbling through my bag for wipes, I shakily blot away the smeared mascara under my eyes and sweat from my forehead.

Walking back to my office, I can't help but wonder, once again, if I'm losing it a little bit.

Desperation and exhaustion lay thick, like a second skin. A sensation I've tried to wash away for weeks. The delivery driver shows up daily with new sleep hygiene deliveries ranging from eye masks to magnesium spray.

These recurring nightmares are causing constant, endless small mistakes and disruptions in my days. My endless energy is winding down after weeks of dream-interrupted sleep, the nightly cortisol surges creating confusion and indecision in my mind.

My therapist thinks starting medication will help once I'm done nursing, but I'm not convinced. Organized chaos has always been my life. Getting diagnosed with ADHD created many "aha moments" for me, including how I used the sweet combination of structure and pressure to *get shit done*. But lately, my organized chaos style of life is dissolving into, well, chaos. And "that look ain't cute, boo," as Alma quoting Cody Rigsby would say.

My phone beeps with an incoming text from Jack. "You coming to your 2:00 p.m. meeting?"

Dammit. This look ain't cute, boo.

It's 2:08 and I'm late. I walk back into the office as fast as my heels and pencil skirt will let me, slowing my pace as I breeze into the conference room.

The only seat left is next to my boss, and Alma looks at me across the room with a small grimace and mouths, "you okay?"

I wink at her and pull out my laptop, quickly closing the extra tabs ranging from a dreamy all-inclusive vacation to an article forwarded over from a new mom friend called "In the absence of a village, mothers struggle most."

"Thank you for joining us, Maggie," Jack says coolly, turning to look at me.

I give a small smile and nod, waiting for the meeting to begin.

Oh, shit. This is my *meeting to run.*

I move to connect my laptop to the projector, making opening meeting small talk as I search for the right cord. Turning my back to the room to breathe deeply—and knowing that creepy tech guy is going to be checking out my ass the whole time—I pull up my presentation.

Say something smart. Say something smart. You can do this. You have a PhD.

CHAPTER SEVENTEEN

I pull into Alma's luxury apartment community after work with Jillian in tow. She lives in one of those made-for-singles communities with a pool, pickleball court, and more. In true Alma style, she is subletting for a fraction of the rent from a friend working abroad for a year.

She didn't have to try too hard to convince me to come to the community bar's bonfire happy hour after the shitshow at work.

Alma's standing in the parking lot wearing something that looks like a backward backpack in the evening light. Jillian squeals and kicks her feet, smiling as Alma opens her door and scoops her up before I can even grab our bags. My eyes fill, and a huge grin spreads across my face as I realize that Alma, my gorgeous best friend, is wearing a baby carrier with the full intention of getting Jillian into it for the night.

"You clearly needed a break. I doordashed this to my place during that shitshow of a meeting. Don't we look cute?" She slides Jillian expertly into the baby carrier and spins, the silver thread woven in the white and gray leopard print gleaming in the dark.

She and Jillian do, in fact, look adorable. Tears stream down my face, wrecking what is left of my perfectly winged eyeliner, and I embrace both in a giant hug, squishing Jillian between us.

"I practiced with Wink before you got here. He might like it more than Jillian does."

The vision of her miniature poodle bouncing around in the baby carrier strapped to her chest makes me laugh so quickly, it comes out as a snort.

"I'm sure he does." Wink's been obsessed with Alma since she rescued him at a dog adoption event last year.

"I assumed you'd be harder to convince to come out tonight. It's been a while since you've said yes to happy hour, but I was ready to do all the bribing once I ordered this carrier."

I don't miss the slight accusation in her voice as she pulls out her phone and flips through a dozen photos of Wink tucked into the baby carrier.

"If you said no, I was going to send you these and call in all favors you owe me. I miss you, Mags."

Sighing, I hug her tight again.

"Come on, I tracked your location and ordered your favorite cheesy tater tots. Stop crying and let's go."

I once again fix my mascara and follow her, with my baby happily strapped to her chest, to the bar.

Alma moves around the bar gracefully—a social butterfly, she seems to know everyone—or everyone seems to want to know the adorable baby giggling on her chest. Alma's right, people *do* love babies at bars. Something about the juxtaposition delights the crowd here, and Alma's gone for a long time with Jillian.

Long enough that I curl into a chair by the bonfire, tucking my legs under me, and send Caden some quick pictures of the two besties in all their glory. Alma's thoughtfulness makes me consider telling her how much the dream about the girl and her brother being attacked shook me, about the man bringing the gun barrel to his mouth has flashed in my mind throughout the day.

How I almost dropped Jillian at the store because I startled unexpectedly when Janis Joplin's "Break Another Piece of My Heart" came on over the speaker system. She was extra squirmy and wearing the most adorable—and slippery—fleece onesie. As I tried to get her back into her car seat, I startled and she slipped in my grip as I was transported back to another time. Another place. Another person. And just frozen there. The powerful wave of recognition forced my mother's instincts to take over and grab onto Jillian's slippery, fleece-covered body as I pulled out of the déjà vu taking over my reality.

Even Jillian seemed to freeze, mid-suck on her pacifier, and stare at me like, "What the hell, Mom?"

Telling someone would feel incredible, would relieve the fear and shame that floods me when my body tenses or my mind wanders to somewhere I've never been, to a life it seems like I've lived before.

Alma finally wanders back over holding a tray filled with tater tots, cauliflower wings, and two bottles of Budweiser.

I raise one eyebrow at her and gesture to the beers. Odd choice given that our usual espresso martinis are specials tonight.

She smiles wide as she thrusts the beer to me enthusiastically.

Well, I guess I would trust Alma to find out how to get me back to happy hour again. She's invested in fun. And I guess I'm lucky she's invested in me having fun at her side.

"But why Budweiser?"

She shrugs and points to the pack of athletic-looking bros at the bar who wave and one tilts his head back, his eyebrows lifting as he gives her "the nod."

Swoon.

"Remember that text from the other day?"

Nodding, I pick out the crispiest, cheesiest-looking tater tot in the pile.

"That's him. Eric."

My head swivels back to the bar, hair catching in the cheesy tater tot I was moving toward my mouth as I openly stare at the incredibly sexy man now leaning with an arm above his head on the overhang of the bar, one leg crossed over the other, sipping from his own bottle of Bud. He's definitely checking out Alma. I let out a low whistle and drag my eyes back to my best friend, who is trying to get her hair out of Jillian's tight fist, before I wipe cheese out of my curls.

"Right? Fucking hot in bed too. He's one of those guys who *loves* his face between my legs." She whispers the last part and covers Jillian's ears.

I let out my loudest laugh—Caden calls it my cackle—and pick up the beer bottle, pressing it to my reddening cheeks and forehead.

"Well, cheers to Eric and multiple orgasms!" I'm still laughing as I take a swig of Budweiser—and almost immediately wretch it up.

Beer mixes with stomach acid in my throat as I rely on my fear and shame of throwing up in public to keep the vomit in the pit of my stomach. Puking in public is almost okay when you're pregnant, but not at all when sober, with your baby, at a bar.

I set the bottle on the ground next to my chair and pretend to look absorbed in Caden's text responses, which consist mostly of thumbs up and a heart for the one of Jillian. My mouth waters and stomach clenches with the need to vomit, but thankfully, Alma's too wrapped up in tickling Jillian and making flirty eye contact with Eric to be worried about my odd reaction.

I head to the bar to grab a seltzer to rinse the taste of beer and vomit from my mouth—and to give myself a moment to process the flashback that flooded me as I sipped the Budweiser. I was hyperaware of each second of that sip of beer. The cold curve of the beer bottle on my lips. The weight of the beer shifting as it flowed down the neck of the bottle and into my mouth.

I wasn't myself sipping from that beer bottle—I was a seventeen-year-old girl dancing and carefree. But as soon as the beer hit my stomach, all I could see were flashing lights and blood. The flashback overwhelming me to the point I almost puked. I wanted to puke—like the girl in my dream threw up her entire night of beers.

Alma locks eyes with me when I return with a seltzer for both of us, and I'm *this* close to giving in to the urge to tell her how bad it has gotten lately. To spill these secrets and let her tease me and then force me to call my therapist… but I really don't want to ruin our night out together.

"You okay?" she asks, glancing at the beer on the ground and water in my hand. "I can grab martinis if you'd rather—"

But she never gets to finish that sentence, and I lose my opportunity to spill my messy secrets because Eric walks over to us and sits down on Alma's other side.

I get a different type of vision of how Alma's night is going to end now that Eric has split off from his pack of friends and is bumping shoulders with her. Someone is getting lucky tonight, and it's not me. Well, at least it's not me with a sexy man between my legs. But my fingers will do since Caden's away.

Jillian seems to sense the change in energy as she fussily glares at Eric. He's one of the few people here not enamored with her.

"We should get going. Your tiny best friend is ready for bedtime."

Alma blows raspberries on Jillian's round belly as she pulls her up from the carrier and over to me.

Eric wraps his arms around Alma, helping her get the baby carrier unclipped. Jillian gets a good whack on his forehead as she's lifted up. I smile a little and wiggle my eyebrows at Alma.

She smirks at me and then slaps my hand away as I reach for the carrier. "No way, mama, this is mine. Now Jillian can come hang with Auntie Alma whenever she wants and her mean mommy can't stop her."

Drowning in this woman's nurturing, tears fill my eyes again, and I hug her tightly, not letting go until Eric starts to look antsy behind her.

"Have fun tonight," I whisper to her and pat her butt as we pull apart.

Squeezing my hand, she picks up her beer and turns to Eric, glancing over her shoulder as she calls back, "I always do."

As expected, my phone glows in the night with a text from Alma requesting coffee in the morning.

ALMA

Put extra espresso in it. That man wore.
Me. Out.

CHAPTER EIGHTEEN

Alma's been distracted by Eric and has let me off the hook for happy hour for now. There's been little time to fill her in on my latest traveling *into* my dream. I thought this might turn into her first serious relationship in a long while, but she's having too much fun keeping it casual while she's all in on her professional goals.

"Who needs emotions when you can have multiple orgasms? I'm deep in my compound interest era. Relationships will have to wait," was her last reason for not wanting to get too serious with him. Alma's flippant nature around relationships hides the deep need to provide for herself and her future family. Her greatest goal is financial security, to weave her own financial safety net to avoid ever returning to the hard knocks of a life living paycheck-to-paycheck like her parents.

Alma comes across as a happy-go-lucky, hardworking professional woman, but she's putting every penny she earns to work paying off her student loans and saving for a mortgage. One of our first overshares was her asking me how much I was putting into my 401k and grabbing my hand in horror when I replied, "um, 0%?"

"Not even the company match?!" she shrieked in horror as I

blinked rapidly at her. Alma coached me through changing my health insurance and maximizing my tax savings for daycare and Jillian's future college. And now I willingly save money by packing my lunch and sitting with her rather than getting delivery.

People are noticing my jumpy, bordering on erratic reactions. I'm blaming my strange behavior on lack of sleep and Caden's travel schedule. Alma's covering for me, sending me "See you in 10?" texts to make sure I show up to meetings and upping the wins I do manage at work.

Caden and Alma are still sure I'm okay, that I haven't developed postpartum psychosis. Even after I told them about the flashback with the beer bottle at happy hour.

But I'm not sure I'm still okay. Because this has gone beyond "new mom hard" and into something beyond explanations or understanding, especially for Caden.

His patience is wearing thin… he wants to be supportive, but his frustration grows with each yawn, every note he sees me make about the dreams.

Caden's curt nods and deep sighs are the only signs of how annoyed he is—not with me, but himself. He's desperate to fix this, and he can't. How can he solve a problem I can't explain?

LATER THAT DAY, I go home and reverse all the motions that got me out the door that morning. Dress and heels to leggings and a nursing tank. Unpack lunch boxes and bottle bags. Handwash the endless pump parts and milk bottles. Reheat dinner. Eat. Fill up the bottles with fresh milk and relabel each one. Nurse, burp, repeat while snuggling with Jillian. We watch *Jane the Virgin* in bed until I put her to sleep.

As I brush my teeth and watch the eucalyptus leaves on the branches in the shower rustle in the breeze, I can't help but think of my mom. The deep longing and sadness from earlier today have thankfully stamped out my fear from the gunshot dream.

How long can I make this tube last before it's empty?

Sometimes the same tube of toothpaste will last for two more weeks before it's gone. Two weeks before I need to InstaCart another. That's a long time to stretch a couple of bucks. My mom would tell stories about being achingly poor in her twenties. She could barely afford toothpaste and maxi pads. She had a skill for getting every bit out of a tube of toothpaste, for figuring out how to get by.

I wish I'd asked her more about the hard times in her life when she couldn't even afford toothpaste instead of rolling my eyes as she squeezed and manipulated the tube of sparkly blue toothpaste. I wish I had asked her more about how she learned to survive.

CHAPTER NINETEEN

Opening the door of the apartment, I pause, listening to see if Jeremy is home or not. Silence. I head directly to the closet, my tips from waitressing burning a hole in my pocket.

"I freaking earned this tonight," I whisper to myself, going into the closet door to tuck the latest bit of cash into the pocket of a fancy purse.

The beaded evening bag is hidden in the sleeve of a winter jacket in the back of the closet. There's no reason Jeremy would ever need to go in there. Would never even occur to him to look at my winter coat when he was sober, let alone half-cocked like he usually is lately. Jeremy doesn't know about this stash of cash, and he doesn't need to. I almost have enough to leave.

But something about the closet makes me pause again and listen. Something is off. Wrong. I try to be optimistic as I notice his clothes moved around the closet.

Maybe he made it to work today.

I do mental math, pushing clothes in the closet out of the way, figuring out how much cash is squirreled away and how many more extra shifts at Chef's I need to pick up before I can leave.

Hairs on my arms stand up as the all too familiar panic starts to creep up my spine. Some of the boxes in the corner have been moved around.

"No. No. No. No. No," I whisper as I slowly reach for my coat sleeve. But I *know. A little part of my brain has already registered that the coat has been moved around, just a little bit, and I know. The zipper lower than I left it (Exactly ¾ of the way zipped. Every. Single. Time.)*

Alarm bells ring in my ears as I slowly reach my hand to the jacket and the sleeve pressed up against the dingy closet wall. The uncovered lightbulb flashes as my hand touches the sleeve, like a sign from the universe that this moment is monumental.

I squeeze the sleeve, and my hand squishes the overstuffed nylon between my fingers. The tips of my fingers meet through the layers of fabric.

No.

I move my hand down and squeeze again. The hiss of air pushing out from the stuffing and nylon under my grip fills the air.

No.

One more part of the sleeve to go. But I know it won't be there. I give it a half-hearted squeeze anyway. And then I grab at the coat, ripping the hanger off the closet rod, clutching it in my fist while my heavy, desperate panting fills the air. The smell of my sweat fills the stifling closet.

Wait. Maybe the bag fell on the floor. Okay. Of course.

It just slipped out of the sleeve and fell onto the floor.

Crouching down, I search through the bags, belts, shoes crowding the floor.

But no. The bag is gone. Fuck. Fuck. Fuccccccck. He has it. Could he have it? *He has to have it. Nothing else is missing. The cash is probably half gone by now on rounds of beer and whiskey at the bar.* Where the hell could he even be?

Through the red sheen of rage in my eyes and fiery acid in my belly, my survival instincts began to take over again. My ragged breathing slows and catches in my throat as a new realization dawns on me.

If Jeremy knows about the money, then I have a totally different problem on my hands.

Jeremy is unpredictable. And unpredictable means dangerous. He's unpredictable when drinking on a good day, let alone on a day when he has just uncovered a secret pile of cash his wife has been hiding from him. How many lies have I told to keep this money hidden?

In sheer desperation, I methodically search every inch of the apartment. The shelves made from scrap wood and cinder blocks holding what's left of our record collection, whatever he hasn't pawned off. Under the bed. Through the piles of dirty laundry and trash on the floor. As I lift up a wet towel gone mildewy with age, I wonder how these piles of smelly clothes and empty chip bags became my life.

When I ran away from my parents' house in a fury of rage and right into Jeremy's waiting arms? Those arms that were only a few short months away from pushing and shoving me during drunken fights. Little did I know there would even be drunken fights. Before we ran off to the courthouse and got married in a blaze of young love, we had only ever gotten drunk and fooled around. Danced. Sang to the moon on the roof of his car in a field.

My fingers continue to fumble around the clothes on the floor and slide in and out of pockets, not finding a single coin. I'm about to give up when I come across something in a pocket of Jeremy's coveralls from work earlier this week.

The all too familiar fear races up my spine. My body freezes in place, ears pricking for any sounds around me, my breath quickening. I'm on edge and ready to run far away from whatever is in this pocket.

Alongside the fear, a nostalgia-like recognition of this small space between before and after takes hold. Unlike the past, this time I have a little more control, a choice. I can put the coveralls down. I haven't found anything. I don't know anything yet. I can just as easily not know.

I sit back on my heels and consider the choice in front of me, sorting through fear and anger and exhaustion.

What do I want to do? What do I want to know? I can still set the coveralls down and walk away or take control of my life and deal with whatever is happening in this pocket. This is my life. MY life. Not Jeremy's. Not my brother's. Not my parents', but my life.

It's a choice to know *but not* know. *Just like my sister when her husband's home late, and she can smell another woman on him. His excuses don't quite add up, and he's quick to dismiss her concerns. But it's easier for both if she decides to believe him. See? You can* know *and not* know *all at the same time.*

So, yes, I know but I don't know. My feet start to fall asleep and my legs cramp as I squat down on my heels, holding the coveralls. As soon as I move, the choice will be made. Know or not know?

All this circular thinking won't stop whatever is going to happen next. I can't bury the future under denial and rage from the past. I'm tired of choosing to be scared and angry. I've been trying to leave for months, and this may be the reason to go.

My hand slides into the coverall pocket, letting the last few seconds of knowing but not knowing *slide through my consciousness like water. I swear the air pressure in the room changes as I slip my hand into the pocket, and my fingers touch the syringe.*

Pop.

The pressure releases, and the room starts to spin as I close my hand around the syringe and pull it out of Jeremy's pocket. The ugly, sad truth of his addiction sits in my hand. The dirty needle of the syringe bursting my bubble of denial.

Pop.

If Jeremy is using—or, I guess, since *Jeremy is using—my money is as good as gone.*

Money doesn't buy happiness, but it sure as hell buys options… and heroin. And I'm out of options, and Jeremy is shot up on heroin.

CHAPTER TWENTY

Caden gently but firmly shakes my shoulder and whispers the sweet words all moms want to hear in the middle of the night: "Wake up. Jillian's awake and hungry."

Watching me with wary eyes, he passes over our fussing baby. "Are you okay?" Concern softens his sleep-rough voice as I use my miraculous octopus-arm skills to shift pillows, hold Jillian, unhook my nursing tank, and latch her on all in the soft glow of the phone screen telling me it's 2:12 a.m. My feet are asleep and my calves ache, just like in the dream.

"Sure, babe, why wouldn't I be?"

I massage my calf with my free hand and watch his cautious expression relax with the lie. Jillian's been sleeping in longer stretches, and my milk flow is a little heavier than usual. But baby girl is happily gulping down her mama milk as fast as I let down. I scramble to find a diaper cloth but settle for a tank top from the dirty clothes pile next to the bed—does it count as a pile if the clothes are technically everywhere in the room?—to catch the extra milk flowing from my other breast. Something else I'd love to have known about prior to having a baby: breastmilk can flow from both breasts instead of neatly *only* out of the nipple in use.

"You don't have to pretend, Mags. You kept saying 'no, don't know. No, don't know,' in your sleep. You repeated it a few times. And earlier, you gasped so loudly you woke me up. I assumed you were awake reading one of those fairy smut books and was going to tell you to go to sleep but you already were. I didn't want to wake you up, but you seemed kinda... unsettled. And then J woke up."

With a long sigh, I stare at him for a solid minute, not breaking eye contact, as the new dream floods back to me.

Well, fuck.

And he's right—I don't have to pretend. Not with him. Not right now.

"It's that dream again, isn't it?" he says quietly, looking anywhere but at me in the dark bedroom.

"It's... it's a dream but not *that* dream," I explain.

He rolls toward me, leaning on his elbow and plays with Jillian's toes as she nurses.

"I thought you were making progress with your therapist? Things have seemed better lately. At least better to me."

"Therapy did help. It is helping. I haven't dreamt about the girl in the bar in a while." I conveniently leave out the flashbacks, but I'm technically not lying. "This wasn't the same dream. There's a woman searching for stolen money. This man shoots himself in the mouth," I trail off.

Heavy silence settles around us.

He takes a big breath, and I immediately know what's coming next. The argument that has existed in the air between us for the last few weeks, ignored because we got heated last time. Too heated.

I move my hand off Jillian's back and put it in the air between us like a stop sign. "No, I'm not having this conversation now. I'm not going to stop breastfeeding Jillian because I'm having weird dreams."

"Weird dreams" may be the understatement of the year.

"You said so yourself that the pregnancy hormones gave you psychedelic dreams. Maybe letting your hormones go back to normal without breastfeeding will help. Maybe you'll stop acting crazy."

The tension in the room rachets up. There it is. That word.

Caden holds his hands up in front of him, as if trying to pull back that word.

Crazy.

"Sorry, Mags, that was too far. But, seriously, how can I help you stop obsessing about the dreams?"

"I'm not going to stop breastfeeding because I'm having bad dreams," I repeat. "Yes, I'm exhausted and stressed and all of that might be contributing to these dreams. I get it. You're worried. It seems like a fix." He tries to interrupt, but I roll on, "These dreams are slowly taking over my life. You're right. I do need to pull back from them. Need to cut off the grip these emotions have on me."

He nods briefly, but his next words promise that this conversation isn't over.

"Mags, it feels like you're coming apart at the seams, about to explode sometimes. You're an amazing mom. You worked so hard to be a good mom. Life would be so much easier for you if you could shake off the hold these dreams have on you."

"I'll take the day off tomorrow and rest while she's at daycare. Relax. Sleep." I mentally roll my eyes at these "self-care" activities while simultaneously wondering how my boss will deal with my "sick" day. What I need is a revolution around nurturing mothers, a sisterhood, a village, and, at the least, excellent government-funded daycare—not to hold the Warrior II pose while trying to focus on my breath but trying not to pee my pants.

"Okay, but I'm not the bad guy here. I'm worried about you." He takes Jillian to burp her and change her diaper like he used to when he was on parental leave.

"I know, babe, I love you." I settle back down in my blankets *knowing* but *not knowing* that the dream was far from over. This dream was about to get much worse as I fell into a fitful sleep with the promise of a day alone ahead.

The familiar hand tightens around mine and pulls, guiding me right back to the filthy apartment I just escaped…

CHAPTER TWENTY-ONE

I stand behind a woman staring at an apartment door, squeezing keys tightly. Her hand shakes as she holds them in front of the lock, frozen in the hallway. My eyes water from the stench of body odor and urine.

She turns around suddenly, and I jump out of her way, pushing into a neighbor's doorframe, while she walks to the phone in the hallway, dialing quickly and turning as she faces away from me, her wary eyes watching the apartment door and stairwell. I smile and give a small wave, unsure of what I'm doing here, but wanting her to know I'm not a threat. The hand in mine squeezes gently, as if reassuring me I'm okay in this dimly lit, peeling wood-paneled hallway.

She glances my way again, and I turn around to give her privacy as she urgently whispers, "Jeremy should be at work, but what if he's not? I should have waited for you to come, too." Fingers drumming on the phone base, she pauses, listening. "I just have such a bad feeling right now. Something's going to go wrong." She nods as if deciding, "Okay, yes, you're right. I'm going to run in, get my shit, and call you back in five minutes. If I don't, call the police." She quickly hangs up and strides purposefully to the door.

"Are you okay?" I ask as she shoves the key into the lock hard enough to make it jam for a second.

Ignoring me, she takes a big breath, turns the key, and pushes the door open.

We both freeze as she steps in the room, my nervous system and all my instincts screaming "Danger! Danger! Danger!"

She leaves the door open. I follow her when the hand in mine squeezes and pulls me forward.

The apartment is a dump. Trash heaped in corners of the room, dirty clothes in piles everywhere (well, that's a lot like my bedroom, to be fair). She holds her hand in front of her nose to avoid the smell. I get the impression she's saying goodbye as she sighs deeply, tears rolling down her cheeks. Pulling grocery sacks out of her purse, she heads to what I would guess is the bedroom given that it's a tiny apartment and the bathroom door is open next to me.

Time is moving in a weird way. I'm not sure if we've been in the apartment for five minutes or five hours. She pushes open the bedroom door and freezes. I do too. A scream sticks in my throat as the shock from finding someone in the apartment rips through me. She seems equally shocked but hides it better than me.

"Hey, maybe we should go," I whisper to her, even though I know he can hear me too. We're close enough together in this shithole of a room that we could hold hands.

They both ignore me as their eyes lock. He doesn't look surprised to see us, well, her, and is ignoring me completely. Or maybe he's too high to be surprised if the glossy look to his blown-out pupils means anything.

"Jeremy… what are you doing here?" she says softly, her tone achingly sad.

Jeremy's sitting on the edge of the bed, arms resting on his knees, like he's been waiting for her.

He slowly stands up. "Baby, why wasn't I enough? Why are you running away from me? From our life together? We could have had it all. This was our dream."

He gestures around the room with his hands, and I almost don't see it for a second, the flash of the gun in his hand.

"We need to get out of here. Now!" I shout at her, but she seems frozen in place, my pleas doing nothing to get her moving. Fear and indecision making her a statue.

I try to leave the room, but that hand, that damn hand, grips tightly and won't move. Now I'm stuck as well, witnessing whatever is to come. I wonder how many more minutes until whoever she was on the phone with calls the police. It has to have been five minutes, hasn't it?

"J-Jeremy?"

He takes a step closer to her, to us, and she takes a slow step backward, back into the living room, one step closer to the front door that I left open.

"Don't go, baby. Don't run away from me again."

"What are you doing?" She sounds sad and scared.

"What were you doing with all that money, baby? I found all that cash in the closet. I used it to buy this," he said as he holds up the gun and waves it in the air. Thank God he's pointing it at the ground and not at us. "I was gonna keep us safe."

"Safe? From what? The only thing that is making us not safe is you, Jeremy. Heroin, seriously? Life was hard before that shit, Jer, but we could have been okay. But not now. Not with this."

He angrily waves the gun around again, stabbing toward the ground with the barrel to end each sentence.

"I know. I fucked up. Again. And again and again and again. It's all I ever do. I take something great, like us, and fuck it up." Using the gun, he gestures back and forth between us as he talks. Sweat starts to pool under my arms and slides down my chest.

I watch her lick her lips as she begins to speak but he cuts her off. "I'm done being a fuck up, baby. I wanted to love you enough to save you. To save me. For us to make it."

Jeremy's emotions are rapidly shifting across his face, his voice sounding more and more unstable with each word. "But we never had a fucking chance, did we? You're tough, baby. You're going to survive. I was never going to come out of this life okay. I tried. At least I hope I did. Maybe I gave up a long time ago and hoped you would carry me along with you out of this shithole. But you left me. You left me, God dammit. You broke my heart."

Tears run down his face as he mournfully looks at this woman he's accusing of breaking his heart, not realizing he has already broken hers. He's saying goodbye. Maybe he's going to let her, us, walk out of here without using his gun on her.

I slowly back up as he and the woman stare at each other with sad eyes. She starts to speak again, "I'll always love you, Jeremy, but we can't—"

WHAT THE FUCK.

One second, the woman is speaking, and the next, Jeremy's head is splattered on the wall behind him. But his body is still right here, crumpling onto the floor. He lifted the gun to his mouth and instantly pulled the trigger. Neither of us have

time to react, to scream "Stop!" before the noise of the gunshot and smells of
gunpowder and blood fill the room.

I reach out to grab the woman and pull her back, to protect her, but my arms
move right through her, and I stumble back in my shock. Right. It's a dream.
This is just a dream. Ears ringing, I watch as his body collapses onto the
floor. Heat burns through me as I try to remember to breathe, blood pooling on the
floor around Jeremy. Bright red splatters of blood stain the wall behind him,
sliding down the poster of Janis Joplin.

I'm frozen in shock. Like if I don't move, none of this will have happened.
But it has happened, and five minutes must have finally passed because the police
burst into the apartment yelling questions about a gunshot. Whoever she called
must have made good on their promise to call the police.

As if the enormity of the situation has finally broken through to this woman,
she suddenly starts screaming and sobbing, turning to run into the hallway and
away from the bleeding-out body of her husband on the ground.

Huge, guttural wails spill from her soul as she leans against the wall for
support. I move to stand by her, pulled by the invisible hand guiding me through
this dream. As she slides down the wall to the floor, I do the same, slowly
collapsing under the weight of what has transpired in front of me in this dream,
tears streaming down my face.

A few apartment doors open and people peek their heads out, but this isn't the
type of building where neighbors ask questions. Too transient. Too many eviction
notices pinned to doors. Too much fear. The doors close just as quickly as they
open once they see the police, locks sliding back into place.

I sit next to the sobbing woman outside the open apartment door for what
feels like hours. I guess it's not like I could leave if I wanted to since I'm
technically still asleep and dreaming. An arm that I can't see wraps around my
shoulders and squeezes and a feeling of warmth and rest bubbles around me, as
if the spirit wants to provide a sense of comfort in this hell. Police officers ask
lots of questions, search the apartment, and eventually take Jeremy's body, and
his gun, away.

"Where are you taking him?"

"City morgue. You can come down and say goodbye if you want. That's
where the funeral home will need to pick up the body."

"Who's gonna call his mom?" she asks.

Looking at her like she's the one on drugs, he slowly says, "Aren't you his wife, ma'am? Usually, you would be the person to make those calls."

She stares blankly at him for a few seconds too long and nods.

"Oh, and we can save you the trouble of making a trip downtown. Let's go ahead and swab your fingers while you're here. The detective over there will have a few questions for you to make sure there's no foul play but this looks like a suicide."

She nods again and holds her hands out while the officer swabs them for gunpowder and peppers her with questions that she answers in as few words as possible.

How did they meet? High School. When did they get married? Not even a year ago. Where did he work? He didn't. Not regularly, he picked up labor jobs when he was sober. How often did he drink or use drugs? Daily? Was he often depressed? Yes. Had he ever tried to commit suicide before? No?

Her answers get softer and shorter with each response, starting to end in questions as if she can't trust her own memories. Not sure who she was married to or how she ended up in this hallway with her dead husband being carried down flights of stairs.

Was he connected to his family? Mentally stable? Angry you left him? How did you end up here today? Was he dead or alive when you walked in? Did you know about the gun? The drugs? The depression? The intent to shoot himself? Did you know?

Did she know?

"Did you know what you were walking into today?"

My hand is squeezed and held tight as the woman takes a long inhale, and all in one breath answers the officer's final question.

"When I walked into the room, I didn't know who the gun was for—me or him. I don't think he knew who the gun was for either. I don't know why he shot himself instead of me. When did he even get a gun? He stole money from me to buy it. And the heroin. He started using at some point and that's why I finally had to leave last week. He had a... a needle in his pocket and I knew. It was the beginning of the end. But that was a week ago. I didn't know the end would come so soon."

As she finishes, the hallway starts to waver and fade along with the voices of the police officers around us. My time is up here. Whatever I was supposed to see is over.

The grip of the hand holding mine loosens and a kiss presses into my hair.

CHAPTER TWENTY-TWO

I wake with tears pooling in my eyes, my heart breaking in my sleep in my own dark, cool room with soft sheets on my clean bed, floor littered with the debris of a baby and working parents—diapers, suit jackets, a pair of heels. Cluttered in a full of life way rather than despair. Soft waves from the sound machine lulling everyone but me into a deep slumber. I watch the curtains flutter in the breeze as I'm instantly and thankfully transported from a squalid, stale apartment back to my real life.

"Well, shit," I whisper urgently, breathing as slowly and deeply as I can into my belly, trying to regulate my shaky breaths, not wanting to wake Jillian.

Should I wake up Caden or let him sleep?

I wrestle with craving his support and knowing one of us needs more than a few hours of rest.

My side of the bed is wet with sweat and tears. I swear I can smell blood but that must be impossible. There's no way I'm going back to sleep anytime soon. My heart is beating too fast from the adrenaline of the dream, the heaviness of this overwhelming sadness sitting on my chest, weighing down each breath.

I'm sad for me, for the confusion and fear alive in me right now, and for this woman who watched her husband kill himself. For the girl in the first dream. These stories are devastating to me, and it's not my life. Or at least not this version of my life.

Who could live through something this sad, tragic, and be okay?

The desperate urgency to feel clean pushes me out of bed, to shower. The sticky feeling of dried sweat and blood clings to my body, to my cheeks and shoulder where blood sprayed on me in the dream but refuses to appear in the mirror.

I never quite make it back to sleep. I keep getting sucked into an anxiety spiral of *how does this end?* while I wait for Jillian to wake up for breakfast. Remembering how quiet Alma was last night, I send her a text, "Hope all is good over there! Seems like you and Eric are keeping each other busy." I'm hoping the stream of kissy face and heart emojis following my words lets her know I'm teasing.

I rally by blowing out my hair, but gasp and drop the blow dryer in the sink when I glance in the mirror and see my mom looking back at me. Blinking, frozen in shock, the image blurs back to my exhausted, puffy eyes that no amount of makeup will make look perky. I look like I was crying all night, and I guess I was.

I shove the hallucination down into that pocket of my gut where all these dreams live, all the signs I'm not okay stay hidden. I focus on how I'm going to respond to the well-meaning but slightly condescending ask of "Are you okay? You look tired," from my colleagues.

I need a solid answer because I can't snap back, "Of course I'm tired! On top of having a baby, I'm being sucked into my dreams and maybe slowly losing it." I timidly glance in the mirror one more time, relieved I only see myself looking back. No mom in sight.

I ignore Caden's pointed look at my work bag on the counter, all promises of a self-care day broken because I forgot about the grant proposal due today. "Next week, babe, I promise."

On the way to work, it happens again. I catch a glimpse of myself in the rearview mirror and swear it could be my mom.

"Okay," I tell myself. "This is okay. You're tired. It's a weird trick of light. Your brain is exhausted, and your hair does look a lot like hers."

I end up throwing my hair in a ponytail—so much for that blowout—before I walk into the office because I can't handle catching another glimpse of my mom's soft green eyes and swishy brown waves again.

I'm not hallucinating. I'm exhausted, not crazy.

"I'M EXHAUSTED, NOT CRAZY" is the mantra I silently repeat during meetings, while I respond to emails, and on my frequent trips to the office coffee pot. I even write repeatedly in a notebook to the beat of the pump during my afternoon break before Alma pops in to hang out for a few minutes.

"How you doing, Mags?" she asks as she settles in next to me at the table.

I look over at her and deadpan, "Just peachy" with a sarcastic thumbs up.

"Listen, Amanda was a dick at lunch and everyone knows it. She's just jealous and catty. Jack, who is not known for being Mr. Empathetic, even called her out on it after you left."

"Alma, she looked me right in the eye in front of a room of colleagues and straight up said, 'Do you feel like you're throwing your PhD away since you became a mom, Maggie? You're just not so... on it... since Jillian was born.'"

Alma winces at hearing Amanda's comment repeated. "Yeah, like I said, it was a dick move."

Tears well in my eyes as I look at Alma, the real reason for my shame over the comment spilling out of my throat in a rough whisper. "What if she's right, Alma?"

Amanda has no idea she jabbed a knife and twisted in my most vulnerable wound since giving birth.

What if all I am now is a mom?

"Oh, Maggie, you know she's wrong. We all know. And she just let everyone know how intimidated she is by you by insulting you like that. It's almost as bad as when she met Caden and her tongue practically fell out of her mouth and she asked how you managed to snag a man like that."

Remembering that encounter makes me laugh just as Alma intended and breaks the tension. Alma starts to tell me about her latest brilliant inspiration when a police car, lights flashing and sirens on full blast, flies by our office. I'm instantly hit with a flashback to that first dream and jerk suddenly in my chair, surprising Alma, who accidentally knocks over a freshly pumped bottle of milk. I immediately start crying while Alma jumps up to grab the roll of paper towels.

"Don't worry, Maggie, no use in crying over spilled milk."

I *know* she means it playfully, but her flippancy enrages me, and I lash out, my emotions still dysregulated and barely tempered after the embarrassing lunchtime incident.

"Don't even, Alma. You don't fucking get it. I'm getting sucked dry to make this milk and now it's wasted. Fucking gone."

"You have a freezer stash at home, Maggie!"

"That's not the point, Alma. That's not the fucking point."

I grab the wet paper towels from her and heave them into the trash can after wiping up the last few drops, willing something, anything, to make me feel better. She slips her hand into mine to comfort me, but she has no idea how triggering it is after all that has been happening with these dreams. How could she? I'm a locked chest of secrets, and the pressure is making me want to explode, pounding inside of me, building up each second that goes by, and I'm not okay.

And then, suddenly, the pressure is too much, her comfort overwhelming me. I finally explode. At exactly the wrong person. Alma.

"Stop. STOP. You can't joke or hug your way out of this. You can't understand how much *pressure* I'm under every second of the day to be okay. To not fuck up. To prove myself. To not feel like I'm losing my mind."

Alma lets go of my hand and takes a big step backward, grabbing her bag with one hand and the door handle with the other. I unconsciously reach out for her hand, recognizing with horror my mistake, fresh, sharp tears forming at the loss of her hand in mine. Her resigned, angry eyes feel worse than the waves of grief from my D-MER letdowns.

"No, Maggie, I don't understand, but I know you're not losing your mind. I'm going to give you some space before you say something we both regret right now. You haven't seemed like yourself lately. I'm getting worried about you."

Alma's parting words almost split open the raw, aching wound deep inside of me where I've been pushing the hard, unsolvable pain, cutting too close to where my sadness hides. A place I can't go, can't feel, because I don't know how I will ever come back again. How to move on once the fear and grief tumble out in waves, drowning me.

She closes the door behind her, leaving me with one less bottle of milk, a messy argument to clean up, and my nursing bra hanging open.

My head drops to my chest, and fresh tears fall in the spilled milk.

SITTING in the rainy traffic on my way to pick up Jillian after work, I call Caden to let him know I'm running late.

"Don't worry, babe. Dinner's ready. See you when you get here."

We end the call quickly, and the news comes on. My eyes get heavy and droopy with each whish of the windshield wiper, the newscaster's voice creating a soft droning in the background. The warmth of the car is my undoing, and I start to nod off.

I jerk my eyes open quickly and rub them, cracking the windows to let the fresh air wake me up and switching the news to Brandi Carlile on blast. I try to sing along to stay awake, but it's not enough to drown out the sirens as multiple police cars and ambulances fly by me on the side of the highway. I freeze, once again stunned by the flashing lights against brick walls, gleaming off a puddle of blood. A hard gust of wind blows through the window, shocking me back to reality. I slam on my brakes to avoid hitting the car in front of me.

My hands and teeth shake hard, and I struggle to put my blinker on and maneuver to the side of the road. The horror of my actions —or reactions—almost causing an accident on the highway because of my freefall into a flashback sits in the bottom of my stomach. I was consumed by the memory of Craig's head being bashed in by a brick. The blood. The lights. The sirens.

What if Jillian had been in the car with me? What if I forgot to fully secure her car seat, or if a latch was loose? What if the airbags deployed and hurt her? Or a car slammed into *us* from behind?

Scenario after scenario of how that flashback could have caused a tragedy flip through my imagination, sending me to the verge of a panic attack.

What if that happens again? What if I hurt someone because I can't control these memories?

I breathe slowly, grounding myself with each of my senses and fighting off the extreme need to panic building under my chest.

Why am I having flashbacks?! It was a *dream*. Okay, one I've dreamt at least a dozen times. That I was somehow guided to by… what? A spirit? A ghost? An invisible hand? Each one sounds more implausible, impossible, than the last.

It is why I startled and scared Alma earlier and why I froze at lunch the other day with Caden. "Break Another Piece of My Heart" came on as he got up to get us more coffee, and I simply froze. My heart pounded in my chest, whooshing in my ears, as cold fear raced through my veins followed by the hot shame of knowing I was deeply fucking up in my current reality, all while trapped in a flashback to a *dream*.

The flashbacks, bad dreams, and momentary lapses in connection with the present moment have all become my little secrets. Caden doesn't know how little sleep I get between nursing Jillian and relentlessly being pulled into dreams. I came close to telling him when we were at lunch, but he looks at ease now that I'm supposed to be better. Adrenaline and caffeine are my unsustainable life source, and my body can't keep up with this crushing pressure inside of me.

Just when I'm getting better, when I think the dreams are gone, I wake up sweating and gasping for air, pulled back into the chaos of my mind and out of a dream.

As I park in the daycare parking lot, I realize that Janis Joplin is in both dreams. Odd. Head down as I type this revelation into my Notes app, I hurry into daycare, running late. Again.

I WAKE CRYING, the sound of my tears blending with Jillian's own wails. Both of us comforted by the ritual of nursing, I hold her close and dry my eyes with her swaddle blanket. It's getting harder and harder to avoid being pulled into a grief that is not my own. The tragedies in these dreams are woven into me on a soul level, and I can feel the hopelessness in my bones.

Alma has noticed that I seem "off," as she put it. I apologized for my overreaction and surprised her with a little treat from our favorite bakery near the office, but she seems to think I'm still mad at her—that this is why I'm "off"—why I always say no to her invites out. She even gets pouty about not being able to use the baby carrier again. I tried to tell her that it's not her, it's just that I'm drowning. Drowning in needs and obligations and milk. She rolled her eyes a little and let out a big sigh. She doesn't say it, but she's over me complaining. Her invites out have slowed way down, and she's spending a lot of time with Eric.

Good for her. I think.

Knowing I owe her a little bit of efforting, I text her the new seasonal ice cream flavors that dropped overnight from our favorite shop. Maybe I will even open up and tell her about the flashbacks, the hand pulling me into dreams that keeps me entwined with these tragedies.

ME

See you at lunch? My treat <3.

ALMA

You can absolutely buy my love with ice cream. I'm in.

My smile is huge and reassuring. I haven't pushed her far enough away that she won't let me bribe her with ice cream.

A second text pops up, causing a giggle that accidentally wakes Jillian enough for her to open one eye and glare. "Sorry, baby girl," I whisper and kiss her forehead. Now, it's time for me to go back to sleep so I don't whine about it all day tomorrow, per Alma's orders.

I LEARNED EARLY in my career that my health and wellness are not important in this capitalist, patriarchal society. I've been implicitly and explicitly trained to know it's better I show up to work and pretend to be fine than use a sick day. So, I'll play my part and show up to work. Break my promise to Caden about that self-care day. Look exhausted. Push my mouse around, respond to emails, and smile at Amanda. Trade dry shampoo and lactation cookie recipes with the other new moms. And always smile.

When women stop smiling, the questions and whispers start. If I can stay pretty and smiling, *and* laugh at the dumbass jokes of my male colleagues and let the sexist comments about other women roll off my back—women getting heavier or looking tired or being bitchy. It's always the judgment you know is spewed out to create the boundaries and expectations and limitations you must perform to, meet, and accept to be "okay" and "safe." To be left alone and overlooked. So, I smile, and I fake-laugh at their dumb jokes, and then I put my headphones in and do my job enough to be overlooked as competent and pretty and smiling and agreeable.

I can't wait to call them on their bullshit as soon as I get a good night's sleep.

My fake smile slips when I round the corner to the reception desk at work to meet Alma for ice cream and overhear my name in the break room. I pause outside the door and listen, even though I remember Alma's sage wisdom shared over margaritas during my first week back from work after maternity leave. "Other people's opinions of you are none of your business, Maggie. Of course you have haters. You're like this uber productive woman with a PhD. You out-hustle them, and they hate it."

I winked and responded, "That's Dr. Uber Productive Woman to you, Alma," which then became my nickname. Until suddenly that wasn't true anymore. I was struggling to hit the productive benchmark now, let alone uber productive.

And that's the topic of conversation in the break room that I'm accidentally eavesdropping on.

"She just looks so, like, unhappy and sloppy now. And just rushing everywhere."

Someone else chimes in, "She doesn't even try to make it to happy hour anymore."

A male voice says, "Okay, but can I have three breaks a day to go sit in a room by myself? That'd be the shit."

And then, like the hero she is, I hear Alma pipe up.

"Relax! Yeah, she's tired. She's got a baby at home and her husband is almost always gone." Alma talks over a male voice. "Yeah, that's not your problem but she's still running laps around you in team meetings, and that *is* your problem." She interrupts the same male voice again and says, "And don't you *dare* even suggest that she could smile more. She's not here to make you feel better about yourself. She's here to do research and she's the best at it."

Alma's last words trail off as she turns to head out the door and bumps into me standing to the side of it, tears shining in my eyes. She links arms with me and spins me to the door. "Let's go, boo. You owe me an ice cream."

Smiling wide, my cheeks hurt while I laugh. "I owe you the whole ice cream shop, Alm. Thanks for having my back."

Pulling me in for a hug, she kisses the side of my head, much like I kiss Jillian's, and whispers, "Always, Mags. Always."

CHAPTER TWENTY-THREE

Giggling with delight, I throw my arms around Caden's neck. He lifts my heeled feet from the ground in a tight hug. A black, pointy heel hangs from my toes as I bend one knee, clinging to him as he kisses me, eyes gleaming and a smile pulling up a corner of his mouth. He surprised me, and he's proud of it. My favorite dinner is laid across the table for an impromptu date night at home. Caesar salad, French fries, and prosecco.

So basic. So delicious.

Spinning me, he places my feet back on the ground with another kiss.

"Alma texted and said you had a rough day at work. Something about 'whiny boys' and you deserving a celebration dinner for not losing it today. I was thinking your favorite dinner was the least I can do. I'll even bring it to you in bed if you want."

I break out my cackle at the way Alma not-so-subtly influenced Caden to spoil me after today's hellfire.

Bending to pick up the evidence of my mind's chaos that went flying out of my tote during Caden's spin, I'm grabbing my journal when a hand playfully smacks my butt, causing the journal to fall back to the ground, almost in slow motion. I scramble to grab it before it falls open, knowing the drawings and words spilled across the pages will ruin the playful vibe Caden carefully curated tonight. I snatch the journal, grabbing at slips of paper blowing away from my fingers in one of those strange breezes.

We really need to have this checked out.

But the thought flies away as I slam the journal closed just as Jillian ensures we haven't forgotten her with a wail that startles us both out of our flirty trance.

Fight averted.

Caden has been trying hard to be supportive, and Alma went out of her way to make sure I'm cared for tonight. He and I both need a light-hearted, sexy night to connect, not to mull over my latest theory that the women in the dream are actually one and the same.

He knows I journal about the dreams, outline my theories, search for answers. I've added a layer of academic rigor to my analysis to find something, any tiny detail that will unravel the hold these dreams have on me, on our lives.

Stories that feel like memories pour onto the pages of my notebook, creating a world in which these women from my dreams are becoming real to me. At some point in my writing, I combined the two women in the dreams into one. I don't know if they're the same person, but it felt true at 3:00 a.m. one sleepless but dreamful night, and I rolled with it.

After writing about this woman for months, she seems so familiar. Waves of nostalgia and longing for her hit me when I'm reminded of her during the day. When I journal now, words pour from me onto the tiny screen of my phone, from my hands as I write with pens—on my laptop, with random markers on old meeting agendas I find in the room where I pump.

This woman's stories want to be told, to be freed, and they flee from the tips of my fingers to the screen. Words flow through me in the same way milk falls from my breasts and into my daughter's hungry mouth. My daughter is blossoming and growing and thriving from milk from my body, and my creativity is thriving from these torturous dreams taking over my nights. But I'm not convinced about my sanity.

Over dinner and a glass of bubbly, I feel more like myself than I have in weeks, and Caden's here for it. We joke and debate and flirt, the vibe in our home feeling much more like we hoped for, dreamed of, when we became parents.

Caden puts Jillian in her bassinet and carries me upstairs to do the same. He sets me on my feet, and I jokingly push him into bed, his brows raising as if to question my hurried motions. Giggling, I climb onto the bed and fall into his waiting arms, sinking into the playful connection and looking forward to more.

Later, when Caden's satiated smile glows through the film of exhaustion coating my eyes, this moment feels simple, easy, happy.

PART II

CHAPTER TWENTY-FOUR

And then, suddenly, I'm not happy. Days turn into weeks of survival mode, barely getting by. I'm not okay. Real life is getting harder and harder. I want to flee to my quiet space to write and create and fall into these stories I'm telling. To get these stories out of my body. I long for the spirit from my dreams to come back. To grab my hand and pull me through to her world again.

My desperation to go back is overwhelming. I'm drawn to the spirit's presence, her safety. She's a light in the dark I'm constantly drawn to in the chaos of my mind, and even if I'm not safe, I'm connected to her.

If I can't be in the dreams, can't call this woman back to me, then I've chosen to obsess over the dreams, writing each one out as I remember it, buoyed by snippets of memories collected from random slips of paper found in the diaper bag, on the kitchen countertop, and around my workstation along with the notes from my phone and journal. Reading the dreams in their entirety helps details stand out, immerses me back in this other world, other lifetime. To try and figure out why it feels so familiar, why I'm so drawn back to that alley, that bedroom, over and over.

To see where I fit in.

My rarely used home office now looks like I'm the main character in *A Beautiful Mind*, much like when I'm deep in a new work project. Once, Alma jokingly tossed me a ball of yarn to track my thought process across the sticky notes spread about the conference table. She brought the ball of yarn in simply to mess with me and was beside herself when she finally got the chance.

Now I'm using that yarn to organize the memories, flashbacks, and theories that I've collected from the backs of receipts, bar napkins, bits of paper torn off meeting agendas, all waiting to be turned into organized chaos with this string.

Alma would be so proud. Andddd maybe a little nervous.

Through it all, I smile. I smile and lie. Deflect. Compliment. Ask questions.

It's enough for now. Enough to avoid too many questions after the sidelong glances and "Just seeing how you're doing" texts. Enough for Caden. For my boss and my coworkers. For me. And for Jillian. She doesn't have to see the shell I'm turning into each day while I try to survive this pull to be away. To be asleep. I'm not sure if my writing is madness or inspiration. Dangerous or glorious. Maybe all of it is true. The ultimate both/and.

But I show up for Jillian with love, tenderness, and milk in my few waking hours with her. Just like I promised myself, my unborn child, at the fire ceremony. I would always mother her, love her, beyond all else. I don't want her to feel like I often did with my mom, like she was present but not there, even when she was right next to me. Jillian deserves to know, to feel in her bones, that she's seen and loved.

"You're doing it again, babe. You're drifting away."

Sighing, I continue washing pump parts, wrapping up the tasks of the day so we can have time to connect before he leaves again tomorrow.

"Maggie, you don't have to do it all. You've got to stop this Wonder Woman routine. It's killing you. Especially if you won't, if you can't, let go of these dreams."

He gently wraps his fingers around my wrists, soapy hands and all, pulling me toward his chest and wrapping me in a tight, warm embrace.

"You are so smart and determined, babe. But maybe there's no answer to be found, no puzzle to be solved, with these dreams. Putting so much weight on a hidden message, on this mystery dream woman, is causing too much pain in our lives."

Leaning into his chest, I breathe with him, co-regulating with his steady, calm heartbeat.

"Everyone else seems to be able to do it all."

Everyone else seems to be able to stay sane too. Why can't I?

"You're not just doing it all, Mags, you're lost in an obsession. You don't have to get through this alone, babe. You're an amazing mom, but I'm losing you little by little, day by day, to this… compulsion. I miss you."

I miss me too.

But when I'm sitting at my desk later, listening to Janis in my earbuds and sending emails like I'm supposed to, I'm wondering if I'm already a little bit crazy. The dreams won't go away. The compulsion to write won't stop. These words need to exist as much as my lungs need oxygen.

The pressure mounting inside my brain from all these words is explosive. Sometimes the words appear in small drips, as if they're simply leaking out and can't be held in anymore. Like when I wait too long to pump, and the drips of milk from my nipples bead onto my nursing pads while listening to the same people share the same ideas for the same problems at work.

But I stay in my seat, knowing the rolled eyes and whispered snark will fly if I leave a meeting early to pump. And just like my milk, I can't keep these words in. Scribbled notes crowd my meeting agendas, pop up as reminders in my calendar, and flow while I type emails, zoning in and out of reality. I caught myself before I sent a colleague an email that contained a full paragraph about the woman being cornered by her dead husband's dealer at work. He wanted her to settle his debt to him for his last few deadly hits of heroin. What if I'd sent that? How could I explain it?

And even more than trying to explain, I was desperate to go home and add this new detail to my wall, to connect the string to where this thread fit in the expanding web being woven around my sanity.

Have I lost my mind enough that now I believe this is okay, or am I connected to myself enough to know I'm still okay? That I haven't crossed that line?

This might be as close as I can get to experiencing what an addict might feel. Drinking or drugging to be okay enough to function in their day-to-day life, but knowing they're not truly well or rational when they're drinking and drugging. Stuck right in the middle of lucidity and madness.

Stuck in the in-between of reality and dreams.

So I let go of trying to convince myself this isn't happening. That it will end. *That I want it to end.* I don't want to give up the high these dreams are giving me. I crave this connection with the women in my dreams if only to fuel the burning of their stories in words and sentences and paragraphs all over my mind, work, computer, phone, and house. I'm addicted to them. A hyperfocus that has given me tunnel vision.

I can't pull myself away from these dreams and have simply stopped trying.

I constantly jot down notes about grief, gunshots, lost dreams, and finding hope, searching for the thread that must be woven through it all. Some connecting point from beginning to end that will make all of this make sense once I simply uncover it.

And it must exist, because if it doesn't, then I may just be losing my mind.

Caden has stopped asking questions after our conversation at the sink. He has seen me go through this type of deep obsession before, looking for answers, facts, strategies to pull seemingly impossible solutions out of thin air.

It's how I became Dr. Maggie after all.

My doctoral research looked a little like madness too. Handwritten notes spread across the large windows of my office-turned-Jillian's nursery. Research articles strewn in piles. Index cards taped to the wall, outlining my dissertation.

But this time feels different. My worry that hiding each new detail means I know I'm obsessed. Addicted to the feeling the words, this woman, brings my heart and nervous system. What looks like chaos to everyone else feels like peace, calm, to me. So I leave my web of analysis uncovered on the wall of my home office for all to see.

A conversation I overheard at an Alcoholics Anonymous coffee hour long ago floats up in my mind. "You know you have a problem when you start to hide things from people you love, who love you."

On some level, I know I'm not okay and don't want to worry Caden and Alma. To prevent their pain, I hide these stories of love, grief, addiction, shame, anger, joy, and family.

I smile and I lie and I dream and I write.

And it is fine. Fine like an "I'm standing in front of a dumpster on fire" fine. Fine like getting pregnant and having a baby in the middle of a pandemic fine, but fine nonetheless. And is fine better than standing in front of a dumpster on fire? Fine seems to imply that mediocrity is okay, preferred, safe. For the first time in a long time, I'm more than fine.

I'm free.

I'm connected to the deep fire of womanhood in my bones, like when I was pregnant with Jillian.

I'm more than fine. I'm soaring on the wings of women before me, feeling the wind under me and the fires of resiliency, determination, and survival as these words pour from me.

And I'm probably fine, but most likely not okay.

CHAPTER TWENTY-FIVE

And then the dreams get worse. I can't hide that I'm not okay anymore. I don't want to hide anymore. I want to leap into the arms of my village, of Caden and Alma, and unravel.

The dreams have started pouring out of me at night. I mumble and moan in my sleep. Softly. Loudly. Tears leak from my closed eyes. Fists and arms fly under the blankets while my mind is in another place. I smell blood and beer and gunpowder while I sleep and wake needing to scrub the dreams, the invisible hands, off my body.

Caden's worried. Whispering on the phone with Alma worried. Reaching out to my therapist worried. Suggesting I take time off work worried.

Caden's a good man trying to find a good compromise. Trying to stop the love of his life from losing herself to postpartum depression, as it is now being called during the whispered phone conversations. On the verge of postpartum psychosis.

One Sunday morning, Alma comes over under the guise of brunch plans but links arms with me after our initial hug and pulls me onto the front porch bench swing of my and Caden's small two-story home.

She starts off ominously, her voice shaky but eyes clear and full of love. "Mags, we need to talk…"

"Oh my god, Alma! Are you holding an *intervention?*" I cry.

"Maggie, this has been going on for months. The dreams aren't going away, are getting worse. Don't you think you should make sure you're okay?"

Caden must have walked outside while I was staring open-mouthed at Alma. He reaches for my hands, and pulls me into his chest. He runs his hands down my arms and circles his thumbs over my tight fists in his palms. "My mom said that it sounds like you might wanna think about if this isn't just depression or anxiety… What if it's that one where you start to make stuff up in your head?"

His unspoken "and hurt the baby" lingers in the air between us.

"I'm fine, Caden." *And I am fine… but I'm also making up stuff in my head.* "Stop telling your mom that I'm going crazy. You're making her nervous. She thinks I'm going to hurt the baby."

Caden's pause says more than his denial that comes a few seconds too late ever could erase. "Babe… She… It's just been a lot but, of course. You aren't going to hurt the baby."

"Oh my god, Caden. You're worried I'm going to hurt Jillian?!" My voice rises dangerously as my eyes narrow, and I push his arms away. "You seriously think I might have postpartum psychosis? What about you, Alma? Is that why you staged this intervention?"

Postpartum psychosis is the scary diagnosis. The one when they start to think you'll hurt your kid—and you just might out of fear and hormones and rage. That's the diagnosis where the world has failed mothers over and over again by not legislating social support networks or universal healthcare, including mental health support. The one where they might want me to spend less time with Jillian "to keep her safe." And then I won't be fine.

I start to think of how thoughtfully, carefully Caden has been acting over the past few days. Of Alma's texts coming in like clockwork to make sure I don't trip up at work again. The gentle, loving way they have each supported me in the past months as I've lost myself to these dreams.

Alma has been just distracted enough with Eric to be placated with reassuring text messages and check-ins at work… until now.

And Caden? Caden doesn't call me crazy. But he slowly and carefully moves around me. Speaks to me in a soft voice, like he doesn't want to startle me.

Caden moves a lot like he was suddenly dropped into a cheetah's zoo enclosure (do we not call them cages anymore??) and came face-to-face with the fierce, black-spotted animal. The zookeepers (handlers? prison guards?) leave and there you are, watching and waiting. Something you felt safe with before, when the bars (sanity?) separated you from the power of the very animal (person) you're now facing (in your living room). The cheetah could lie at rest or swiftly strike out. Most likely, the cheetah will strike from rage and resentment and fear rather than hunger. Because that's what happens when you've been locked in a cage. You lose yourself.

Until the cage is opened, and you're free.

CHAPTER TWENTY-SIX

The intervention works. Alma and Caden convince me to take a day off that turns into a long weekend at an Airbnb to relax and reset. Or to hit the bottom of my deep dive into these dreams so I can finally swim back up to the surface, to the rest of my life that has been waiting in the wings.

Caden wisely suggested stretching the day away to three when his face was still between my legs, kissing up my thigh after my orgasm shook a thousand yesses out of me. Made it easy to give him one more. An easy "yes" to take a few nights off hiding the havoc inside my brain from him. "Yes" to the space to safely let go, and figure out what's going on without work emails and Slack messages and pump breaks interrupting.

Because I don't feel safe to let go, and no one feels safe around me. No one—including myself—understands what is happening. But I still can't sleep through the night because of my baby and insane dreams and a husband who sleeps in the same bed as me in fear of the next wake-up. He won't move to the guest room if I won't let him take Jillian with him. So here we are.

I fill Alma in on the details of my getaway during our next "pump and chat." As I chug water and eat lactation cookies to try to build up a sufficient freezer stash for Caden, Alma gushes over the Airbnb listing he found, pushing over another cookie from the grocery tote bag she carried in with her.

"Maggie! You didn't say it's a *treehouse*. Like a literal house in a tree." She gives a low whistle as she swipes to the hot tub. "Can I come with you? Please? I promise you won't even know I'm there. I'll pack your favorite snacks."

Laughing, I shake my head and throw a cookie wrapper at her. "Alma, no, the whole point of this weekend is for me to be alone and be done with these dreams."

"But I'll bring wine!"

"No, Alm, just no." I giggle.

Pouting, Alma squeezes my hand and pushes my water bottle to me. "I'm glad you're going, Maggie. You haven't been yourself since these dreams started. Maybe you can figure out what this is all about this weekend. It will be good to have you back if you do. I miss you."

My eyes well with tears, and I squeeze her back. "I miss me too, Alm, I miss me too."

"No crying!! Not today! Not yet at least. I need to talk to you about something."

I still, sensing that Alma is gathering her words carefully when she would typically just vent stream-of-consciousness style to me.

"Last night, when Eric and I were having sex… the condom broke. We didn't realize until afterward. I almost called you, but didn't want to wake you in case you were finally getting some sleep."

I grab ahold of her hand and nod, not wanting to interrupt.

"I stopped at the store and picked up Plan B. I've decided I'm going to take it to try and prevent an accidental pregnancy."

Then Alma picks up the grocery tote bag and spills its contents across the table between us.

Bottles of sparkling water, popcorn, and trashy magazines pile on top of nail polish and lip balm. New pacifiers spill out from the bottom of the bag as she upends it next to my whirring pump.

I lock eyes with her over the pile of distractions between us. The reason for this drugstore stop spilling out of the bottom.

"Oh, Alma. I'm so sorry this is happening. I'm grateful you told me. Are you okay?"

"Yep. Sure, yes. I just wanted to talk to you about it first," she says decisively, nodding just in case I wasn't convinced by her words.

The box of Plan B pills sits in the middle of the table between us.

In lieu of a hug, I squeeze both of Alma's hands across the table. Then I twist open a sparkling water and start to open the box.

"The sooner the better." I pause, pill in hand for her.

Tears immediately well in her eyes as she comes around the table to give me the most loving, awkward hug with my pump bottles between us.

"Wait, Alma, hang on. Let me unhook before you spill it all. I'm just about done anyways." I set the pill down and unhook myself. Pulling her into another hug, she starts to cry, and words tumble out.

"I didn't know how you would feel about this now with Jillian. Like, what if you changed your mind after growing a baby inside of you and now I want to stop one from growing inside me? What if this could be Jillian's best friend?" Alma takes a deep breath and gives me another squeeze.

I hold her close, just like I would want my own mom, my own chosen sister, to do to me.

"No, Alma. My choice is not your choice. You get to make your own. Always. And we both know how hard this has been for me. Dreams or no dreams. I would never wish this type of hard on another woman who wasn't all in for it."

And in true Alma fashion, she hugs me one more time and then lets me go, but not before I press a kiss on her hair. Picking up the pill and energy drink, she faux-cheers me and quickly swallows it down. The relief on her face is clear. She's made the best choice for her.

Suddenly, I'm the one crying. Like her flood of emotion broke the dam holding mine in, and now I'm reaching for her and crying. I can't let the secrets about the dream spill out, but I can pour this truth into her for her to hold lovingly just like she's holding me.

"I'm afraid I'm losing myself, Alma."

"Oh, Maggie, I know, I know." And she does. She needed me to be there for her today like she was there for me in the hospital. No judgment, all love.

Alma has held me time and again. Whenever I've needed a stand-in mom to cry or celebrate with me, Alma has been by my side handing out gold stars and boxes of Kleenex every time. She's been by my side as my body and mind came apart—from woman to mother—and as I try to forge myself back together again.

I'm grateful to have the opportunity to do the same for her today. To not have pushed her away so hard that our friendship can't bounce back.

And this is why I'm desperate to tell Alma how much chaos these dreams are causing in my mind, how much the emotions, the mess, are leaking into my life. She would hold my hand and stand by my side as I pulled myself back together and sorted out my mind.

But now's not the time to expose the extent, the impact of these dreams. Alma needs to focus on herself and needs me to support her.

At least that's what I tell myself as I tighten the hold I have on the words desperate to escape, to ask for help.

If anyone could do it, Alma could help me. Alma would hold me and listen to me talk about how my mind is pulled apart by this crazy dream and then help me put myself back together again. I want to trust Alma, and myself, enough to tell her, but I don't know how.

CHAPTER TWENTY-SEVEN

My body is already abuzz with anticipation of space and solitude. Expansive, luxurious open hours—days!—to reflect, think, ponder. Time to roll down mountains of trauma and into valleys of emotions and memories. To smolder and burn and flare. To feel and heal.

Letting these dreams, these stories, burn will break them down into ash and to be blown away in the soft breeze of my breath on each exhale. Forever defining me but no longer controlling me. Manipulating me into someone I don't recognize, don't want to be.

Mothers need space and time for our thoughts and words and dreams to morph from mineral and bones into gems, making "you'll never be alone again" feel more like a threat than a promise. Creativity doesn't blossom in the micro-pockets of alone time I get between feedings, naps, and snacks. My brain is full of half-formed fossils and stalactites from the slow drip, drip, drip of energy I get to myself.

But whenever I bring up this need, I get shut down. People don't want to know my truest thoughts, my biggest needs; they want to hear what they want to hear. And what they want to hear is that I'm a happy, peaceful, glowing mother who can shoulder all the world throws at me. The impossible dualities constantly thrust upon mothers. A girl boss and trad wife. SAHM but more interesting than "just a mom."

Mothers are constantly making impossible choices to balance these unbearable dualities.

"Yes, of course I can work late tonight and come in early tomorrow."

"Of course I can find last-minute childcare. I can't lose my job."

"Of course I can work a double shift and hope my baby is safe at home with my boyfriend/grandma/sibling because I can't afford to lose my health insurance."

"Of course I sent my sick kid to school and nursed my own illness with over-the-counter meds to stretch my sick days because there are simply never enough."

Of course we continue to weigh impossible risks and benefits and pros and cons and hopes and dreams and fears and finances. Of course. Of course we're fine.

Because capitalism and the patriarchy thrive on women being "fine."

Alma got fired up at our most recent girls' night while listening to me outline the pros and cons of the latest white noise machine that promised to help Jillian sleep for more than a three-hour stretch.

"Maggie, the world is feeding itself on your soul. Capitalism, the patriarchy… all they want are your dreams and brains and wisdom and intuition. Like it's bad enough as a woman but when you became a mom, you're constantly stressed and overwhelmed and impulse-buying shit on Amazon to solve a problem. But Amazon doesn't sell what you really need—a village, community."

I was a little dumbstruck by her insight and in awe of her wisdom.

Mothers are continuously put in hard situations with hard choices until we collapse under the weight of it all. Until we simply lay down and give up. Until gems of ideas and passions and dreams are crushed not into diamonds, but into dust and cobalt to make the next generation of smartphones. Or the latest holiday décor item in the Target Dollar Spot.

I know my credit card isn't the superpower I need to pull myself out of this all-consuming dream, but a best friend who loves and supports me like Alma? A partner who strives to believe me that motherhood feels impossible *and* cooks dinner? They are my superpowers.

So, I freeze my milk, love on my baby, and kiss Caden before I go to the Airbnb. I pack my journal and art supplies. My oracle cards and phone charger.

Alma came through on her promise of snacks. "Maggie, you never know how thirsty you will get in that hot tub" was her response when I asked her why a *box* of wine.

I prep myself to spend the weekend writing and drawing and dancing and feeling these stories and emotions right out of my system. Like an exorcism of my soul but in the most divine, embodied, feminine way.

Because this is a last chance. A final straw. An exit-only door. If I don't come back more than "okay" and "fine," there will be consequences.

Caden hasn't said anything specifically, but the last conversation was unfinished. An air of expectation bubbled between us. This is the end of the road for this chapter of life. The chapter where I slowly lose my mind after giving birth must end. That we're starting a new chapter, together, where I emerge from this weekend as the happy mom we both assumed I would be after the drive home from the hospital. That I will, once again, be me when I come home.

"Or else" lingers in the air until I close the trunk and climb in the car to drive away to my treehouse, where all my problems will be solved.

Hope has me breathing in the pine-heavy smell of winter in the wood as I walk up the snow-cleared ramp to the tree house and open the door. I giddily set up the box of wine with a full glass on the hot tub and text Alma a quick pic. Then another to Caden of the view out the window, thanking him for his thoughtfulness as I unpack the charcuterie snack board he secretly stashed in my cooler bag.

Sipping from my glass, I settle into some journaling on the extra-large couch, stretching my legs in front of me under a luxuriously soft throw blanket. I light a candle and set my intentions for the time away to "heal myself" with an oracle card pull.

I can't help but begin to hope this might be the fresh start, reaffirmed by the card I pulled from the oracle deck of goddesses from around the world. As I stare down at Brigid, the Celtic goddess of fire, I know I've made the right choice to be here. To trust my family to support me. That I'm ready to move forward and break the hold these dreams have on my soul. The universe has told me so.

Because Brigid, goddess of fire, is also the goddess of healing. The goddess who first burned away my fears of motherhood, who forged my belief in myself that I can do this. I feel an innate sense of comfort seeing her name again, given she is part of my motherhood origin story at the fire ceremony so many months ago. She helped me decide to become a mother and can now help me *be* a mother. The mother I yearn to be, without the weight of this obsession around my neck.

Then I immediately fall asleep on the couch, pressing my fingers comfortingly into my tattoo while being pulled into a new dream.

CHAPTER TWENTY-EIGHT

"Next stop..."

I shove my notes for my job interview back into my bag when my stop crackles over the intercom. After dropping the newspaper the kind priest gave me earlier back on the seat, the backs of my thighs burn as they slowly pull from the sticky train seat when I stand and work my way to the doors. Just me and a few others are on the train this early in the day, including a man wearing an oversized flannel jacket. He looks like a homeless hippie who didn't quite make it through the 60s in one piece.

The insides of my legs chafe from rubbing together in this heat, and he's wearing a flannel? My stomach clenches and brow furrows as I consider him. He looks up, and our eyes meet for a few seconds too long, the wild glint in his eyes a little too familiar to feel safe.

I glance away and see two other passengers who look like they're heading to work, an elderly lady and a younger man in a suit. He has the look of a boy who is starting to fill out into a man in a suit that is not new and has had at least one (if not two or three) owners before him. Freshly shaved and sitting straight up, he looks both exhausted and happy in the way young adults do when they are new to freedom. The elderly woman looks like she's the best type of grandma who always brings treats like fortune cookies and popcorn back from the city for her grandkids.

I mentally mark them as "safe" and my shoulders settle when I take a big, deep breath. A few more seconds and I'm off this train and away from this strange man.

The other two passengers don't seem to feel the tension in the train car. She's knitting (because of course she is), and he's staring off into the distance, fidgeting with the end of his tie. Even though I try to convince myself I'm okay, that I'm safe, I can't help but move in front of the train doors. I'm getting the hell off as soon as we pull into the station. The hairs on the back of my neck are tingling, telling me to "GO!"

The crowded train platform comes into view. Full of city workers, coffee vendors, and homeless people, many of them Vietnam vets home from the war but with nowhere to call home anymore. The businessmen move with intention, suit jackets slung over their arms in the heat, and women in practical shoes race up the stairs to beat their bosses into the office. Why do the women always look like they're rushing? A little too nervous? A little too much like they have something to lose while the men move like the world is theirs and they just have to swagger in and claim it?

I glance around the train car as we slow to a stop.

The train doors open. I lurch forward, my foot about to land on the platform, when a hand grabs my arm hard. I cry out as I'm pulled back onto the train through the open doors. Stunned, I stumble back into the chest of the wild-eyed man, crying out in surprise. He shoves me back onto my feet, and I stumble backward. Scream stuck in my throat, legs frozen in place—I can't obey my body's panicked command to RUN!

He wraps his hand around my elbow and pulls me back from the door, keeping me unbalanced and at his side as he pushes me farther back into the train car, pulling out a large hunting knife from under his jacket, the blade glinting sunlight off the wickedly curved tip.

Luckily for them, the young man doesn't freeze and grabs the elderly woman's arm. He clumsily pulls her onto the platform, her knitting having fallen to the floor of the train car, while the man holds my arm tighter, locking me into place at his side. The young man's shouts echo down the platform.

"Get back!"

"Don't get on that train!"

"Call the police!"

My world shrinks to the man and his knife, my eyes blurring and sweat breaking across my brow, my back, my whole body.

I sway for a second before I regain my balance, trying hard to slow my breathing and failing. Now is not the time to pass out.

No one else gets in this train car. The doors close, and the gap of safety narrows between them along with my vision. I've gotta breathe. BREATHE. This man is unhinged and waving his knife in the air between me and the doors. Talking too quickly and quietly. I strain to hear over the roar in my ears and the cacophony of train whistles but can't make it out.

The train slows down sooner than usual for the next stop, halting in the train yard rather than the platform. The train doors open, and the tracks swell with people and then empties again as police officers guide them to the safety of the station. The man grabs my arm again, wrenching it at unnatural angle behind me. Any movement I make to get away threatens to break my arm, and he uses this to his advantage, pinning me to him as a human shield. He presses the wicked tip of the knife into my side.

"Don't even think about it," he whispers in my ear. "Fuck. Too fast, man, this is too fast."

This is officially "a situation."

The immensity of what is happening sinks into me as I take in the now empty train station. Not just of passengers, but coffee vendors, station workers, and the usual homeless people asking for spare change at the bottom of the stairs. Empty. Quiet. This man stopped the morning commute in Chicago. He's a storm rolling in over the lake, and not only am I missing an umbrella, I'm in its direct path.

Oh, God. The knife.

Fuck being afraid. Being afraid has never helped me before.

No time for fear as he stiffly holds his arm straight out, pointing his knife wherever his eyes go. I freeze when his gaze swings around to me. My eyes widen as I see what is happening outside the train car, and he swings back to the windows at the movement.

Police officers approach the car with guns drawn. The man's wild eyes narrow and his jaw tightens as he holds the knife higher and points it out the windows at the police. A dozen police officers outside the train simultaneously lift their guns and point at the train car. He reaches out and grabs me by the arm and pulls me close to his chest, pressing the blade to the column of my throat. I inhale sharply and pull back hard as he turns me around the train car, making sure the police see that he has his knife pressed to my throat. Hard.

Now I do pee a little.

"Don't fucking move," he says.

I stare straight ahead and nod, piss running down my leg and pooling around our feet.

"What are you doing?" I ask, voice quivering. "Why are you doing this?"

He glowers at the knife still pressed to my neck, a thin red line from where he has pressed hard enough to cut. When his eyes meet mine again, he suddenly seems to deflate. Shoulders falling, a sigh escaping his lips, he holds his knife to my skin but not as hard, the pressure fading with his conviction.

"It's all too much, man. It's all too fucking much. Someone's gotta pay for how this all turned out. They took everything, man." He looks at me with sad, lost eyes for a split second before his anger takes back over. "I lost my brother, my best friend, my fucking soul over in Vietnam, and you know what I fucking came back to? Judgment. Guilt. Shame. No fucking support. I'm about to get evicted from my goddamn apartment. I can't find a job. I can't sleep. I've got these fucking nightmares spinning around in my head. No one wants to fucking help me. They all just want me to disappear and be fine. I'm not fucking fine."

Why aren't the police doing something?

Police officers shift slightly outside the train, guns drawn but not approaching the train car. A trio of officers in the back are talking and gesturing back and forth with their hands, arguing. One of them looks up, and I swear our eyes lock across the train yard.

"Help me," I mouth as tears fall down my face.

My eyes catch on a man dressed in black behind the trio, hands moving swiftly around a cord… is that a rosary? Beads slip swiftly through his fingers, lips move in prayer, as he watches the train car intently. Is that the priest from earlier?

"The government, that war ruined my fucking life. Now I'm going to show them what they created over there. A fucking monster. A hopeless, broken monster." A sob breaks on the last words as he points out the window with the knife, spinning around as he tries to keep an eye on all the officers outside the train. "A fucking monster. That's what she called me. And she's not wrong. I went over there knowing I might not come back—but I didn't know I would be

ordered to do shit that you wouldn't even believe. That war, man. It consumed my soul."

His grief wrecks me. Empathy and pain for this man and his life squeeze my heart as fear for myself locks my limbs in place, holding my neck back from the blade resting on my skin.

How can I get away from this man? I'm not this weak. I can't die here after everything I've survived.

"My friends died in horrific ways. And for what?! We were trying to protect our families. Our countries. Pawns in a fucking game we will never win. Our lives—and the Vietnamese lives—were just thrown away into the jungle in one fucking game of Risk no one wanted to lose."

He breathes deeply and shudders. Then he sounds more resolute when he speaks again.

"But I lost. And I need people to know what happened over there. I'm not broken, not crazy—I need people to listen. My shot on this earth may be done— but there's still hope for all my army buddies. We need help. They need help.

"Do you know what happens when I hear a car backfire on the street? I almost piss my pants. Sometimes I do. My girl surprised me one night and I lashed out. She surprised me with a goddamn birthday party, and I lost it. I was back in the jungle and just lost it. What kind of life is this? Why doesn't anyone care? Someone's gotta fucking listen and do something."

Well, I'm certainly listening. The hot whoosh of his breath on my neck and skin, his words combined with the fear and wild glint in his eyes are making my stomach clench. His feral eyes dart from window to window.

He looks like someone who knows his life is about to end. This sad man, who left all his hope behind in the war, shouts out his demands, pleas, prayers.

The sound of breaking glass suddenly destroys the spell of the train car. Time moves slowly, seconds stretching as glass shatters, his knife drops to the ground, his body close behind, blood spreading from his head.

Glass shards sparkle in the sunlight like the glitter of broken dreams and lives falling to the ground.

And then as if sound finally caught up to the horror in front of me, the warped bang of a gunshot fills my ears.

CHAPTER TWENTY-NINE

I sit up suddenly on an unfamiliar couch, heart thudding, mouth dry, soaked around my chest. One of my engorged breasts is stuck in the armhole of my twisted tank top, both nipples dripping milk. Eyes scanning the room to place where I am… The treehouse… The woods.

Why am I wet?

"Oh, snap," I mutter, moving my soaked shorts away from my thighs.

Oh my god—I peed my pants.

Cheeks burning, I hesitantly look out into the woods, overwhelmed momentarily by the quiet, intense dark. As a child of the 90s scary movies, I know a thing or two about dark woods and lone women.

Fake it till you make it. My favorite professional motto. Whether it's bravery in the dark or statistics or motherhood. *Just fake it till you make it.*

Forcing myself to move, clean myself, and turn on lights, I poke around in the kitchen looking for a pot for stovetop popcorn. I thumb through my phone as I wait for the oil to heat, slowly shaking the mason jar of organic kernels in my other hand. No messages from Alma other than a thumbs up to my arrival texts.

Maybe she's busy or *gasp* honoring my space this weekend.

I miss her bombardment of silly memes and random thoughts about her day.

I drop the kernels into the pan after the oil heats up, then melt copious amounts of grass-fed butter to top the popcorn—because what's the point if not to be a little indulgent in life?

I'm so extra sometimes, and I love it.

Still thinking of Alma and her distance lately, I crouch down to search in the lower cabinets for a popcorn bowl when the first kernels give a loud "pop."

Surprised, I jerk back and hit the crown of my head on the cabinet, knocking my bun out of place, and feel that familiar pull of a flashback to a life that isn't my own.

The kitchen fades in and out as my vision spins and I lose my balance, falling to my side. I have no business experiencing flashbacks to these women's lives. I'm tired of hearing a loud noise and being sucked back to the apartment where that man shot himself. Or seeing flashing lights on a building and feeling sick to my stomach, like it is *my* brother lying on the ground in a pool of blood around the corner.

This time, my brain quickly jumps back to the glass shattering on the train car, and the all-too-familiar panic returns as cortisol and fear surge in my veins.

I jerk up from the floor and flick off the stove, letting my body slam into the cabinets. The wood pushing into my back makes me feel dull pain instead of just helpless and angry. I lean against the cabinets, my head falling into my hands as tears slowly stream down my face, a slow drip… drip… drip as my nervous system realizes it is fully overwhelmed by these dreams. These nightmares. This life.

Then, as if my body realizes I'm not going to shut down the tears, that she has my full permission to let these waves of fear and anger and rage pour out, waves of sadness and shame and frustration and overwhelm rush through me, followed by the helplessness that my life isn't my own to live rising.

I picture a grief-filled rainbow streaming out of me, blues of sadness, purples of grief, and reds of anger, all tinged dark with shame. Once the pressure to hold it all together is lifted from me completely, the ribbons and strings and barbwire holding all these emotions break their hold and allow the emotions to flood out, spilling over the boundaries and compartments and walls that I spent months building and reinforcing with layers of fear and guilt and ego and ambition.

This whimsical treehouse in the woods. Being alone and responsible for only myself for the first time in months. I'm completely undone. As if the world feels my turmoil, clouds roll in, and a storm erupts in full display across the large windows. Trees sway in the wind, and lightning cracks across the sky.

I cry and cry and cry. Tears squeeze from my eyes like a rag twisted over a sink. Snot runs down my face and almost chokes me as I gasp for breath between sobs. Mascara runs down my cheeks, staining my sleeve as I wipe my face, curling into a ball on the floor.

With my grief and shame set free in my surge of tears, rage and anger cut through, raw and sharp-edged after being suppressed for months. I kick out at the pots and pans strewn around my feet. Throw the dish towel as far as I can with as much fury as I can muster at a dish towel. Stomp my feet on the ground. Jump up and slam the soles of my feet into the floor. Resist all urges to slam the cabinets and throw the pots at the windows as the rage whirls up from my feet, through my limbs, and streams like light out of my fingertips.

The sheer emotion lights me up from within as I continue to sob and cry and scream. Primal screams from deep in my belly, from the throats of the women in my dreams. Sobs of pain and fear and rage and helplessness. I roar from the deep guttural place in my womb where I communed with myself and God while giving birth.

Until my throat is raw from the fire of my rage, and I'm panting through my mouth because my nose is stuffed and swollen from crying.

And then, my body starts to shake, slowly at first but then almost violently, as I'm curled up on the floor. My fingers start to twitch,

and then my arms and my chest. The shaking moves through my
hips and legs and feet. Strong, full-bodied shivers roll through me
and feel like rage evaporating from my cells. I give in to the shaking
and let my body process these massive waves of emotion in its most
primal way.

The front door slams open in a gust of wind, and cold air flows
in and around the kitchen. Pieces of paper blow around me onto
the floor, and the sounds of rain and thunder echo across the room.
The wind cools my hot skin and dries the tears and sweat from my
face.

As my shaking limbs still, emptiness slowly creeps in and the
rage dissipates, like bubbles from a bottle of champagne set free
when the cork pops. An outburst, a riot, a cacophony of chaos at
first and then, a quiet settling to golden calm. I unchained my
emotions and finally let myself feel. Pushed out by lightness and
expansiveness, my jaw unclenches, belly untwists, releasing the
anxiety and fear that had it tight for months, maybe years.

*Is this what calm feels like? Is it peace? Do other people feel like this all the
time?*

No wonder they like it so much. Constant fight-or-flight is
burning my energy, using my soul fire to tend the flames of my
trauma responses-turned-personality traits. Holding in this pain has
cost me dearly, emotions buried deep, the root cause of internal
chaos in my life.

Instead of using all my energy to push these feelings down,
down, down to work and parent and solve the problems of
#adulting, I suddenly have nothing else to focus on except for me.

No pressing needs. No crying. No one trying to sex me up. No
questions. No nursing—but I should pump soon, especially if that
box of wine keeps getting lighter. Just me and popcorn and wine
and processing the shit out of these dreams so I can move on with
my life and back to handling my actual, real-world problems. Life
was already full before the grief and trauma from these dreams
swept into my reality.

Curling onto my side and resting my head on my arm, I choose
to ignore the pile of papers for now.

How would I have spent the past few months if I could "just be okay" like everyone wants? What joy would I have found? What other problems? Would we be planning Jilly's first vacation? Our first solo night away? To get a dog? Maybe even those chickens Caden wants?

A million things could be happening instead of the worry and fear and time and money being poured into making me "okay."

My swollen eyes blink slower and slower as I curl into a tight ball on the floor. Exhaustion is creeping in, and it would feel good to let it take over right now. I wasn't planning on falling asleep here on the kitchen floor, but I hadn't planned on freaking the fuck out here either.

What if all this happened? What if all this is true? Who could survive these things?

Then I slip right out of the treehouse and into sleep, curled up on the kitchen floor, barely noticing the hands that wrap around mine, pulling me back to the chaos of the train.

CHAPTER THIRTY

Time slows and then snaps back into place. The echo of a gunshot thrums through my head. I try not to step in the broken glass and growing pool of blood in the train car.

A police officer forces open the train car doors with a crowbar and climbs in, gun drawn, scanning for more threats. I'm intently focused on the barrel of the gun and don't notice the woman from my dream on the ground and the second officer at her side until he's picking her up. He moves quickly to the door and jumps, already running by the time both feet hit the ground.

I leap out of the train car, following them to a waiting ambulance, almost slamming into a priest praying the rosary. "Excuse me, Father," I cry out, pulling my shoulder back to avoid a collision. Our near miss doesn't faze the priest as he continues, his rich Irish accent giving the Latin prayers a musical quality as it rings out over the frightened murmurs of the crowd.

My mind is still catching up with my body as the reality of what has just happened crashes into me as jagged fragments of terror and fear, sadness and blood. Like memories I never made invading my mind.

The razor edge of a knife pushed into my throat.

The low whistle of a bullet, the high-pitched sound singeing my ear as it passes me. Then a wet popping sound as the man's head explodes.

His. Head. Explodes.

Next to me.

On me.

On her.

The woman is passed over to an EMT waiting by the ambulance, who instantly peppers her with questions. "Are you hurt? Ma'am, are you hurt? Can you hear me?" Her eyes rove around the train yard, dilated and confused as if she can't process how she got from the train to here.

Just like every other bystander in the train yard, I watch hands move over the woman, inspecting her for injuries, asking her the same questions repeatedly, hoping this time she will respond. "Are you hurt? Can you hear me?"

I wince as an arm I can't see slips around mine, pulling me forward. The hand squeezes until the points where our skin connect grow hot, and I suddenly feel as if I'm inside the woman in the ambulance, her thoughts whispering in the shadows of my mind.

"Can I hear you? Yes, I can hear you, but how can I answer such a basic question as "are you okay" when a piece of something soft and pink is on my sleeve? When red circles of blood blossom on my blouse, my skirt, my legs, my face? When I can't seem to get myself to speak?"

Eyes that are not my own are locked on a soft, pink piece of brain on her sleeve as the horror collapses onto her. A dense pressure pushing me down like a heavy fog, making me smaller and smaller. Compressing me and filling me with tension and fear. Her emotions are warping my presence in this realm. She's deeply, primally afraid. My vision, her vision, narrows into a smaller and smaller circle before tunneling. I might pass out.

I gasp as the hand lets me go, and I'm whisked back into my own body, grounded on the grimy platform, the chaos and noise racketing up around me.

The woman starts shaking as the EMT moves her arms and legs, fingers and toes. She winces at the burn of the alcohol wipes as blood and brains and pieces of debris of a man who no longer exists are gently and methodically removed from her skin. She's poked and prodded for cuts and wounds as the EMT tries to sort out what is her blood and what was his.

I jump in the back of the ambulance as the doors are pulled closed. She keeps shaking as her jacket and blouse are removed, the closed doors protecting her from the news cameras on the platform. I press my body against the wall to stay out of the way, no matter that no one seems to notice me, to see me. A glance out the window shows me that the priest I almost collided with is still praying, head bowed and creating a split in the wave of officers and train yard workers moving around.

Quick, efficient movements by the EMTs shift her body this way and that, bandaging wounds that wouldn't stop bleeding and removing pieces of glass from her hands and legs, jagged reminders of falling when the gunshot blasted into the train car. Hands move her shiny brown bobbed hair around, searching her scalp for cuts and debris from the Veteran's shattered body. Gloved hands pluck pieces of pink from her hair, like picking raspberries from the bushes by my house growing up. Her eyes widen and jaw clenches as we all watch in horror as a piece of tan skin covered with short brown hair is removed from her locks.

With that, her shaking gives way to full-blown shock. As her breathing turns ragged and stuttered, wool blankets are wrapped around her shoulders. Held there as she gasps for breath and puts her head between her knees. The door is suddenly pulled open, and the police call the EMTs out of earshot for an update. After scanning her eyes and laying her down on a stretcher, both EMTs quickly jump out of the back of the truck and, just as quickly, the woman sits up.

Grabbing a jacket from a hook on the wall, she pulls it on over her bra and slips out of the ambulance door, moving to the hidden side of the vehicle and away from the eyes of the watchful police and pedestrians. Everyone's attention is on the man's body being loaded onto a stretcher, in the opposite direction of the ambulance.

I chase after her, but she's too fast. Too desperate to escape. I'm about to run up the stairs after her when I'm held in place by a hand on my shoulder. I watch from below as she disappears into the crowd at street level, the priest's chants ringing in my ears.

CHAPTER THIRTY-ONE

My shoulder and hip dig into the hard tile of the kitchen floor as I come back into my body, eyes slowly blinking open. I'm flooded with memories of the woman's fear, and my mouth starts to water while my stomach suddenly contracts. I make it to the kitchen sink just in time to throw up.

I rinse out my mouth with water directly from the faucet, watching vomit drain into the garbage disposal. I quickly change into dry clothes, throw my hair back up into a ponytail, and grab my laptop. I need to record these new details from the dream quickly.

I sit down with a can of sparkling water to wash away the taste of another woman's terror and quickly type—details of the interview, train, hope, despair, knife, gore. When I'm finished, I'm exhausted and empty. Open. Lighter.

I'm whole, and empty.

Most of all, I want to be held by my mom. But the version of my mom I remember when she was sober, functional, healthy. Not the woman in the memories unveiled after Jillian was born. I want her gentle, soothing touch and unwarranted understanding.

The mom who sat on the couch and brushed my hair after bath

time, unraveling tangles and life woes while *Seinfeld* played in the background.

The mom who taught me breathing exercises in elementary school when I couldn't sleep through the night, installing a tape player by my bedside to play meditations to lull me to sleep, counting one, two, three, four, inhale…

The mom who understood the pain of being ridiculed for "being ugly" in 6th grade and scheduled a glow up with her favorite hair stylist. Who understood that I simply could not take swim class during the school year because of my curly hair and stayed up all night outside my school to sign me up for summer swim classes.

I want to not have to make sense, to not be fine, to not be okay. I want to be held while I fall apart, trusting that the arms holding me will still be there as I put myself back together.

I want—need—the version of my mom I remember… not the woman in the flashes of memories that pursue me relentlessly since Jillian's birth. Memories I pushed down for decades seem to be bubbling to the surface, and I'm powerless to repress them now.

The mom who hid liquor bottles under the bed. Who called from jail after getting arrested for a DUI. Who I had to hide my pain medication from after surgery when I was fifteen.

Caden never met my mom, but he's not convinced she would have been the village I need now. Since she's been dead for over twenty years, she doesn't get to control whether she would have been sober or not when Jillian was born. I get to create the illusion —delusion?—that she would be the best version of herself.

I get to write the version of my mom who would be here for me now, and I choose the best in her.

I text Caden a string of emojis that I hope says something like "Love you, babe! Life is good!" instead of what I'm thinking.

Great weekend here, babe. Lost my shit in the kitchen. Almost destroyed some cabinets in a rage. Then fell asleep on the floor and got pulled into a new dream. How's the baby?

I sink into the couch with my popcorn and flip through TV channels, settling on black and white reruns of *I Love Lucy*. My mom and I used to eat microwave popcorn and watch this show when I was little.

I can't wait to share this with Jillian. I'll snuggle my baby girl and tell her how I used to do this same thing with my mom. But did I?

A longing for tenderness squeezes my heart as I think of my mom. Did she hold me in these moments? Did she pull me close or just let me be nearby while she decompressed? I remember climbing onto the couch and snuggling up to my mom, but now I'm not sure if I remember my mom always holding me back. She may have been physically present but emotionally checked out, tolerating, but not reciprocating my affection. Was she touched out? Exhausted at the end of the day? Or was it something more?

Rolling the stem of a wineglass between my fingertips, an unasked question that lingers in the shadows of my mind since Jillian was born drifts up from my newly expanded consciousness. The space was made for it to be considered after my rage and fear were released.

Was my mom happy? Joyful? Hopeful?

Her eyes always looked distant, a little sad. Like she was there, but you better hold on tight in case she decided to flee. Like she was watching for the moment when it all fell apart, and she needed to run.

She seemed fragile sometimes. Like things beyond her control were coming for her, and she wasn't sure she could handle it. Like this time, it just might break her.

But other times, I remember her bringing such joy to the world with a laugh that threw her head back and her mouth wide as the sound poured out of her and into the universe, lighting up the world around her. Lighting up everyone around her.

I always thought her pain, her fragility, made me stronger, but I'm realizing that her fragility made me *have to be* stronger—and my awareness of the difference between those two experiences is squeezing my chest so tightly that my breath catches. Pushing down the flood of new, old, memories, emotions, is exhausting. Before all the hard of pregnancy, hormones, and a new baby, I could shove these realizations away with a quick scroll or work. But now, the harder I resist, the harder the truth pushes against the crumbling walls holding it at bay.

As if entering the liminal space of childbirth shattered the walls I built to protect myself from my reality for decades.

The truth, hard, heartbreaking memories were held at bay by pure strength of will, pure survival instincts… the harder I try to push these memories away, the more my reality, my truth, pushes back. Fissuring my walls. Pressuring my weak points.

And then childbirth shattered the walls, and now I'm flooded with these thoughts and revelations and drowning in the trauma.

Sitting with my glass of wine, enjoying the breeze and sounds of nature through the open window after the unexpected winter storm, the irony of this moment isn't lost on me. Growing up, the adults in my life never drank alcohol—anywhere. Home, parties, restaurants. La Croix, water, coffee, Diet Pepsi, or Diet Coke depending on which aunt's house I was at, and that's it. No bottles of beer, Irish coffees, or glasses of wine to be seen. An interesting reality of being a child of a sober mother.

A little snort escapes at how different Jillian's life is right now, being paraded around a bar by her Auntie Alma.

She won't be wide-eyed the first time her grownups order drinks at dinner like I was during my first dinner with my college boyfriend's family. Auntie Alma and I enjoy our espresso martinis at brunch too much. My friends drinking at college parties never fazed me, but watching *my boyfriend's mom* casually sip a margarita made my mouth fall open, caught off guard by the confusion and dissonance of the moment. Alcohol held a distant, yet defining role in my world. Playing at Alcoholic Anonymous pancake breakfasts and understanding that everyone at that table had sad stories leading up to these moments of laughter, including my mom, makes for an odd but empathy-building childhood.

Whispered conversations of my mom's "before" would pause when I walked into Gramma's kitchen, aunts and uncles surrounding the table with mugs of coffee and bowls of chips between them. *Before*. When my mom was sober for good (until she wasn't).

Sometimes, the whispers held hints of why my childhood was spent attending AA meetings instead of playdates. A dead husband. The weeks I lived with my aunt as a baby while my mom was in rehab. A broken nose.

Whispers I had long forgotten by the time I was pregnant with Jillian... until now.

My own "before" stories peek out from dark hiding spots in secretive corners of my mind, breaking through only after I gave birth to Jillian. As if the pregnancy hormones lured each memory from its cave to be seen, understood, healed. As if the D-MER, the hormones, opened the gates and each ugly memory pushed to be released into the light.

To be seen. Felt. Healed.

Nightmares of crying babies and runaway moms plagued my early months of pregnancy, leaving me tossing and turning in the dark. These are the original nightmares Caden remembers. Along with how I was able to move through them, heal from them. After waking up with tear-streaked cheeks too many nights in a row, I found a therapist. Her clear, calm voice still rings in my ears these months later, "Could these be memories rather than dreams?"

Nausea tightened my stomach and made my mouth water while I let that thought sink in. Sobbing, arms wrapped around my chest, I knew that *I* was the child, the baby, in those dreams. Too painful for my own memory to let them be known until now.

My mom running away from me as a toddler, crying on the porch in a heavy diaper, watching her robe fly behind her like a superhero as she fled around the corner of our townhouse.

She ran away. My mom ran away from me.

Fear and abandonment still curl tight in my chest under my ribs, searching for a reality where this isn't true. When I wasn't abandoned by the one who was supposed to keep me safe.

Rubbing my fist over the center of my ribcage and breathing deeply, her pain when she ran from me flashes in my mind. Eyes wild with desperation as she disappeared around the corner. That gleam would flash again in her eyes when she relapsed for the last time when I was sixteen.

I calmly told my therapist, "I can see how it could happen, that desperate urge to flee."

She made that humming sound and tilted her head while she waited for me to continue, to walk myself to my own healing.

"The mother in me can empathize with the overwhelm, overstimulation. Feeling alone and lonely and unsupported "

"How does the child in you feel about it?"

"I don't know. That feels too dangerous consider."

That wild, feral look is becoming more and more present these days, haunting me from the eyes of people in my dreams. Of the boy with the bloody hand and shirt outside the bar. Of the husband when he shot himself. Of the man on the train with the knife.

In my own eyes when I wake in the middle of the night and stare in the mirror, not recognizing myself, terrified that I'm losing control.

That one day running will be my only option too.

CHAPTER THIRTY-TWO

I spend the rest of the weekend diving into dreams, reconstructing my outlines and theories across the spacious dining table. Buoyed by new details from the dream at the train station, I analyze the dreams in their entirety to help details stand out.

To see where I fit in.

When I step back from my work, I could be right back in my home office. My brain feels like I've turned it inside out, and all the details, theories, wonderings I have stacked up are now laid out on the dark wooden table in front of me. The organized chaos soothes my nerves and reminds me that I know how to do this. I know how to solve problems.

I know how to heal.

I text Alma a picture of the chaos on the table, making sure nothing stands out as "too much" in the picture.

I caption it, "Where's that ball of yarn now?" and press send.

I follow the picture with a string of laughing emojis. Relief floods me with the brief, but honest connection that comes with looping Alma into my mind. Feeling like I can share all this with her.

The soft woosh of paper moving quickly across the counter fills the air as I work to place each detail in its proper sequence, like chess players speeding through the final moves of a game.

Nothing makes sense. Each dream is tragic, each life-altering. I use a different color marker to show where I was pulled into the dream, trying to make sense of that sensation. If it was simply a new element to the dream or if I was *pulled* into that reality.

Circling the kitchen island, my mind catalogs each scrap of paper as if it were a puzzle piece, clicking different details together and apart again. On my third trip around the island, my eyes blur the paper rows together, and then a new thought slowly starts to form. What if I look at this as one long story instead of three separate dreams? If she might be the same person from the first two dreams, it's not a stretch to wonder if these dreams are about one as she grows from a girl to a woman, from a sister to a widow to a hostage.

There's always been something hauntingly familiar about the woman.

Have I met her before in a dream? Could I have been her? Caden and I half-jokingly theorized timeline hopping, but past lives makes so much more sense.

I cover the floor-to-ceiling windows of the treehouse with this idea, my dry erase markers flying as I make connections across dreams and realities. I start with the dream about the young girl at the bar whose brother gets his head smashed by a rock. She was young, still in high school. The beginning.

Barely fazed by the pinging notification of Alma's text response, I outline the second and then third dream on the windows. Nodding, I step back and admire my work—my theory seems plausible. I've detached my emotions from the outline. Dr. Maggie is analyzing a problem instead of sleep-deprived mama drowning in chaos. I can't analyze my way to healing, but it feels damn good to not be in a flood of someone else's emotions and flashbacks right now. I know how to analyze. How to find the sticky point where the process is getting held up.

Suddenly ravenous, I warm up pasta and scan my phone. Alma's response of a quick "haha" makes me pause. I stop myself from asking what—or who—has her distracted. Usually, she would bounce on an opportunity to tease me, and I used to do the same.

THE SUN SETS, taking away the lighting for my window outline. I grab a box of markers and a legal pad. I'm exhausted but not done, and the urge to know more beckons. I can tease out more of my memories through art.

I've started to think of these dreams as *my* memories instead of dreams. Maybe I've dreamed the stories enough that they've woven in with my memories—or were they always mine somehow? Memories that were being drawn up and out of my unconscious by postpartum life? Hormones, no sleep, high amounts of stress… all forcing me to grapple with my own fears and pain… breaking down the walls I've painstakingly built around my past, my emotions, for decades.

Why does it feel true that this woman's story lives inside me? That some version of me has in fact experienced these deeply devastating events one after another? I'm exorcising these traumas out of my skin, bones, muscles, my cells, and DNA with each swipe of a marker through art or analysis. These dreams—this woman—feel part of me.

Am I losing it? Or is this is what deep creativity feels like? Art and words and stories deeply embedded in you, and to remove them from your being and put them out into the world feels like an exorcism—or birth.

This thought floats around my mind as I draw. I let the idea that these are my stories, just not from this lifetime or timeline, travel through my legs, my arms, right out of my fingers and onto paper. I'm barely conscious of my movements as my hand moves fluidly across paper, drawing, drawing, drawing.

The creative flow trickles to an end as a thought settles firmly over me, and I can't shake it.

What if I let it all be true for a minute?

What if…

These are my stories. These stories are woven into my soul, my bones. My past lives?

I'm the woman.

The woman in the dream was me.

Could I have been…

The young girl watching her brother bleed out after having his head smashed in by a brick?

The bride with a drug-addicted, suicidal husband?

The woman held hostage on the train?

What if this woman was me?

Just in a different timeline.

Or a different life.

My breath catches in my throat.

Could this be true?

As if whatever, or whoever, is pulling me into dreams is guiding my work, sketching out detailed scenes from each dream.

A ghost sounds absurd at first. But so does the idea of a past life. Or timeline jumping. That these stories might be playing out on different timelines of my life is wild to me. None of this would have been plausible a few months ago, but what is possible has greatly shifted after the months I've spent relentlessly dreaming, almost crashing cars, and ruining relationships over flashbacks. Not to mention being pulled into dreams as an invisible bystander to this pain and trauma.

Flipping through the papers, I pause to admire how the simplicity of the drawings allows new details to stand out.

Talk about a flow state. I don't remember drawing any one of these.

A brick covered in bright red blood.

A train car at a station.

A pair of white sneakers splattered with blood at the bottom of jean-clad legs. Fat tear drops splattered around the edges of the paper.

A syringe and gun drawn in stark black and white.

A building with a puddle of blood outside it. *Is that a name on the front of the building?*

A purse with its contents spilled on a hard orange plastic chair.

Something that looked like a mirror, maybe in a bathroom? A blurry drawing of a woman's face stares out from the mirror.

"It cannot be this freaking easy," I murmur, organizing the drawings by dream, connecting them to each row on the kitchen island. Drawings from the pub in one pile. The suicidal husband in the second. Anything related to the hostage situation on the train in a third.

Some seemed like they could fit anywhere. A typewriter. A pair of platform shoes. Pizza. A sewing machine. A beer bottle. A window with broken blinds. A door with the same cross as my tattoo on it. Those became a fourth pile.

Details emerge as I look at each picture more closely, in the context of their dream. The name of the pub is clearly visible: "O'Malley's Pub" written across the front in block letters, shamrocks scattered across the background. A date in a newspaper on the train seat. A building on a street corner.

Excitedly, I realize these are all new details. New pieces to add to my puzzle on the kitchen island.

The sun glows magenta beyond the trees, the first colors of a winter dawn. I'm suddenly exhausted and pulled to sleep. This is all too much, yet not enough. This weekend has torn me wide open, and I need to put myself back together before I go home.

I can't show up at home after a weekend away in worse shape than when I left. The whole point of this weekend was to deal with whatever is causing these dreams and turning my life into a nightmare. If nothing changes, Caden's unspoken ultimatum still looms—get better or else... else what?

It will be hard for me to say no to anything Caden suggests after this weekend. We're both out of ideas and energy to get me back to "okay." And I do want to be okay. More than okay. I want to be joyful in this gorgeous life we've created together. This time away was supposed to be *the* fix that would help me get some control over myself. Over the chaos these dreams are inflicting on me.

And if it means stepping into a version of reality that most would scoff at? I'm here for it.

Because answers are in those drawings, in that outline. I've created the precipice to "more." The cliff I need to jump off to be free.

But first, I need to sleep. I pass the still damp couch on the way to the bedroom and roll my eyes. Maybe this will turn into one crazy story in a few years. The time I wet the couch.

Too late—or too early—to FaceTime with Jillian, I dive under the covers, and for the first time in months, I sleep deeply and dreamlessly.

CHAPTER THIRTY-THREE

Notifications light up my phone, reminding me that today is the day I'm supposed to return home a renewed woman. Caden texted photos of Jillian—a smiley one and one of Gramma out to lunch with the two of them. Jillian is pressing her tiny fist to her mouth in the primal sign of baby hunger, and my breasts instinctively swell with the feeling of an impending letdown.

Whoops, not again.

I hastily stand up and realize my shirt is already soaked from sleeping all night. The sweet scent of warm milk envelops me but will quickly turn rancid if I don't rinse the sheet out. I don't want to be charged for leaving my bodily fluids all over the Airbnb.

My breasts ache with the need to release this milk. I pump first, postponing dealing with the rest of the mess—both in the kitchen and in my life.

A wave of relief hits me when I see a new text from Alma, but concern takes over when I read her unusually succinct words.

ALMA

Are you free next Tuesday afternoon?

Usually, this would be followed by details on the latest yoga studio or happy hour that she wants to lure me to, but something about her tone and utter lack of exclamation points and emojis makes me respond right away.

ME

I can move a meeting if it's important.

Her response pops up immediately.

ALMA

Yes. Please.

I use the last few minutes of pumping to reschedule my meeting —I don't want to forget later. Because in all reality, my ADHD brain will not remember to do this important task again after I put my phone down… until Tuesday morning. This time away has shown me how focused I've been on myself these past few months. It's one thing to be losing my mind from dreams and motherhood and a whole other one to abandon my closest friend who has shown up for me in the most patient and hilarious ways.

Rubbing my fingers over my tattoo and breathing deep, I give myself a pep talk to strategize the next few hours while my stomach growls in reminder that I need to eat to keep up this energy. "Okay, screw cleaning up. The next few hours of focus are worth more than my cleaning fee."

The growing, slightly desperate need to look at the drawings makes me work faster as I shuffle papers on the counter and thoughts in mind, tossing my belongings into my bags. When the timer beeps and signals my lunch is ready, I'm packing up the unused nail polish and face mask. Not a real mom night away without trying to do *all the things*.

Holding a steaming hot slice of pizza in one hand and a sparkly pink marker in the other, I start comparing my notes and pictures with the outlines on the windows. I need to wash away all evidence of my foray into *A Beautiful Mind* territory before I leave, but I don't want to miss any details. I muse over what to investigate while I chew.

Details in the first dream seem simple. I write down the name of the bar—O'Malley's Pub, a brick building on a corner—and that Janis Joplin was playing and seemed to be a newly released song.

What year did "Piece of my Heart" come out?

The gun and syringe drawings are from the second dream. Not as easy to find a suicide listed in a city paper with no town, name, or date. And the hard truth is that this story is probably another sad tale of a young, poor drug addict who took his own life—an event that wouldn't be newsworthy in this age of opioids, but was it then?

More details come up from the third dream to research. The hostage situation would have been big, and on the L, in Chicago. If the dream is like reality, there had to be coverage from local newspapers and reporters. Maybe the name of the hostage would even be listed? The thought of knowing the name of the woman haunting my dreams makes my heartbeat pick up.

One drawing of the train has a number on it and the phrase "NWI Express." I may live in Ohio now, but I grew up in Northwest Indiana and know this is the train line that shuffles people to and from the city. Nostalgia sweeps over me as I shuffle through these reminders of my hometown.

Time is flying. I hastily pack up the last of my belongings and set them by the door. I want to spend a few minutes working on my list. I'm sure I forgot something, but I shrug it off to #ADHDtax and start a Google search of the bar in the first dream. I can't resist the need to know if any of this is true. If O'Malley's Pub exists, then I need the drive home to process. What does it mean if I'm timeline jumping between different versions of myself? If the bar doesn't exist, then I'm back to where I am now—a dreamland with no connection to reality unmooring my world.

I type "O'Malley's Pub" in the search bar. I'm sure it can't be this easy, but if it does exist? Then Maya's talk of timeline jumping feels more plausible today than it did on the beach. Like the true academic I am, I prep myself for disappointment, to trust in the research and what was reality until the first dream shook my foundation.

With five minutes before I need to be out the door, the search loads. A zip of electricity flies down my spine as results fill the screen. The thrill of seeing that the pub exists quickly morphs into a sense of "duh" as I realize the screen was full of O'Malley's Pubs from all over the country.

Papers start to rustle as the unseasonably warm morning turns windy. Wanting to avoid a repeat of the night, I pop up to close the window and regroup.

The hostage situation was in Chicago. What if I start there?

Reminding myself of the next steps in my research process that I know by heart, I add "Chicago" after "O'Malley's Pub" in the search bar. Time to narrow down the funnel of results.

I quickly scroll through the newly loaded page. A few O'Malley's or versions of the name listed in Chicago fly by. One at the bottom of the screen catches my eye. Not in Chicago, but in Hammond, Indiana, where my mom grew up, near my hometown. The article covers the owner's retirement and closing of O'Malley's, an Irish pub originally opened in 1960.

Okay, this place has been around for a long time.

I plug the address into Google Maps and realize with a shock that the location of the now-closed bar is within walking distance of Gramma's home.

Well, fuck.

Puzzle pieces of information move around my mind, clicking this new detail into place.

As quickly as the thought comes, I text my aunt about O'Malley's. No point in questioning my flashes of intuition at this point in my journey.

ME

> Do you know of O'Malley's Pub? I know this is random, but I just read about this old Irish pub that was close to Gramma's house in Hammond.

Not a lie, but not the whole truth.

She obviously doesn't understand the sense of urgency in my careful yet casual words and doesn't text back the immediate response I'm craving.

The knock at the door means my time in this whimsical treehouse is up. I quickly gather up my piles of paper and then answer the door. While I pull the frozen milk bags out of the freezer, the owner helps carry my other bags to the car.

"I hope you got what you came for. Mother Oak has a way of caring for our guests in ways we could never imagine."

I pull my head out of the freezer and turn to the woman with joyful, riotous red curls surrounding her face and warm smile. "Mother Oak?" I ask, confusion wrinkling my nose.

"Oh, you didn't you see on the listing? Well, we call the tree this home is built around Mother Oak. She has a type of magic that draws in people seeking answers and embraces their spirit, pushes them forward in their quests. Sharing her energy with others is an honor for us."

Smiling, I realize why Caden sent me to this particular rental home for the weekend. I was craving a mother to hold me through this journey, and he found me one.

I grab the final totes and walk out the door, waving goodbye to Mother Oak and thanking her spirit for caring for me.

"Enjoy the drive home," calls the woman with twinkling eyes as the breeze blows her curls away from her face. "Maybe we will see you again soon!"

"I can't wait to come back with my daughter one day, to introduce her to Mother Oak," I call, waving as I pull out of the driveway. My heart swells with gratitude for a partner who is learning to believe in magic with me, who goes out of his way to care for me and meet my true needs.

For a woman who shares the magic of her Mother Oak with the world.

"Annnnd I left all those notes on the windows." I sigh and press my palm to my forehead as I drive away. "Well, I'm probably not getting my deposit back anyway."

CHAPTER THIRTY-FOUR

I try to catch Alma on the phone on the drive home to ask about this mysterious hold on my Tuesday afternoon of next week, but she doesn't pick up. I'm debating calling a second time, but that would be the ultimate bat signal of "EMERGENCY" and this is not that.

After voice-texting her that I'm in the car for a few hours if she wants to catch up, my mind wanders back to past lives and timeline jumping, letting each possibility play out on the rolling hills of Southern Ohio. And debating with myself about the pros and cons of updating Caden on my new theories.

Is it more normal to have visions from past lives in your dreams?
Nope.

What about glimpses into other timelines playing out somewhere in the universe?

Hard no.

Am I making this all up?

No. Maybe. Probably not.

As much as Caden has supported me over the past months, he is ready to be done exploring this liminal space. He doesn't want more theories about past lives. Caden wants his best friend, his wife, back.

The farther I drive away from the cabin, the more I sound like I'm making excuses for my mental instability and not accepting the actual reason I could be in this situation—postpartum mental illness. These theories seemed ripe and juicy in the treehouse, but shrivel with each mile I drive.

But now that I'm in the car, back on the road, can I go home and say to him, "Hey, the weekend was wonderful, super restful. Lots of time to reflect and process and journal and draw. And now not only have I slept for the first time without dreaming in months, but I'm more convinced than ever that the dreams might be glimpses into my other timelines playing out. Or maybe a past life. And not just any past life, but my past life."

Caden's going to hate this new development.

Ugh. I need more time to think this all through and research, but time is up. Caden and Jillian need me to come home and be present and happy. They both deserve a mom and partner who joyfully returns for snuggles and milk and sex. And I want to be the person who gives them what they need, to show Caden I'm not losing it and motherhood isn't too much for me like he sometimes believes. Like I sometimes believe too. To give him, both of us, hope that his partner is going to be okay.

I tap the brakes as I pass a sign for a psychic off the side of the road. The sign glows in the window, probably in the living room with the smell of grilled cheese and *Wheel of Fortune* on an old TV in the background while a lady smoking a cigarette half-heartedly reads tarot cards.

But who else to indulge in a conversation around past lives and visions than a small-town psychic? This might be my first and last opportunity to talk freely about all this drama, with someone who might believe in past lives and timeline jumping. With someone who might not think I'm losing my mind when I describe how I'm pulled into dreams while I sleep.

Deciding to trust my intuition once again, I quickly turn into the driveway. I won't have another chance to do this once I'm back in the carousel of daycare, work, and bottles.

Besides, what have I got to lose at this point besides $50?

Okay, this home doesn't smell like grilled cheese. More like incense and store-bought rotisserie chicken mixed with vape smoke. A fan whirls in the background as the blades oscillate across the room. Times have changed since Alma and I got tipsy and dropped in on a psychic on a work trip.

I settle at the silk-covered table in a room cozily lit up by candles as the woman who answered the door introduces herself as Carmela.

"Do you come with a specific question or are you looking for a general reading?" She asks as she shuffles her well-loved tarot cards.

I can't shake the sense that Carmela had been expecting me as I ask for a general reading. No need to just hand over all the details right away.

"You look tired. Deeply tired. Do you have a small child at home?"

I nod and sigh.

Will it always be obvious that I'm bone-deep exhausted?

"May I?" Carmela asks as she reaches for my hand.

I nod. As our hands touch, a small shock zings my fingertips, moving up my arm. Static electricity? Or my body's reaction to being touched for the first time in three days. I was touched out before I left, but I didn't comprehend the space I've had in the past few days until it was just taken away.

Carmela's eyebrows lift, but she only purses her lips. She runs her fingertip along the lines in my hand and then lifts her eyes to mine. "You have a baby at home. A daughter. A daughter born into a legacy of trauma and hope. She's a piece of your heart."

My breath catches. "A piece of my heart?"

No. Well, yes, she *is* a piece of my heart, but what are the odds that she would use that exact phrase?

Carmela pauses at my reaction, watching me intently. She shuffles the deck of tarot cards and then sets it on the table.

"Please cut the deck," she says softly. I slowly move the cards before she lays them out. Silently, her eyes scan the cards before she looks at me again and lets loose a long sigh.

Carmela points to the first card, the Five of Wands, in the layout. "I see pain. Hopelessness. Helplessness. Lost chances snatched away as quick as a gunshot. Green eyes hiding sad emotions during happy times. So much grief in your past, your legacy."

I know enough about tarot to know my spread of cards is holding hard, sad truths that I don't know if I'm ready, or want, to hear. My mind is screaming to pick up the pieces of rubble around me and rebuild walls that lay in pieces, to protect myself from what's to come.

Jillian's gorgeous green eyes under her soft baby lashes fill my mind. Her eyes turned from brown to green over the past month, much to my delight. Protected fiercely by Caden and me, her biggest problems have all been milk-related. Loved and safe now, will she one day be sad in a world that demands she pretend to be happy?

The fan flutters my hair as Carmela's eyes suddenly glaze over as if she's staring off into the distance.

"You're headed the wrong way, baby cakes," she says softly.

"What did you call me?" I whisper.

Carmela shakes her head. "I'm not sure. Sometimes I get overcome with thoughts during a reading and let them flow. I don't know what I'm saying until I'm done, and I rarely remember."

No one has called me *baby cakes* since I was a little girl. It's a nickname I almost forgot about until I was rifling through old pictures and found a note from my mom that had probably been tucked in a lunchbox or under a $5 bill after school to buy ice cream with my friends. "Have fun, baby cakes. Love you."

Hearing that nickname again feels proof to the world, to me, that my mom *did* love me even in her pain and addiction.

Carmela continues my tarot reading, interrupting my thoughts about my mom. "You have great sadness from the past clouding your future. The bloody path leads the way to healing, to home."

I peer at her curiously, trying to understand the vague words.

"Until the sadness is unearthed and a life reclaimed by a woman onto herself, the blood and pain will continue to soak through, generation by generation."

I nod like I understand, but the hairs on the back of my neck rise. While I may not understand what's happening right now intellectually, my intuition seems to have no problem connecting with Carmela's reading.

Blood soaking through generations? That seems dramatic and frustratingly unclear. I may have been secretly hoping Carmela would try to sell me a "How to Stop Seeing Past Lives and Prevent Timeline Jumping 101" handbook.

She asks about my relationship with my mom, and I tell her I don't have one; she died when I was sixteen. Carmela looks at me strangely, tilting her head to the side.

"Interesting. I swear both a mother and a daughter spirit surround you. Someone wanting to hold you and needing held. Pieces of a heart needing to be made whole. The spirits of those who have passed usually feel more... far away."

Carmela continues with the reading, tired, subdued, like her intuition had fled the building. She talks of financial security, needing to nurture myself and rest more, and leaning into strength, into a soul that is not my own.

"I get the sense you are in the middle of a great love story."

As she picks up the tarot cards and returns them to the deck, I walk to the door with fewer answers than when I walked in. I didn't even ask her about timelines and past lives, and now I just want to get back to the familiar comfort of my car.

My hands tremble as I open my bag to pay, dropping bills on the floor in my race to get out of here. Pain spreading through generations sounds too much like Jillian being impacted.

Suddenly, she lifts her hand and says, "Don't worry, baby cakes, Jillian will be okay. You're lookin' the wrong way."

She pauses, cheeks turning pink, flustered by her words. Looking at me curiously, she asks, "I haven't a clue why I just said that, but does it make any sense to you?"

"My daughter's name is Jillian," I respond begrudgingly.
Carmela nods.

"Okay, that makes sense. The spirit… spirits? shadowing you wanted you to know that, wants you to know you are loved."

CHAPTER THIRTY-FIVE

I arrive home to much fanfare from Jillian and Caden, both excited to see me and my body for different reasons.

I already know I need time away again after only being home for an hour.

Next time can be a weekend with Alma instead of losing my mind solo.

Alma's away for the week at a professional conference, and our text thread has been suspiciously quiet. Chalking her distance up to the chaos of work travel for now, I assume we will catch up next Tuesday, as planned

After a few nights of dreamless and restful sleep, Caden's relief is apparent in the smooth plane of his forehead, the easy smile in his eyes, the way he stands behind me when I pour coffee and rests his head on top of mine, wrapping me up in a gentle, loving hug. I lean into his embrace and relish this calm. It hasn't been this easy between us in months.

"I've missed this," I whisper, loving the warmth of his chest and arms on me.

"You're sleeping better, babe. No more tossing and turning, screaming out in the night. You haven't even hit me in my sleep since you got back."

I turn my head to kiss his scruffy jaw, smiling at the morning scratch of his beard. Ease and peace are simply more accessible with more sleep.

I sing along to the radio in traffic again, and I didn't even jump when an ambulance, lights flashing and sirens blaring, drove by our office. I simply blinked and paused, waiting for a flashback that never came, but it's not as if I'm totally okay either. Parts of the dreams seem determined to stay around, quiet on the sidelines, not willing to disappear completely.

The urge to tell Caden about how Joplin songs are the new background music in my earbuds at work or what I hum while I nurse Jillian is there all the time. As is the pull to show him the outcomes of my insatiable desire to draw scenes from the dreams and research each new detail that emerges from my art, like clues waiting to be unearthed from my unconscious. What am I searching for? Closure? How to access my alternate timelines? A lost cause?

My life, being released from these dreams, feels just out of my reach. Like there's a puzzle piece missing, and if I could just find it, all would be well. I would be well.

While I'm spiraling in my thoughts, Caden's hands start to roam under my robe, sliding up my tank top and under the waistband of my shorts. He presses kisses into my hair and down my neck, pulling me more tightly against his chest.

I quickly see where this morning could be going and let go of all thoughts of talking to him about the dreams. Instead, I lean into how good he feels pressed against my back, especially as his fingers start to work their magic in the waistband of my pajamas. The other perk of being more well-rested is that I enjoy this sexy as hell husband of mine and sink into the connection we both deeply crave.

HURRY UP!

I adjust the pressure on the pump as I glance at the minutes ticking by on the clock. I need to meet Alma, but I'm a little grateful for the extra minutes to look over my notes. I may not be dreaming anymore, but I'm consumed by this search for more details, this quest to discover the meaning of the dreams.

Desperation pulls at my fingers to scrawl my findings all over a giant whiteboard to see how they connect, but then I would need a hiding place for it. Instead of putting my notes back up on the wall at home, I've organized them into a binder. Either to protect Caden or keep it a secret from him. I'm not sure which is more true; maybe both.

My need to hide the binder with all my artwork, stories, and research makes me feel as if I'm doing something wrong, something shameful. But since people will judge me if they know about the binder, what it contains, and because I'm not doing it because of that judgement, I'm in fact not crazy. Because crazy people do whatever they want without caring about other people's feelings or opinions, right?

No idea. My mind is a tornado of circular thinking. I'm spiraling and throwing around stereotypes to justify my behavior, to protect Caden and Jillian and maybe myself from whatever the truth may be right now.

Could I have postpartum psychosis? Am I jumping timelines? Seeing past versions of myself?

So many questions. So few answers.

I almost wish that hand would come back and pull me into a new dream, one where I can ask questions and get answers, finally.

Two more minutes until I need to be out the door. Maybe I will send a second text to my aunt about O'Malley's?

She never responded, and while not out of the norm, I'm done waiting. Rather than push her for a response, I Google the bar again, imagining my mom growing up in this area, how she could have walked to the bar from home.

Or from a friend's.

My mom and Gloria, her best friend, could have gotten in all sorts of trouble at that bar together. They grew up a few houses apart on the same block.

I can message Gloria.

It's been years since we've spoken, but what's the worst that could happen? Impulsively, I swipe open the messenger app on my phone and search for her. Our last messages are over ten years ago and full of miscommunication and painful emotions. That conversation didn't exactly end badly, but there wasn't a ton of love either. I make sure I front-load my greeting with lots of hellos, how are you, and how are your kids, before I jump into the reason for my message.

ME

> Random, but I was wondering if you remember O'Malley's Pub in your old neighborhood in Hammond? It's come up in some of my research.

I'm getting good at partial truths these days. I couldn't think of a valid reason to justify the ask, so I leave it at that. Gloria helped raise me during my most awkward years. Why try to ease the tension of this unexpected question?

I wait a few seconds to see if her icon lights up to indicate she opened the message, but nothing. Who knows? She may ignore it completely or tell me to go away. That's what happens when you break up with her son decades ago and then never talk to anyone in your hometown again. I now understand that as the self-protective trauma response it was, is, but that doesn't help get me answers any faster.

I need to leave *now* or else I'll be late to meet Alma. I can't mess up whatever this afternoon is by being late, like this is a test, and one I desperately don't want to fail. Alma's quiet distance yet insistence that she needs me today is so out of her norm that the least I can do is be on time.

Silencing the alarm that means "*LEAVE NOW,*" I shove my binder and phone into my tote as I run out the door.

CHAPTER THIRTY-SIX

"Oh, Alma." Lips pressed together in a tight line, hands clenched on the steering wheel as I maneuver around the crowded sidewalks of the green building on a busy corner downtown. "I guess Plan B didn't work."

I've missed my constant connection with my best friend over the past week. The pull to send her a picture, a funny story, to ask how she's doing has been on the tips of my fingers. And now I understand why. Sometimes Alma isolates herself when she's scared, overwhelmed. Even from me.

The sidewalks are full of people shouting and waving signs with messages that claim to be "pro-life" but feel full of hate and fear as women cover their faces with their bags and push into the door of the nondescript building.

A hand pushes a paper onto my car window while I wait for a group to move so I can pull into the parking lot. "Your baby loves you" is in large block print pressed against the glass. The paper pulls back as soon as my car crosses into the parking lot.

I grab my phone to message Alma that I've arrived when someone in a pink "volunteer" shirt taps on my window. I almost give them the finger before they hold up a sign attached to the back of a clipboard that says "I am a volunteer with the CLE Women's Clinic. Would you like support getting into the building today?"

Now that feels more pro-life, pro-love, than whatever is happening on the sidewalks.

The heightened emotions surrounding this building feel volatile, on the verge of chaotic, like one push and the protesters could turn into an angry mob waving torches and hunting witches rather than harassing women making hard choices.

I hope they feel the same way about all the men who make excuses not to use condoms.

I shake my head and find a spot to park next to Alma's older model, black two-door car. Head down, staring at her phone screen, she's frozen in her seat.

Thank goodness I was on time.

My heart breaks for her, and I hate that she even drove over here alone. I fire off a quick text.

ME

> I'm parked next to you. I'll meet you by your car door.

I see her read and register the text as her shoulders drop and she adjusts the hood of her oversized sweatshirt, already pulled up over her face. I glare at every protester shouting at me, immediately becoming the protective mama bear and friend that Alma needs, and open the door. "Hi, Alm, I'm here. Are you ready to go inside?"

When she looks up at me, I see the same "I need my mom" pain flash across her eyes that she must have been seeing in mine for all these months.

"We can do this, Alma. Together. I've got you."

I hold her hand and take her bag as she gets out of the car. Wrapping my arms around her, I hold her in my arms as we walk into the abortion clinic.

AFTER PAPERWORK AND VITALS, Alma's brought to a room for an ultrasound. Our vibe is off, and even the ultrasound tech can feel it. She gives me a side-eye look. "Alma, would you prefer to have your ultrasound performed alone?"

Holding my breath, I step back to give her space to decide how much she wants me to be involved. I'm happy to sit in the waiting room or hold her hand. No matter what has been happening between us, she needs me, and I'm here for her.

She grabs my hand and pulls me into the dimly lit room with her. "This is my best friend. I need her with me."

The ultrasound tech nods and closes the door behind us. Weird vibes and all, I stand by Alma's side, squeezing her hand, as the ultrasound wand moves across her flat belly and pauses on a heartbeat.

"You're like five weeks, aren't you, Alm?" I whisper as the tech measures and estimates gestation.

"Yeah, I haven't gotten my period since I took that Plan B," she whispers back miserably.

"You two must be close. That guess was spot on. Five weeks, two days. Would you like a copy of the ultrasound?"

Alma looks stunned by the request. I answer for her. "I'll take it. You can figure out if you want it later." I gently tuck the tiny square of white film into a small pocket of my purse as we silently watch the heartbeat on the screen flicker for another intimate, vulnerable minute.

I glance at Alma and realize tears are streaming down her cheeks as she lays back on the exam table. Grabbing a tissue, I wipe her eyes and pull her up. She pushes my hand away but then pulls me into a tight hug.

The amount of information thrown at us is overwhelming considering I just found out that Alma is pregnant.

This early, Alma is given the choice between two simple and safe abortion procedures—surgical, a procedure performed at the center, and medicinal, taking several rounds of medication at home over the course of a few hours. Both are highly effective and safe for women. Alma opts for a surgical abortion.

"I can't leave here knowing it might not work. This is hard enough as it is. I won't be able to relax until I finish the medication at home."

As she discusses pain management options, my eyebrows fly up and my mouth opens and closes as I stop myself from interrupting, waiting for Alma to have her questions answered before I blurt out my own.

"What version of reality is this that someone is offered a medical procedure with just ibuprofen? Women have abortions with less ibuprofen than I take for a migraine."

The patient advocate explains. "A lot of women don't have a choice. It's the only option for pain medication if she needs to drive herself home."

Stunned back into silence at that response, my heart breaks for the women alone in the waiting room. *Why is Alma even considering ibuprofen?*

"Alma, you know I'll drive you to your appointment and be here with you, right?"

She nods without looking at me and asks more questions about recovery.

When the patient advocate leaves to check on our waiting time to see the doctor and sign the 24-hour notification paperwork, I reach over and take her hand. "Thank you for letting me be here for you today. I'm so sorry I didn't know. I wouldn't want you to be here alone."

"Well, that makes one of you, Maggie. Eric just Venmo-ed me and texted some nonchalant shit about me 'handling it.'"

My head rears back as I choke out a gasp. "That's beyond awful. What a—"

Alma angrily interrupts. "Yeah, well, I wasn't even sure if you were going to show up. I was terrified sitting in that parking lot with those people screaming awful shit at me about being a baby murderer."

"Oh, Alm, I'm sorry. Of course I was going to show up."

But even I hear the half-lie in my voice. There was absolutely a chance I wouldn't have shown up since I kind of thought we were just meeting for lunch and would have expected Alma to understand that I forgot/was too tired/had to get Jillian.

I've expected a lot from Alma lately without giving much back to her. The guilt I felt when I pulled into the parking lot and realized how much she had been dealing with alone lately pulls at my heart.

I reach for her.

Alma puts her hand out between us and shakes her head. She keeps it there as she lays into me, revealing the true stress I have put on our friendship.

"No, Maggie. There was every chance you wouldn't show up, and we both know it. Every chance you would have gotten distracted by pumping or forgotten or made up some excuse about how motherhood is the *worst* and you hate it and can't be expected to do much of anything anymore with your friends."

Her words land like bombs between us, painful truths being thrown at me in this building that seems to heighten every emotion.

"I'm your best friend, Maggie. I need *you* and not the miserable version you've turned into since you gave birth. I mean, do you even *like* Jillian?"

Recoiling as if she slapped me, I slide as far down the bench as I can from her. Even if her anger at Eric and emotion around being pregnant are influencing her words, she's not wrong about how I've shown up, or not, for her as a friend lately.

"Alma, I—" I don't get out much more before the door opens and the patient advocate walks back in.

"The doctor is ready for you. You can follow me." She pauses and looks at us more closely. "Doing okay in here?"

We both nod and stand to follow.

"Do you need a few minutes?" I start to say yes, but Alma cuts me off.

"No, I'm ready. Thank you."

She confidently walks out of the room, and I follow, catching up to her and linking my arm through hers.

"I'll go to the waiting room if you want, Alm, but I'm one-thousand-per-cent here for you."

The sincerity in my eyes must shine through because she squeezes my arm with hers and leans her head on my shoulder.

"I know, Maggie."

Alma and I compare calendars and pick a day for her abortion. She opts for a surgical abortion with the strongest pain medication available. We both block off the whole day and put in personal day requests before we leave the clinic, so we (I) don't forget when we (I) get home.

The silence in the waiting room makes the conversation we need to have awkward. For a room full of people, the quiet is unnerving. Almost everyone is staring at their phone with tight brows and slight frowns on their faces. Stress. Money. Time. Love. An inordinate amount of unmet needs and bodies squeezed into this room.

The crowded waiting room caught me off guard. The advocate explained that every patient must meet with the doctor at least twenty-four hours before their abortion because of state law, and this doctor works at four other clinics around the state. With so few doctors willing to sign waiting period forms, his time is scarce, and appointments take hours to make the most of his one afternoon here.

"Alma, do you want to talk? I need to apologize for being a shitty friend. I'm sorry I haven't been here for you lately."

She lets out a long sigh. "I can't do this right now, Maggie. Not here. I'm okay. We're okay. I shouldn't have unleashed on you in there, but I stand by what I said. The truth is that I need you to be a better friend right now. I need my old friend back."

"I know, Alm. Today is a massive wake-up call for me."

"You and me both, babe. And as much as we need to have this conversation, I'm ready to go home."

We walk out of the clinic and hug next to our cars. The last few protesters pace slowly up and down the sidewalk, and I can't help but wonder how much further their energy would go volunteering as foster parents than standing on sidewalks yelling at women. Pouring love into little ones instead of anger into mothers.

"I love you, Alma. Call me if you need me tonight, promise?"

She nods. "Can I have that ultrasound picture?"

I press the small photo into her hand. "I'm here for you no matter what you choose."

"I know. Love you too."

She climbs into her car and gives me a small wave as I stand next to my car, between her and the last few protesters on the sidewalk, and watch her drive away, sending up a little prayer for love and support for her.

Her taillights disappear around the corner as a rogue thought pops into my head.

How can I give Alma her "old friend" back when she doesn't exist anymore?

Old Maggie disappeared when Jillian was born. Alma needs that version of me, but she's gone. I will never have the same amount of freedom as Alma does right now… My energy and time and love will always flow strongest to Jillian and the millions of new obligations (both amazing and awful) that come with motherhood.

Alma can't understand this because *I* didn't understand it until now.

And while I can't be the "old Maggie" that Alma wants, I can show up better as the "new Maggie" we both need.

A protester yells to get my attention and takes a picture of me with his phone.

"Oh, fuck off," I mutter and flip him off as I climb into my car to go pick up my baby.

CHAPTER THIRTY-SEVEN

The night doesn't go much smoother as Jillian screams in her witching hour and dinner goes up in flames on the grill. Tonight is the first time Caden seems to be flustered by parenthood. I smile slightly and take Jillian from him as he tries to salvage dinner with no luck.

"It's okay, babe. I'll order delivery. It's been a day."

Caden tosses burned meat in the compost while I order delivery of our favorite stressful day treat, the Dragon & Phoenix from the local Chinese restaurant.

Sighing deeply, I take the liberty of opening a fancy-ish bottle of wine to go with our chicken and pork, the cork popping easing some of the stress from my afternoon with Alma. I pour him a glass because my husband is almost as worried about my best friend—and pissed at her ex—as I am.

Caden's typical self-restraint is holding him back from calling Eric out on his bullshit. "I can't believe he's sleeping around if he's not ready to step up and at least be a mature participant in the consequences."

Given the topic, my small smile feels inappropriate, but I can't hold it in.

This man is dreamy when he's standing up for women. Who knew my love language was feminism?

Then I almost snort my wine up my nose when he continues.

"I mean, don't bust a nut without a condom if you can't deal, ya know?"

I nod somberly in agreement, trying not to choke on my wine at this unexpected rant from the usually cool-headed Caden.

"I get he doesn't want to be a dad, but he doesn't have to be an asshole either."

The doorbell rings, distracting Caden from the rest of his rant, but that was enough to make me fall in love all over again with him.

After Jillian is asleep and our dinner on the couch is cleaned up, Caden switches from comedy replays to one of his shows with too much gratuitous violence for me. Craving time with my binder, I go upstairs and get in bed.

Rather than think about my afternoon with Alma, I work on the next task, finding dates and locations associated with the different pictures and dreams. Time to Google.

What year did "Piece of my Heart" by Janis Joplin come out? 1969.

What year did O'Malley's Pub close? 1998.

Does Chef's Diner exist in Chicago? Not that I can tell based on Google and Yelp. I'm not even sure that's the real name of the diner or just what the woman called it in my dream.

Maybe reddit will have some answers?

So far, the past life theory fits. I was born in 1984. These dates would give me time to die as the woman in the dream and be reborn again as myself...

I pause and do a mental double-check that I haven't accidentally eaten a weed gummy. I can't believe I'm considering any of these ideas as real possibilities.

Okay, back on track.

When did the NWI Express run? It's basically been running for the past fifty years or so. What if I Google hostage on the train?

Hmmm. Okay, there are more hostage situations on trains that I thought, even if I try to keep it to the NWI Express.

I synthesize my keywords and even go onto the dreaded second and third pages of the search results. Eyes starting to droop, I'm about to wrap up for the night when I realize most of the newspaper articles are coming from the Chicago Tribune. I update my notes and tuck the binder away for the night.

I love on Alma by text message and then put my phone into sleep mode. I tried to get her to stay with me tonight like we used to before Jillian was born, but she passed. Her last message was, "I promise I'm not mad at you, Mags, I just need some space tonight. Coffee tomorrow, promise."

We both have a lot of adulting to do right now, and I don't envy her.

IGNORING the growing number of unread emails in my inbox, I pull myself out of the rabbit hole of searching for hostage situations and make a map of the locations of Chef's Diner, O'Malley's, and the train line. Last night's research led to some new details. My hastily and poorly drawn map stretches across two states—Indiana and Illinois—in an area familiar to me. After more reddit searches when I should have been working, I found the diner location.

I inhale sharply as this realization settles down on me. I've been on this train before. I've walked around Gramma's neighborhood and most likely at least driven past the corner where O'Malley's Pub used to be, maybe even while it still existed. Chef's Diner was torn down way back in the 80s and is now a Rock N Roll McDonald's that I grew up going to with my mom.

If this was me in a past life, am I just wandering the same path over and over? Walking in the shadows of these tragedies each lifetime?

I can't narrow down the hostage situation. I've already taken a guess and limited my search to only those which occurred prior to 1983 (hell, might as well make sure that there was time for me to die and be reborn between the hostage situation and my conception). I search one more time using the specific stations of the train route, putting my fancy PhD to the test.

I'm about to give up when my eyes snag on the first lines of text from an article dated August 16, 1980. An unidentified woman was taken hostage on the NWI Express L train at a downtown station by a Vietnam Veteran.

This must be it.

My muscles tense up as my adrenaline and fear skyrocket. I straighten up in my chair, eyes flying around the office, watching my colleagues have seemingly normal workdays. I've been tensely bent over my keyboard all morning, pouring copious amounts of attention into this research. I decide to simply give in to the flow today and catch up on work tomorrow. I'm out of my mind with the extreme coincidences taking place, but quickly coming down the other side to wonder what the fuck is going on?! How am I dreaming of real-life events I know nothing about? The eeriness and supernatural vibes of this whole situation make me start to shiver. My shoulders tense and my teeth chatter as the full realization of what is happening settles over me.

Just then, Alma stops in front of my desk. I may be lowkey avoiding her and the uncomfortable conversation we're due for today.

"Hey, Mags. Pump break?" she asks as she picks up my pump bag.

Well, I guess this is happening. "Yep, let me send off this email real quick."

We're unusually quiet as I close my computer down and follow her to the pump room, as if I've been called to the principal's office. Alma's about to lay into some hard truths, and I need to hear her out.

She waits until I'm hooked up and the pump provides a rhythmic background noise to cover this conversation from anyone walking by.

"Listen, Maggie, about yesterday…" Alma pauses, and the irony of her pregnant pause isn't lost on me. She breathes out through her nose and continues quietly. "Thank you for coming with me yesterday." Then, her words burst forth as if she's been holding them in during our short walk to the break room. "You aren't the reason I want to have an abortion."

I breathe in sharply as she says those painful words again, but this time I'm less reactive than yesterday.

"I want to have an abortion because I don't think it's the right time for me to become a mom and hundred-per-cent the wrong time for Eric to co-parent. I'm not sorry I said what I said yesterday, but I should have said it differently. You don't make motherhood look miserable. You just seem unhappy in it. I miss you. I miss our friendship. The past months have been lonely without you."

I reach out for her hand and squeeze, trying not to move my chest too much and break the suction of the pump. "I know, Alma. I'm not okay. I haven't shown up for you or Caden or even myself lately. Jillian seems to be the only person who is happy with me right now. And you've been beyond patient as I work through the fire storm of these dreams. Sometimes, it takes some real talk from my favorite person to show me how far things have gone."

I grab a cloth diaper to dab at the tears trickling down my cheeks. "This is all much harder than I expected, and I don't know how to ask for help or what to even ask for help with so I complain and get some attention that feels like a cheap version of nurturing. It's fucked up." I take a deep, shuttered breath. "And I dumped all my unhappiness on you in one nasty resentful heap. That's not what you needed yesterday. I'm here for you, always. I love you, and I'm sorry, Alma."

Now we're both crying and hugging and laughing because our hug is causing the pump bottles to lose suction and make quacking noises. We are a chaotic hot mess, just like we're supposed to be together.

"You know I'll be by your side next week, Alma. There's no way I would let you go by yourself if you want me there."

"I know. It's why I needed you at that appointment with me

even though I was mad at you. And you better bring the good snacks and tell that man of yours to get the guest room ready. Auntie Alma's recovering with her besties in style… a *Love is Blind* marathon and ice cream in bed. Get the good milk out for Jillian. We're popping bottles after this is all done."

My laughter sends tears down my cheeks as I text Caden because he will in fact get both bottles and ice cream ready for us without any questions asked—and he will know to splurge on the fancy ice cream too.

"Alma, do you still have that baby carrier?"

"Of course. Why?"

"Why don't we take Jillian to the Vintage Market this weekend by the lake? Brunch too? We've gotta go before Jillian's nap, but we can squeeze it all in if we leave early enough."

Alma nods enthusiastically as I continue. "Besides, we need to come up with a plan to create lowkey chaos in Eric's life with that five-hundred dollars he Venmo-ed you. I still can't believe he said 'use it for an abortion or diapers, dealer's choice.' I can't even!"

"Yeahhhh. He's not the ideal man to have both a condom break with and then Plan B fail." Alma covers her mouth with her hands and lets out a soft groan. "I mean, I never thought I would be in this situation, but—"

"I know, Alm. It's okay. You're okay. Motherhood is more than just having a baby. It choosing how to, or not to, bring life into this world to love and nurture, not the consequence of a broken condom. You and your baby, when—if—you become a mom, deserve all the love in the world."

CHAPTER THIRTY-EIGHT

Caden's text pops up after the live stream announcing my latest research findings about the positive impact of community around teens with challenging backgrounds and hard family lives.

CADEN

Babe, you were so good! You sounded fucking smart talking about statistics. Hot.

He ends his message with a stream of emojis ranging from hearts to eggplants, making my cheeks turn pink and warm. Everyone is benefiting from me finally sleeping through the night. My boss even gave me a thumbs up as I passed him on my way to the pump room.

I wave off a last-minute invite to lunch with colleagues after another round of congratulations and lock myself with a celebratory Malley's chocolate bar and my binder. With the whoosh, whoosh of the pump in the background, I can finally do what I've been waiting for all morning.

Gloria's response waits for me in my messages. I wipe my sweaty hands on my pants as I tell myself—again—that she probably doesn't know anything. Messaging her was a shot in the dark. As I start to read, my shoulders tense and rise up to my ears, and I squeeze my phone hard enough to make my knuckles turn white while I scroll through her general hellos and updates. My breath catches in surprise, and my world tunnels down into only what is on the small screen when I read her words.

GLORIA

> I don't know how to say this gently, so I'm just going to say it. O'Malley's was an old Irish bar where your Uncle Craig got hurt. I don't think you're supposed to know this. Your family never talked about it after those first few years and just pretended he had always been that way. That he had been born like that and that's what everyone was told after a few years. It got easier and easier as the neighborhood changed, and his friends moved away or started their own families.

> It was like that bar fight never happened and Craig had always been slow, or at least that's what your grandma would say to people who asked. Maybe it was easier to pretend that he had always been that way rather than that he had once been this incredibly kind and smart man with a better future than he lived. I don't think it was easier for Craig, though. Every time I ran into him, he was so angry. His future had been stolen away from him, but everyone else was pretending it was all okay.

My mouth hangs open with bits of chewed up chocolate in it as I process the long stream of text. I set my phone down hard, sliding it away from me across the table.

My Uncle Craig?! What?! Is she talking about Uncle CoCo?!? The man I nicknamed Uncle CoCo because he was always drinking Coca-Cola when I was little? It was his thing. He always had a red can, and I always wanted a sip. The story is that every time we

visited, I would call out "CoCo! CoCo!" and it just stuck until he
died years later… Until he killed himself years later.

*I never got a chance to see the man's face outside the bar. I didn't recognize
him under the blood and bruises.*

His eyes and profile no longer whole, but not quite the shape of
the man I knew either, further altered by the flashing lights from the
police cars. I never asked what happened to Uncle CoCo. Why were
his words always a little fuzzy? What was the scar on his face? He
died when I was too young to know these dots existed, let alone to
connect them.

My initial shock wears off as I finish the bite of chocolate
lingering in my mouth and take a long, angry slurp on my water
bottle. Craig's injury feels obvious now, and my deep focus on the
connections between this message and my dream means I don't
immediately realize the pump is now sucking on my dry nipples. I
unhook the tubing but leave the pump on. The noise will dissuade
anyone from knocking on the door.

GLORIA

Maybe I shouldn't tell you this. Your family
needed to let the bar fight go into the past.
NO ONE talks about it anymore. Maybe that
was easier for your grandma, but she's gone
now. They're all gone. So I guess it's okay
for you to know. Who are you even going to
tell?

> Your uncle snuck your mom into O'Malley's one night after she got into a blow-up fight with your grandparents. While she was inside dancing, he hit on some prep's girlfriend. When the guy saw, he shoved Craig out the door and into the alley for a fight. It was a totally unfair fight. Craig against this guy with all his friends. It got out of control too fast. Your mom's cousin came out just as the guy picked up a brick and smashed Craig's head, but it was too late. No one even got arrested. It was their story against Craig's. And he was poor, passed out, covered in blood. Life was never the same for your mom.

> Craig was her protector. Her best friend. And then she had to be his. It wasn't fair but I guess that's fucking life, man.

Her final message is loud and clear.

GLORIA

> Don't tell your aunt I told you all this. I don't want her stirring up shit.

Pulling on my bottom lip, I stare at the text on the screen, trying to sort out what I remember being told about Craig and what I'm reading now.

As if Gloria can sense my presence on the other side of the screen, she starts typing again. More text fills the screen. Maybe she was waiting to see the notification that I'd read her first messages before sending more. Maybe she's ready to pour this whole story out after years of holding it in and doesn't give a damn about the consequences.

GLORIA

Never mind. Tell her. Someone's gotta grieve
for this mess. That night was supposed to
be fun, but instead your mom lost her future
right there with Craig's. There was so much
blood. Even the next day. I went there after
school. People were talking about it... a few
of us wandered over to the pub to see where
it had happened. Craig wasn't too much
older than us. We were all kinda friendly. He
was a basketball player. I don't know why
we went. Morbid curiosity. The blood was
still there. A puddle of dark sticky blood too
big to look like it came from one person. I've
never forgotten all that blood. I still dream
about it sometimes.

Tears fall down my cheeks, and I grab the same cloth diaper I
used a few days ago when I was crying with Alma in here.
How could no one have talked about this? Why is this a secret?

GLORIA

I'm sorry. This is all too much to be dumping
on you. It's too much for me to even be
talking about. I'm getting pulled way back in
the past now. It's all so fucking depressing.
This isn't how you imagine growing old is
gonna be. We were supposed to be hanging
out, listening to Janis, maybe smoking a
joint or two, and watching our kids grow up
together. We weren't from the side of town
where we ever thought life was going to be
easy, but damn, we never imagined it could
be this cruel. Your mom went through a lot.
You gotta forgive her for the way she died.
She tried her best to live, but life kept cutting
her off at the knees. Between Craig and her
first husband, it's a miracle she even made it
long enough to have you.

A low, sad sound leaves my throat as the dream starts to take on
new light. I'm stunned by the emerging details.

GLORIA

> I gotta stop. I've already said too much. I want to say let me know if you need anything else, but I'm not sure I can handle all this pain from the past again. Maybe that's why they never talked about it. The pain just doesn't seem to stop hurting, even after all these years. Love to you and your baby. Your mom would have loved that you named your baby girl after her.

Each word and revelation shakes my body to its core. By the time I finish reading Gloria's messages, full-blown shock is setting in. My body is shivering, but the air in the pump room feels stifling, and I break out in beads of sweat across my forehead.

The room shrinks down until it is too tiny for me and all these revelations. I'm suffocating on memories. My pump bra squeezes my chest too tightly, and I can't breathe. The chocolate and coffee that were pleasurable a few minutes ago are now threatening to reappear. Wet drops fall on my arms as tears stream down my face silently.

Realizations that I'm not ready to accept are waiting on the sidelines outside my consciousness. I can't believe it. I won't believe it. But the gears in my brain keep spinning slowly. Crunching information into facts. Using that same brain that just nailed a huge research project to synthesize these new details. Clicking puzzle pieces from Gloria's message into place to reveal what has been wreaking havoc in my life for these past months.

Why didn't anyone tell me what happened to Uncle CoCo?! Why didn't my mom tell me? How is it even possible that I'm finding out this way? From a dream?!

Maybe Mom would have told me eventually if she hadn't died. She got a GED instead of graduating from high school, but I never asked why. I guess she had to help Craig after he got hurt.

My hands squeeze the edge of the table, grounding myself as my breathing quickens. I don't want to know the other reality settling into my brain, suffocating my senses, threatening to tip my center of gravity.

I push away from the knowledge latching onto my brain with a tenacity I can't fight. The girl dancing to Janis Joplin in the bar. The girl who was ripped out of the bathroom and into the alley to help her brother. That girl would grow up to be the woman who was *my mom*.

And once that thought is fully formed in my mind, I can't shake it loose, no matter how hard I shake my head.

No. No. No. No.

I'm sweaty and hot with desperation to hold on to the stories I've made up about these dreams. My other timelines or past lives. The pain of everything my mom experienced and held secret is threatening to tear me apart from the inside.

Not my past life, but my mom's reality. She was just a girl when tragedy changed the trajectory of her life.

And if that dream isn't my past life, how can the others be? What could the others be?

Short, hot breaths pump in and out of my lungs as grief blooms in my chest. I either need to succumb to the threatening panic attack or howl and shriek like I crave to do. Rage and grief churn beneath my skin, turning me red and splotchy and sweaty.

This pain, and these new details about the trauma in my family, beg to be released from my body. I rip off my pump bra, and I stand there, shirtless with the pump screaming behind me. I'm sweaty and shivering from the blast of what must be the too-high fan, my stomach tied in knots.

I need to get out of here. The feral energy to get out of this office and outside in the open air and light of the sun forces me to move.

I quickly dress as my phone lights up with a new notification. Oh, for fuck's sake, please let Gloria be done. I can't handle any more family secrets being unearthed today.

But it's not from Gloria—it's an email notification from the librarian I emailed about the article in the Chicago Tribune. Another puzzle piece offered by the universe.

I ignore that I asked for this response and throw my phone into my bag.

As I make my way out of the pump room, I stop by my cubicle as calmly as possible to gather up my laptop and car keys. I politely wave and tell Jack I'm heading home to work for the day. I need to leave this building as quickly as possible. He asks if I'm okay, and I give a cheerful, "Yep! See you tomorrow!" and wave as I walk away. My splotchy red face and smeared mascara are dead giveaways that I'm, in fact, not okay. But I'm proud of myself for 1) not running to Alma and pouring out the whole insane story like I'm desperate to do, nor 2) tripping and falling down that damn open concept stairway in the middle of the office building. In my haste to escape as quickly as possible, I threw my bra in my bag. I don't need to trip and fall with my milky boobs popping out of my shirt right now.

The door barely closes behind me before I unleash my huge, guttural sobs into the cold, crisp winter air.

CHAPTER THIRTY-NINE

I squeeze Alma's hand as we wait for the doctor to walk into the small, clean exam room. The smell of disinfectant spray fills my nose. Eyes tight, brows furrowed, she looks at me with what is supposed to be a smile but is more her lips pressed tightly together. Without her signature winged eyeliner and twinkle in her eye, Alma looks like a faded out version of herself in the exam bed with attached foot stirrups. She's undressed from the waist down with a paper coverup, shivering. Ready to be done with this chapter of her life.

Her tote bag of loose sweatpants, a blanket, extra underwear, heating pad, pain medicine, and the largest pads we could find at the drugstore along with multiple snacks and sparkling water sits at my feet. We are prepared for anything with this tote bag. With little under Alma's control, I just stood by and helped as she picked out her essentials for this appointment.

"Don't worry, hun. It's cold in here but the medication might make you feel a little chill, too."

A kind, chatty nurse reassures Alma in between asking how the weather is outside, what shows we've been watching, have we tried the new sushi place in town... all sorts of questions that make today feel less overwhelming. Less scary than the protesters screaming at us as we scurried into the clinic doors, escorted by a pair of pink-shirted college students who met us at the car when Caden dropped us off.

When I pushed him not to drive us, his response was perfectly Caden. "There's no fucking way I'm letting you drive there. Those protesters are always crowding out the women walking in, screaming insane shit. Last thing Alma needs is some rando making her feel bad today. She needs us. The least I can do is drive a car."

The nurse moves trays around the room and adjusts Alma's IV. Alma and I hang on tight to each other, hands clasped, waiting. Waiting for her first journey into motherhood to end as quickly as it began. Waiting for a doctor who risks his life every day to make sure that she has a choice to become a mother—or not.

The door swings open as the doctor walks in, carrying in the low music and quiet chatter from the patient areas of the clinic along with him. He greets Alma, looking her warmly in the eyes and asking, "Are you ready to begin?"

Alma swallows and nods once, confident in her decision. She's ready. I lean over and kiss her forehead.

"You've got this, Alm. And I've got you," I whisper as the nurse pushes medicine into her IV.

I stand at Alma's side and squeeze her hand, grounding her here with me just like she did for me when I gave birth. Both of us stepping into motherhood in the way that is best for us individually. No matter how turbulent the world is outside of our friendship, we will keep each other steady.

Alma cried and grieved last night after we packed this giant tote bag. I know she's confident in her decision. She wrote a letter to the tiny sac of cells that could grow into a baby last night.

Tears streamed down her face as she simultaneously poured love into, and said good-bye to, this sweet soul and explained why this wasn't their time to be mother and child.

She's made peace with her decision and is now simply waiting. Waiting to be on the other side of this door again. Waiting to be in the recovery room. Waiting to become a mother until she can financially support a baby with a partner who wants to be a co-parent and not just Venmo over diaper money.

The doctor takes a seat on the stool near Alma's legs and puts on gloves. "Then let's begin…"

Less than ten minutes later, Alma's abortion is complete.

CHAPTER FORTY

Leaning into the heated car seat, I breathe for a long time before I find the courage to open the email from the librarian. Waiting to read her email has been hard, but if anything can break the grip the dreams have on my life, my sanity, it's Alma's current reality. At least I drove to the nearby Target parking lot in case I lose my shit in my car again and I'm calm enough to handle more news.

The librarian's obviously impressed with herself for locating the incident, but prickly over the lack of details about the hostage. "It's almost like there was nothing to report. No details to be given about this person who was taken hostage. It's unusual. All the other articles from that time interview the victims."

Survivors, I automatically correct in my head as I keep reading. She offers to look through the archives for more information if I want her to. "Just let me know," she ended her email cheerfully.

Do I want to ask for more?

Ugh. It's hard to figure out what I want to do versus what I need to do right now.

The librarian shared a few details that she found from the 1980 article and attached a PDF. Not to my surprise, the shooter was killed by the police while on the train with the hostage. For such a huge incident, it had surprisingly little coverage because of the election cycle.

Closing my eyes, my options play out, and the answer becomes intuitively clear, but annoying. While I *want* to go back to my biggest problem being balancing the working mom circus that is my life, I *need* to learn more about the woman on the train. More information seems the only clear path forward to end the hold these dreams have on my reality.

I ask the librarian to let me know if she finds anything else and profusely thank her.

As quickly as I send the first email, I send her a second. She's genuinely helpful and is asking few follow-up questions, which is great because I lack answers.

I ask about searching for a man whose first name is Jeremy, who was married and probably died in Chicago by suicide in the 1970s. Is it at all possible to identify this man or at least a list of potential Jeremys?

Well at least, I'm finally asking for help. Just maybe not the type of help my therapist suggested.

BY THE TIME I'm home, the librarian has replied to my email. Her email makes it sound like she's hungry for this type of work. She didn't find a ton of new information about the hostage situation, but she combed the Chicago death records and found three different married men named Jeremy who were in their twenties when they died by suicide in the late 1970s.

"We're lucky that I was able to narrow the list down to three!"

We? I guess she's invested now if we've turned into a team.

"I can find the names of the wives in the marriage records, but not until I get back from vacation next week. They weren't married in the city. We need to use a different database."

Dammit. A week? My shoulders slump as I read on.

"I attached the death certificates. The names of the funeral homes that claimed bodies are listed on each record. If you don't want to wait a week, reach out to the funeral homes to see if they have any more information about these Jeremys."

Relief instantly loosens the knot in my stomach as I make a decision, even if Caden's going to hate it. I need to go home to Northwest Indiana for a weekend. There are too many coincidences and bits of information stacking up, and I'm desperate to see O'Malley's Pub, to walk in the alley, to see if I can feel any of my mom on that corner where her life drastically altered course. To talk to someone, anyone, who may have more details. I can't follow these clues from the hidden corners of my mind and bed anymore.

My hometown is pulling at my bones to return, calling me back. I intuitively know this is the right next step. The answers I need are at the end of this journey, and this journey is home.

PART III

CHAPTER FORTY-ONE

C aden had been appropriately horrified by the macabre story of my family's history as I tried to explain how desperate I was to go home. To convince him that I needed to go away one more time. To leave him and Jillian for just a few days. To see these places with fresh eyes and closure from the dreams. Why I was desperate to come and see these places for myself. Fresh memories have sharpened in the months following Jillian's birth, since the dreams began, since the walls holding my childhood trauma crumbled around me in Mother Oak.

"My grandpa died in a house fire. A few days after the fire, Gramma was admitted to the hospital for complications with diabetes and died. She had stopped eating. Maybe she was heartbroken? In shock? Or just couldn't hang on anymore? I don't think anyone knows why, just how."

Caden's jaw had unclenched as he'd squeezed my hand, and I could see his resolve that I was being dramatic about needing to visit soften. Somehow I'd never told him this story in full before. A story from my own *before*. Before Jillian. Before him.

Sharing the last part of the story had felt extra and dramatic, like, "Okay, Mags, now you're just showing off your trauma."

"Then, a month or so later, my Uncle CoCo committed suicide. On Christmas."

Caden had sucked in a breath at that last part and pulled me in for a hug. He'd rested his head on top of mine and stroked my back. Neither of us had been willing to break the silent truce that had formed in that moment, but Jillian had been willing and able to fill the quiet with her wail of hunger. Baby girl was ready for dinner.

"Maggie, does this have to do with the dreams?"

We haven't spoken in detail about the dreams since I returned from Mother Oak. Celebrating Jillian's milestones, supporting Alma. So much life has filled our time that I didn't want to painfully chip these moments back in favor of the torment of these dreams.

I'd used my newly honed skill of half-truths to share what I could without making him worry even more. "Yeah, babe, sort of. I'm desperately missing my mom and think this will help me feel more connected to her right now. Those dreams, my time in Mother Oak, stirred up so many new-to-me memories. Some time at home to ask questions, get some answers. I'll feel more settled after this trip."

True, but lacking in that tiny finding that one of the dreams was about my mom.

SLIDING my sunglasses on against the bright sun, bits of broken sidewalk crunching under my feet, I stand in front of the house built on my family's memories. After a long drive and even longer week full of tension with Caden and at work, I'm finally here.

Memories consume me as I recall some of my last visits to this place.

My first period came a few days before I turned twelve. I remember going to my aunt's house thinking we would celebrate my transition into womanhood but found lots of whispered adult conversations happening in the kitchen instead. The cousins were repeatedly sent outside to play and leave the grownups alone. A few hours later, they told us that there had been a fire in our grandparents' house, and Grandpa had died. The house had burned down.

That was the beginning of the end.

Shooting a quick text to Caden that I've arrived and will check in later, I walk away from the house that had been built on top of my family's broken lives. That year had been full of loss and sadness. Broken relationships today have origins in the smoke and flames of that fire.

I walk the route laid out on my hand-drawn map from this address, my mom and uncle's home when this bar fight happened, to O'Malley's Pub.

I recognize the brick building standing on the street corner, currently a Hispanic convenience store. The red bricks from my dream are now whitewashed. Windows are covered in bilingual ads for everything from fresh tortillas to candy. The new store's name is hand-lettered in crisp black and white. I imagine "O'Malley's Pub" in bright white and green letters curling across the front of the building, tiny shamrocks around the edges, just like in my drawing.

I stare at the building, at the front door. At the street sign on the corner, wondering if it bore witness to the tragedy that happened here. Of the moment that marked a "before" and "after" for both my mom and Uncle CoCo.

For me too.

Would my mom have become an alcoholic without this "before" and "after?" Would that winter when my grandpa, grandma, and uncle died have happened if this bar fight had turned out differently? Would the quick fix of pills and alcohol have been so strong without this alley?

In the briefest answers possible, my aunt confirmed Gloria's details of Craig's injuries. Any hope I had of picking her brain for more was killed when she asked me not to bring her brother up again. "The past needs to stay where it belongs, dear."

But what if the past doesn't want to stay where it belongs? What if the past is consuming my future?

I snap pictures of the street sign and building with my phone
and slowly walk around the corner of the bar to the alley. Before I
can face the literal scene of the crime, I'm pulled into the store as if
my feet are making their own decisions. I can't *not* go in the store.

I open the door, ringing the bells on the door handle. My breath
catches as "Break Another Piece of My Heart" plays over the
speakers. Just for a second as the manager flips through radio
stations. I should be used to these coincidences, these kismet
moments, but my heart still races and my adrenaline spikes.

While long turned into a convenience store, a bar would fit this
space too. Under the guise of picking a few snacks and coffee for my
day of playing detective, I wander around the store and imagine the
dream playing out in this space. The loud music. The dim lighting.

Setting my snacks and coffee on the counter, I look around for
the bathroom. The bored clerk is still flipping through radio dials
and offhandedly points to the hallway in the corner. Checking if the
bathroom looks familiar to the one in my dream wasn't part of my
original plan, but how can I not once I'm here? I walk in that
direction, dodging displays of snacks and energy drinks.

The hairs on the back of my neck stand up, and I press my
fingertips on my tattoo. As I pull open the bathroom door, the clerk
controlling the radio lands back on Janis, and I step inside the
bathroom, déjà vu flooding my body and making me stumble
slightly. I place a hand on the sink to balance myself as my stomach
bottoms out and heart beats hard and fast, echoing in my ears over
the music from the tinny bathroom speaker.

A wild-eyed and tired woman stares back at me from the
bathroom mirror. Eyes shifting too quickly around the room, jaw
tight—the danger my intuition senses from a different time fills the
air, a different decade rather than reality.

Relax, just breathe. Nothing's weird about this bathroom. You're safe.

I start humming along with the Janis song and use the
bathroom. When I step back up to the sink, an electric shock flushes
through me when I put my hands into the stream of water from the
faucet and look in the mirror again. Days have passed since my last

dream flashback, and I'm caught off guard by my mind flashing to scenes from the first dream in the bathroom.

As my head moves up to look in the mirror, my vision bounces back and forth from an empty convenience store to a crowded, dirty bar full of women in 70s clothes and hair, finally settling on the reflection of a girl with green eyes and hippie-long hair singing happily into the mirror. The scatter of freckles across her nose is immediately recognizable because I have the same one. Just like my mom.

Suddenly, the girl glances at the door and rolls her eyes. She must hear someone calling her name and pounding on the door. I can feel the recognition of her name being called in my body as her face changes in the mirror to worry as if she remembers she's drinking underage in a bar. Annoyance shoots up her spine from being bossed around and told to come out. While I can't hear what's happening on her end of the mirror, I wish for her sake, and my own, that it was someone telling her to get out because the police or her dad had shown up at the bar. But I know it's not.

I'm suddenly jolted from my flashback as I shakily realize the pounding on the other side of the door is real. A woman is knocking urgently and saying in Spanish that they need the bathroom now please. I leave, murmuring my apologies in Spanish, and walk outside into the fresh air with my bag of snacks.

One of the oddest aspects of feeling like I'm losing my mind is that... I don't feel like I'm losing my mind at all. That encounter in the bathroom mirror was almost... comforting. Healing. Seeing my mom as a happy teen singing is better than the repressed memories that have been floating to the surface since the treehouse, like of the cheap vodka bottle I had found in her closet right before she died.

So that's what the nighttime orange juice was for...

I stand outside the building, bracing against the wind. As I crunch my popcorn, chasing the dopamine fix this crunchy snack will give me, I consider my two options. Look in the alley, or don't and walk a couple of blocks back to my car and continue on to the city.

I know I must look in the alley. I drove all this way to stand on this specific corner and experience this alley in person.

Why would I not look in the alley? But after what just happened in the bathroom, why would I want to look in the alley?

Avoiding the possibility of ghosts in the alley, I remember my Uncle CoCo as an older man, drinking Coke and smoking while playing cards. A man at least twenty years out from a tragedy that altered his and our family's lives.

Taking a long sip from my Styrofoam cup, I reread Gloria's message about the bar fight. Craig's life was ruined that night. His future distorted by the lies, the half-truths, I've been told my entire life.

I toss my trash in a can outside the store and finally walk over to the alley, pulling my hair back into a bun to stop it from blowing in my eyes.

Well that was uneventful.

Wildly anticlimactic compared to the adrenaline rush going off in my body. A few minutes pass before I trust that I'm not about to nosedive into another flashback in the middle of this alley, among the dumpsters, parked cars, and rubble scattered around me. I overlay the dream against this gray, dirty backdrop and feel a groundswell of grief churn up in me. Grief for the life Craig lost and for what his life had become. Grief for the lies and lack of justice on his behalf.

My mom found her brother here, on the ground, covered in blood.

My grief swells to include her as my eyes catch on a pile of old bricks in the alleyway. No way the same bricks from decades ago, but the sight brings forth a vision of the pool of blood in the alley, police lights flashing off the sheen of a growing crimson puddle. The surprise darkness of fresh blood, not the bright red you'd expect.

I shake my head to clear the memories, and after glancing at my watch, realize I need to hurry to make the train into the city. I take a few more pictures of the alley, of the pile of bricks to compare to my drawings later, and walk to my car.

I leave my car in Indiana and take the NWI Express into the city to mimic the dreams as much as possible during this short visit. I need to make the most of this weekend away from my daughter.

Will the seats on the train be the same hard orange from my dream? Will the déjà vu pull me under again?

Whether by miracle, a massive chain of coincidences, or the practicality of a woman in the 1970s, many of the locations from my dreams in the city are within walking distance of the NWI Express' last stop in the city: Chef's Diner, and two of the churches sent to me by the librarian where a twenty-something married drug addict's funeral occurred in the 1970s. What are the odds one of these men is the man from my dream?

Low.

But what are the odds of any of this?

Even lower.

Of being in the city while Caden and Jillian are hundreds of miles away. Of Janis Joplin being played on the radio everywhere I go. Of postpartum dreams becoming my entire world. Did I dream all of this into existence? Family history and secrets unearthed from my dreams are now on display in a macabre showcase in the cold winter sun.

CHAPTER FORTY-TWO

The train seats aren't the orange from my dream, but a scratched, scarred tan. I switch between watching the buildings turn from industrial to skyscrapers and texting with Alma. The change in structures always gave me a thrill as a little girl when I would ride into the city with my mom, just like now. I text Alma a quick picture of the skyline coming into view, and we excitedly promise each other that we'll come out here together soon. Alma even insists on bringing Jillian and the leopard print carrier.

My relief over Alma's good vibes softens the edges of my guilt for leaving her this soon after her abortion. She slept over for two days afterward, and we alternated between grieving and tricking Caden into getting invested in *Love is Blind* with us so we could all hang out together in the evenings. Supporting Alma's recovery even helped smooth over Caden's tension around me leaving.

Alma swore she was fine when she left for her place this morning, and I believed her. She's sad but resolute, her own relief palpable as soon as we left the clinic.

Kind of like the woman being held hostage on the train. Of the relief and fear she must have felt when that man was shot. Horror over the violence and relief that she lived.

These thoughts take me right to the end of the line and my stop. Brakes squealing, metal clanging on tracks, the train slows to pull into the station, and a flood of remembering, of having been here before, comes over me. Because I *have* been here before, dozens of times as a child, in my own version of "before." But now I feel like I have been here *before*.

Remembering and recognizing feel different in my bones. Time doesn't make sense in my recall of this train platform busy with tourists on the weekend.

Overlooking the chaos of the train platform, I see where the hostage situation may have taken place. Where the emergency vehicles would have pulled in. Where the woman in the dream could have been treated for shock while the police and medics examined the crime scene in the train car and loaded the shooter's body onto a gurney.

The woman could have slipped right back into the crowd after being treated and cleaned up, not wanting to turn her life into a spectacle. Before she even gave her name to the police apparently, based on what the librarian had uncovered. Grainy black and white pictures of a woman's head and face in the train car with the hostage, but nothing too clear or close due to the technology of those times. Dark hair styled in the trendy way of the early 80s. Big-frame glasses in one picture. But the woman had disappeared before anyone could get her name along with my chance of identifying her.

I walk quickly away from the train and to the old location of Chef's Diner. My collar is pulled up, scarf wrapped around my neck, to protect against the bite of Chicago's wind, but it still cuts through the layers I dressed in this morning before I left my car at the station.

While the diner is long gone, a Rock N Roll McDonald's now occupies this piece of prime realty in the most touristy part of the city. I always begged my mom to stop at this McDonald's during our city trips, and she often said yes. I would happily eat an overpriced Happy Meal and stare at memorabilia from musicians long before my time, including an outfit worn by Janis Joplin.

I'm caught off guard by this memory from my childhood

because I'm used to my memories jumping back to the dreams rather than my own life.

Hmm… Janis is woven through both the dreams and my childhood.

As the day goes on, my shoulders collapse in relief as a lightness fills the air, a sense of hope for what's to come. I unwrap my scarf a few loops to let in the little bit of sunshine and warmth that keep finding me between skyscrapers, getting brighter as the day marches on. I walk past a small park full of birds chirping and children playing. While not spring yet, today is quickly turning into one of those sunny winter days that promises warmth and sunshine are not far away.

I wonder if Caden and Jillian have sunshine at home too.

Snow still covers the ground in shaded and shadowed patches, and more will come, but with the blue skies and slight tease of spring in the air, you can almost close your eyes and be surprised when you open them that the ground isn't covered with daffodils pushing out of the earth.

Around me, kids laugh, and strangers smile at each other in that friendly, optimistic way that comes so easily in the first warm days of late winter. A breeze flows around me, not quite warm, but refreshing in its crispness. It's only February 1st, and every Midwesterner knows to expect at least a few more good snows this year, no matter how much today feels like spring is just around the corner. But still, we smile and enjoy the glimmers of the season to come. I'm sure the car wash lines are full in the suburbs too.

I stop at the first of three churches on my walk with the directions Caden put together for me. He wasn't impressed by my hand-drawn map and sticky note itinerary, and, in his practical way, he created a Google Map and dropped pins for me. He printed it out along with zoomed-in pictures of the street maps. Now I can easily find my way between stops or in case my cell battery dies in the city.

At some point between taking care of Alma with me, fathering, working, and our general tension about this trip, he put a fully charged auxiliary battery charger and coffee gift card in my backpack, just in case. A few of my favorite protein bars, gum, and

a water bottle rounded out my "dopamine snacks" as he calls
them.

I'm an adult who knows how to use Google Maps and ask for
help if needed, but this is his love language, and I gratefully took the
maps and directions, and the snacks. We both know that while I'm
fully capable, I probably wouldn't have done any of that. And would
have ended up with a dead phone and desperately thirsty
somewhere. Capable, yes. Organized? Nope.

And in his practicality, he made sure not to ask questions if he
didn't want the full woo-woo answer after hearing me describe some
details to Alma. So does Caden know why I have an urgent need to
visit three churches and a Rock N Roll McDonald's? No. No, he
does not. Nor does he want to.

My conversation at each church is about the same. I explain that
I'm researching my family history and tell a made-up story of a
cousin named Jeremy who committed suicide and had a funeral in
Chicago in the late 1970s. Do they have records that far back, by
chance? This church was written down on some notes. No, I don't
have a last name, but I do have the year of the funeral.

Because computer records from that time don't exist, each of
the sweet old ladies—why always an old lady?—at each of the
church offices promises to do some digging in the old storage rooms
and see if they can come up with any information for me. One
woman is actively watching "her stories" and eating chips while
drinking 7-UP from a can with a straw while making this promise. I
try to keep my hopes up that these stops will be useful, but I've got
doubts. I leave my email and cell number on her grease-stained
notepad anyway and move on.

As I leave the final church office, I walk to the last address on my
list—an old apartment building according to Google. I'm not totally
sure how it's related, but I found this detail on a drawing I drew in
Mother Oak. With no context and just the street address, I had no
idea what to do with this until the dreams seemed to be based in
Hammond and Chicago. The address is coincidentally an old
apartment building located within walking distance of Rock N Roll

McDonald's (or the diner depending on what decade we're playing in).

As I navigate the city blocks, my mind wanders to the dreams. The girl—my mom—in O'Malley's watching her brother bleed on the sidewalk. The young woman in the second dream watching her husband kill himself. And the third taken hostage on a train. Each time, the woman's life and destiny were hijacked by men and circumstances outside of her control. Each time, she was *so* close to taking her life and future into her own hands, becoming fully responsible for herself.

I can't help but wonder who these women, this woman, would have become without tremendous amounts of pain and death in their lives. Without the dysfunction of male rage, addiction, and post-traumatic stress disorder wreaking havoc on her, changing her life trajectory, with every angry outburst of a man in pain seeking to release those huge emotions in dangerous and life-taking ways.

Who would she have become if she could have spent her life thriving instead of surviving?

Who could those men have become if they had been given the support and space to feel a full range of emotions instead of solely anger? If the resources they needed, like rehab and trauma therapy, were as easy to access as drugs and guns? If community surrounded and supported their healing? The pain and quiet longing for more feels so familiar to me.

Suddenly exhausted from my sad trail of thoughts and pity for both me and the people in the dreams, I dunk under an awning out of the way of the other pedestrians on the sidewalk to lean against a brick wall and study my map. I locate myself on it and realize I'm about to reach the apartment building at the address in the dream. In fact, I'm on the same block.

Energized, I push off the wall and start quickly walking down the street. Knowing I'm steps away from the end of this journey, the dopamine of finding this final address seeps into my system. I hurry down the street, almost slipping on the gray slush of half-melted snow. An old, rundown apartment building looms ahead, and the familiar sensation of déjà vu starts to thrum in my body.

Could this be the apartment building from the second dream?

Standing in a pocket of sunshine, I pull my gloves off to take pictures of the building. The brick is chipped and crumbling in more than a few places, with past-due notices taped to the row of mailboxes. Bedsheets are used as curtains in more windows than not, others completely boarded up. The crumbling steps into the doorway are heaped in trash, and a despondent energy radiates from the old, worn-down building.

I've never been here before but immediately feel a sense of home in front of this building. My drawings contain so many details that match what is before me now. Details that faded with time and neglect, like the stonework around the doorframe and cornices around a window. The iron grates over the first-floor windows and main door frame shaped by a curved stone design are identical.

The puzzle pieces in my head shuffle and click into place. In a time of nonsensical answers, I can only be impressed with how well I drew this building.

I look up and down the block for a landmark, an anchor. Something to tell me that I'm in the right place, on the right track. Something to confirm that this is, in fact, the apartment building from the second dream. Because if it's not, what is it? A completely random address I pulled from a dream? The address of the sister the woman was living with? Nothing is clicking firmly into place as I stand in front of the building, looking up at old windows with broken blinds and half-drawn curtains. Until I turn around and look more closely at the ornate Catholic church spreading down the block across the street.

I grew up "culturally Catholic" because my mom always wanted us to be part of a church community and have somewhere to turn for support. A home wherever you were. Somewhere to turn to in troubled times.

Standing directly in front of the apartment building now, I look up at the windows facing the street—and the front of this church. If you lived on this side of the building, your windows would face this church. If you sat and looked out your window and prayed for something more (luck, money, sobriety), your gaze would land on this church every time.

My eyes trace the intricate stonework of the church all the way up to the bell tower. Not a large church, but it has a special presence today as the doorways are covered with fresh flowers and greenery that look completely out of place on this winter day on this rundown block.

I'm pulled across the street to examine the impossibly familiar building more closely. A sign on the door welcomes people inside to celebrate the feast day of St. Brigid on February 1st—today.

Once in front of the church, I gasp. The scripted church name, St. Brigid of Kildare Church, and cross I know well.

CHAPTER FORTY-THREE

A chill snakes up my back as I touch the symbol on the door, the same cross tattooed high on my neck, almost behind my ear, my touchpoint whenever I need to find some calm.

The same cross that decorated the fire temple in Ireland last year to call in the Celtic goddess.

I'm shocked to see the cross here on the door of this church across the street from this address that materialized out of my dream. On a walk looking for the location of a funeral of a potentially made-up man married to a potential ghost of a woman haunting my dreams.

How am I even surprised at these coincidences at this point?

The puzzle pieces swirling in my mind, compounded with the timing of finding this specific cross, is almost too much for me. I stand frozen on the church steps, craving normalcy and for this all to go away while knowing that I need to go into this church and find out why this winding road of coincidences and dreams has led me here.

Not having been in a Catholic church since my mom's funeral, I'm hesitant to enter even with the clear welcoming on the doors for the feast day celebration. It's not like I'll burn up as soon as I walk through these doors.

My cousin used to tease me that the holy water would set you on fire if you had sinned before you dipped your fingers in it, and I developed a healthy fear of bursting into flames if I anoint myself with the holy water inside any Catholic church. Even as a little girl, women seemed to sin with every step in the eyes of the patriarchy, and I'm confident I've sinned repeatedly since my last visit to a church.

Maybe some of my audaciousness comes from knowing that I was born a sin. How much lower can I go? As a little girl, a I heard a priest speak of children born out of wedlock as the product of a sin during a weekly sermon. I blushed deeply next to my mom, wondering how she could look calm while our lives were labeled products of the devil. I was old enough to know I'd been born to unmarried parents, but too young to understand that I wasn't a sin.

My mom had looked on at the priest serenely and then down at me. Noticing my discomfort, she'd squeezed my hand. "Don't worry, baby cakes. That's not your problem. God loves you."

This trip down memory lane fortifies me and reclaims some of that boldness I felt as a little girl in a religious space that was a bit too judgmental for my pint-size liking.

I take a few steps farther into the church and peek through the vestibule doors. While I don't believe in God in the same way as my Catholic mom, I do believe in beauty—and this church is full of it. A true feast for the senses to celebrate St. Brigid, apparently. Bouquets of flowers and the shiny green leaves of dozens of plants fill the altar and line the pews down the center aisle of the church. The scents of flowers and greenery and life and spring surround me and welcome me farther into the building. I turn in a slow circle, admiring the ribbons delicately dancing in the air over archways and bells chiming softly near exit doors to catch the draft of the chilly winter breeze as the doors open and close periodically. This is a church ready for a celebration. This is what a church of love would feel like.

An elderly priest walks cheerfully along the side of the pews toward me. I give him a polite nod and wave as he slows and stops when he reaches me. I feel dreadfully out of place. He offers me a warm welcome to his church in his slightly Irish accent, as if he moved to Chicago many, many years ago but can't quite let go of the lilt in his voice to adopt those hard Chicago "A"s.

"Welcome to St. Brigid's Catholic Church. I don't believe we have met before, but you have come on a most special day—we are celebrating the feast day of St. Brigid as we welcome the first signs of spring in the new year. I'm Father Michael. Is there something I can help you with?"

"This is beautiful," I say reverently. "So much life, so many flowers. It's like a nature retreat in the middle of the city. I wasn't sure what I was expecting when I walked in the doors, but I'm glad I didn't catch on fire either." I inwardly groan at my freefall of words and mumble an apology as the priest chuckles.

"Too many young children were told stories of bursting into flames from holy water if they sinned. It's amusing to watch the younger generation cringe as they touch the holy water on Sundays after what I can only presume was a wild Saturday night in the city."

He gives a quick wink when my eyes widen, surprised by his laughter and mirth.

Father Michael continues with a kind and patient look.

"It does no one any good if I pretend to be unaware of the world around us. We're in an exceptional city, full of opportunities to explore the arts and community, and to test and tempt ourselves. Accepting people as they are is a beautiful gift to give—and especially those who have been marginalized by society, the city, and yes, even religion. I make it a priority to welcome all to St. Brigid's as she would do. I pray our white cloth of welcome stretches over the city like hers did over the countryside. I'm proud that we have a little bit of everyone from each corner of the city attending our church—families, homeless youth, recovering addicts, middle class suburban families, people of all races, colors, and ethnicities."

Now my eyebrows go up at his candidness—I'm caught

unsteady by this priest. All of my assumptions swept away by the breeze gently lifting the greenery around me.

"I'm on a mission to bring religion to the people in a way that is true and honest and meets their needs as they are, loved for who they are. Of the many things St. Brigid represents, she's a mother meeting the needs of all in her family and community. The people in this city need to be mothered, and while I'm an unlikely candidate to be a mother, I choose to care through the spirit of St. Brigid each day."

The tenderness of this priest's words about mothering a community brings me to tears. If we're lucky, to be mothered is to be loved and nurtured for exactly who we are.

How deeply and often I yearn to be mothered, for my own mother, since I birthed Jillian. How many times have I wished my mom was here to share the emotions these dreams churn up? A quiet sob leaves my throat as my deep grief wells in my chest, pressing against the longing.

I miss her so much.

This priest's passion to care for and nurture his community in the spirit of motherhood is too much for me to contain. How much of our lives are we spending trying to meet our basic needs? To be seen? To feel connected?

The gift of motherhood, of holding space for all and filling emptiness with love, is a great one indeed for this church—and unexpected wisdom for me. Motherhood as a soulful responsibility and act of love and not a punishment or obligation is a healing and life-changing framework… and one I need to be more mindful of when I talk about my own motherhood if my conversations with Alma are showing me anything.

Father Michael is obviously used to people having big emotions in his church. He patiently waits as I pull a tissue from my overstuffed backpack and wipe my eyes, collecting myself.

"What brought you in today?"

"Um, I'm not really sure," I mumble, searching for a half-truth that might get some answers for how I ended up here. "I felt compelled to step inside because of the cross on the door. I'm out… exploring the city." This is the briefest explanation I can land on after struggling for a second. "I've seen the St. Brigid cross before."

"Ah, yes, the cross of St. Brigid. It's unique, made of rushes, which she created after performing a miracle. Dynamic in its simplicity and special indeed to represent a woman in the church. She's originally from my home in Kildare, Ireland."

"My family is from Kildare! My great-grandma came here over a hundred years ago. I was just there last year." I interrupt as he smiles kindly.

"I grew up collecting the rushes from local streams and weaving the cross to sell to tourists in Kildare. An early sign I was already drawn to Brigid."

Father Michael motions for me to walk down the center aisle with him. His Irish lilt soothes me into a calmer vibe as he describes the paintings and floral arrangements in the church. We make our way slowly to the altar to look more closely at a person-sized cross of St. Brigid.

"In Ireland, she has a longer history than her fate as a Catholic saint. Ancient Celtic lore says St. Brigid was originally Brigid, a Celtic triple goddess. While not original to the Celts, some say she represents all aspect of womanhood—the child, the mother, and the crone or wise woman. She was a fiery protector and connected to the sun and cosmos, watching over poets, healers, and metalsmiths. Coincidentally and conveniently, the Irish people celebrate her on February 1st, her Catholic feast day, but we call it Imbolc in Ireland."

Surprise registers across my face because he winks at me and continues.

"Imbolc brings the beginning of springtime and daylight with it. I always think today is a day of hope and clarity and peace. The long winter of darkness is moving behind us and brighter days are quite truly ahead… and of course, we're celebrating her Catholic feast day."

He shakes his head a little as he realizes how long he has been talking.

"Sorry to give you a sermon you didn't ask for, lassie," he says ruefully.

I brush my hair over my shoulder to show off my tattoo of St. Brigid's cross when my phone chimes with a text message. Relieved I stopped before telling Father Michael I got the tattoo drunk at college, I start to apologize.

"Sorry, I have a baby at home and just need to…"

I fumble my phone as I scroll through the new texts from one of the women I spoke to earlier. Her texting skills are better than expected given the typewriter in her office as she sends a picture of a faded death certificate, yellow with age. She found a church record for Jeremy Smith, who died March 22, 1977.

> Cause of death was listed as suicide.
> Record shows he was married but I can't
> find the wife's name. Could this be the
> cousin you're looking for?

My hand trembles as another message beeps through.

> Found this address listed in his funeral
> record in case it helps.

Then the text bubbles appear as she continues to type.

I hold my breath as I wait, a sinking sensation clenching at my stomach.

The next line of text lands with a punch, and I cry out.

> 136 N. 47th St. Chicago.

The apartment building across the street.

The priest touches my shoulder as I stare at my cell phone in shock. I'm vaguely aware of Father Michael asking me if I'm okay —of me completely ignoring him as I stare at my phone and wonder how this could be.

This woman apparently isn't done rocking my world as my cell chimes again.

This picture was used at the funeral.

A picture of an old photo appears in the text thread.

As my eyes and brain process the photo, I start to shake violently. My eyes are locked on the screen, and sobs overtake me as my vision tunnels to the smiling woman in the photo.

Taking hold of my arm, the priest pulls me to him. I cry into his shoulder for a solid minute. My shock wears off along with my feral gasps and cries. He murmurs in my ear like a father—or mother—might and slowly guides me to the first pew. I sit and hold my face in my hands as I try to take a breath and find words but fail as I gasp and shudder.

The address. The picture. I cannot make sense of this nonsensical world I've been pulled into by these dreams. As much as I believe in magic and spiritual energy, I much more preferred it when I tried to manifest professional success rather than my mom's wedding photo when she was a twenty-year-old. My academic brain aches from the twists and turns of the past few months, trying to channel Caden's usual reason and control to stop this overwhelm. But this is not a reasonable or controllable situation.

The picture is of a couple laughing and smiling. A smile that reaches the woman's eyes. Her sweet, youthful green eyes are full of love and hope.

The picture is of my mother—long before she ever became my mother.

The address in my dream, scribbled on a piece of paper, directly across the street from me now, belonged to my mom in a different life. A life where at some point she smiled. Like this. Like she was happy. Her mouth didn't just curve into the shape of a smile, but the joy lit her up from within, and with a warm glow in her eyes.

And the man in the picture is without a doubt the same man from my dream, but younger and hopeful and healthier. Before drugs slowly killed him, and he finished the job with a handgun to his mouth.

In the apartment across the street from where I'm at in this exact moment, based on an address I found in my dream.

"What the fuck is going on?" I gasp.

My breath turns shallow, sending me to the edge of panic. Hot, sweaty, trapped in a space that is too large and too small for what is transpiring before my eyes. In my heart. In my mind. I can't put these puzzle pieces together as they turn and shift in my head too quickly, desperate to settle into a pattern, a story that makes sense. The more I try to hold these thoughts still, the more panicked I become at the impossibility of the truth hitting me like, well, a brick.

The overwhelm and panic become too much for me. I don't know what the priest is saying, but not being alone is a gift. He could be speaking in tongues about me going to Hell—but I'm good with it as long as I'm not alone with these crashing, soul-churning waves of realization. I'm violently grasping for a firmer grip on reality and failing.

My mom. The first two dreams were never about me—they were always about her.

I didn't know. How could I not know that my mom lived through such devastating experiences?

I'm swept away in a new thought about how sad and hard my mom's life was before she even became a mother, and the heat and panic rise again. She saw her brother's life collapse around her, and her first husband commit suicide.

No wonder she was depressed—had to try so hard to hold on.

I cross my arms and rest them on my knees while bending over to press my head into my hands.

As I curl up, the pressure in my chest builds with the need to pump, but there's no time for that right now. I'm trying to catch my breath and find my center in this insane spinning world that feels too slippery to be real or of this realm.

As Father Michael gently squeezes my hand and whispers calming words to me, my breath slows, but I'm still sweaty and hot. I pull the hair tie off my wrist and wrap my hair up into my mom bun—floppy and bobbling on top of my head like a halo of dark brown windswept hair.

The cold air chills my skin and dries the sweaty locks of hair on my soaked neck, grounding me in the current space. How long have

I been freaking out in this pew next to an Irish priest at an address I found in a dream?

That line of thought is leading me straight back to panic. I keep my eyes on the simple lines of St. Brigid's cross, the smell of the flowers and greenery brought in to celebrate for her saint's day, her miracle day. I feel the hard wood of the pew under my legs and the breeze moving through the church.

As my eyes sweep back and forth around the room, my head turns left and right. I hear Father Michael gasp as I turn my head, trying to find the source of the breeze to cool myself. When I turn back to him, Father Michael's face has gone ghostly white, and he's dabbing at the sweat breaking across his brow, a little wild-eyed. He gestures with his hand to my neck while his mouth slowly opens and closes, his words stuck in his throat.

CHAPTER FORTY-FOUR

Father Michael is visibly shaken, and he tries to pull himself together in front of me. He places his hands on the pew on either side of him and takes a few deep breaths. These moments seem to steady him as the color rises back to his face and his attempts to speak are productive now.

I hear him whispering, "How could this be?" to himself as he wipes his brow with a fresh handkerchief pulled from a hidden priest pocket.

With one more slow, deep breath, he slowly turns to me. He once again holds his hand out and takes mine, but his grip is much steadier now. He opens his mouth, and his question makes my breath catch in my throat.

"Your tattoo… The cross on your neck. Why—where—um, what I mean is, can you tell me about the tattoo on your neck?"

My eyebrows go up as I tilt my head, confused, as he stares at the faded symbol of St. Brigid tattooed on my neck. He explained the cross to me earlier.

I'm still sniffling and wiping stray tears from my eyes as he gestures again toward my neck.

This time, he forms a more complete thought. "The tattoo on

your neck. The cross of St. Brigid, as you know. You mentioned the cross and not knowing all it symbolizes, but I did not realize you have a tattoo of it."

He pauses, and his face scrunches up as if considering getting something permanently inked on your body without understanding the meaning of it.

"I've seen the cross as a tattoo before. People love the cross of St. Brigid and all she represents. She is a powerful symbol of femininity and how strength, vulnerability, love, generosity, and power shift as women age from young to old, child to crone. But only once before in the same place as you. On the neck, behind the ear of a woman I tried to save a long time ago."

I nod slowly and don't say anything. I also knew someone who had this tattoo on her neck, behind her ear. Just because he has never seen it before doesn't mean it's not common. It might be a little weird if all the women were coming in and showing off their neck tattoos to a Catholic priest.

Not sure where he's headed with this revelation, we seem to have switched roles from strange woman losing it and sobbing in a strange church to shaken, emotional priest storytelling. My curiosity peaks as he continues after a quiet moment, broken only by the sound of his breathing.

"At least I tried to help save her. I've always had the uncanny feeling that I was there more as a witness than a savior. A witness to a woman saving herself. I was never sure why this feeling has stuck with me, or why this tragedy, more than others I've witnessed, has always had a hold on me. I often pray for this woman as I get on the L train each day and hope her life blossomed into all she deserved."

My hands still from pulling at the handkerchief Father Michael handed me a few moments ago.

"The L?" I whisper as I look at him through my puffy, mascara-smudged eyes. "Why the L?"

I've forgotten about the third dream. I was too overcome, drowning in sadness for my mom as a sister and wife that I forgot about the third dream.

Father Michael starts to tell a story of "one of the most

terrifying experiences" he has personally witnessed in Chicago. "Imagine getting on the train, like you do a hundreds of times a year, but this time, you're thrown into chaos and fear and almost lose your life."

My hands start to tremble, and I wrap my arms around myself as a chill sweeps down my spine. The hairs on my neck stand up and goosebumps run up and down my arms as he continues.

"Now mind you, child, this was many, many years ago, but one day in 1980, I had a last-minute meeting at this church. I was working for a parish in Gary and took the NWI Express into the city. I brought a book and the newspaper with me to read. I settled into the back of the train as the seats filled with commuters at each stop."

My stomach tightens and clenches as soon as he says 1980 and the NWI Express. I know where this is going, and I don't like it, as if I'm back on that roller coaster, inching up the steep hill and becoming more and more terrified as I move farther and farther from the surface of the earth. I want to climb off, but there's no way to stop this now. The story has begun, the ride has started, and the drop is coming.

"I happened to notice a young woman get on the train, and her bag spill across the seat next to her. She seemed flustered as I handed her back a few things that fell on the floor, along with my newspaper to read to help calm her. She mentioned, babbled really, that she was going to a job interview and was full of nerves. I told her I would pray for her good fortune and calm nerves today, then settled back into my seat."

My body instinctively leans into the priest, my heart hungry for these little details about my mom before I knew her.

"I don't think either of us could have imagined what kind of luck and nerves she would need that day—and it had nothing to do with her job interview."

Falling back against the hard wooden pew, I stare up at the cross, knowing where this story is headed.

It was my mom. All three women were her.

How did I never know? I wish she didn't have to be so brave. At what point is resilience just surviving bad luck?

"I noticed she had a small tattoo on her neck, behind her ear when she moved her hair back as she picked up her belongings. I only noticed it because it was the cross of St. Brigid. Just like yours. I remember it because, coincidentally, I was heading to a job interview myself for this parish, St. Brigid's Catholic Church. Was her tattoo a sign from God that I was embarking down the right path? I was worried about leaving my current parish because I didn't want to dismantle the community we had worked so hard to build there."

Tears roll down my cheeks. He's telling me the story of my dream—about a woman being held hostage on a train. I could pick up the story from here. I squeeze the handkerchief tightly in one hand and place my other hand, curled into a loose fist, over my mouth to stop myself from interrupting. Father Michael is lost in his own telling of this story. His eyes have lost focus as he gazes across the church at a smaller cross of St. Brigid.

"An agitated man got on the train. One might say he looked angry, but I've worked with enough angry men, especially Veterans of the Vietnam War, to know that anger is easier to put into the world than hopelessness and fear. This man looked terrified, hopeless. At times, a scarier combination than anger and fury. He had nothing left to lose."

"I've learned again and again to trust my intuition, and there was something off about this man. He was a live wire, if you will, seemed like he might try to pick a fight with someone on the train, but I was in no way prepared for what happened next. No one was."

I start to quietly weep as the next scene in the story flashes in my mind.

Words come tumbling out of me, like the first screams as the roller coaster crests the first peak. I blurt out, "He had a knife, didn't he? He took the woman hostage, right?"

Now it is Father Michael's turn to be snapped out of his storytelling and stare at me. "How on earth did you know that, my child?"

"I… I've dreamed about it," I say slowly. "I've been having dreams. Nightmares. Over and over. This… this was one of them. The hostage. The train. Almost dying. The man being shot." I pause to blow my nose. The thought crosses my mind that I'm a hot, snotty mess and probably sound insane. I might as well go all in on my crazy with this priest.

Is this all confidential? Or do we have to be in the confessional box?

"I'm only here because of an address across the street that was written on a piece of paper in my dream."

As I say this, I can hear how insane this all sounds. In-fucking-sane.

Father Michael is staring at me with a look of growing shock spreading across his face as if my hair has turned into Medusa's— snakes slithering in the air and snapping at him—as he continues to watch me with an appraising look.

My eyes widen as he speaks again.

He must not be afraid of turning into stone if he's still walking this journey with me.

"What happened next?"

I take a deep breath. "The man with the knife, he stands up and starts shouting. He was a Vietnam vet. He lost everything in the war… He, uh, wanted people to pay attention, to care about his pain. His loss. So he got on the train and wanted to… Well, I don't know what he wanted to do but he ended up taking a woman hostage, the woman with the job interview and tattoo, and then… then, the police shot him. The woman ran away. Blood and brains were everywhere in my dream. The woman got away, she lived, but I could feel her terror, her fear, the shock. The revulsion of being covered in brains and blood from that man. Her deep, deep sadness."

As I'm talking, my eyes gaze into the distance, lost in remembering how this woman's emotions felt—*feel*—in my body. I almost don't catch what Father Michael says next.

Wonder and maybe a little fear grow on his face. Eyes wide and eyebrows raised, he has been nodding with me the entire time as I tell his own story back to him.

"Yes, yes, that is what happened. How could you possibly know all of this?"

I shake my head and shrug. I open my mouth to try to explain but find all I can do is exhale in one big sigh.

"As I said, I've always felt like I was supposed to be a witness to this tragedy, but... but you seem to have been a witness to it as well... in a dream? The young woman—Jill was her name. I always hoped she had a better life after that. I only know her name from my offer to pray for a blessed outcome on her job interview."

And the roller coaster cars drop over the peak, and we are throttling through the air. My stomach hollows out and drops out of my body and onto the floor. Once again, the blood rushes out of my head, and I'm left lightheaded and clammy, palms sweaty.

"What did you say?" I whisper as he stares at me. Now he looks a little scared, probably because I look like I might throw up at any second in his beautiful church.

He licks his lips and adjusts his seating on the pew. He's probably more used to standing at the front of the room than sitting in the pews. A breeze picks up in the room from the doors opened at the entrance of the church to welcome spring inside.

"I said I hope the woman had a good life after the train—"

I shake my head almost violently and interrupt. "No, what did you call her? Her name?!"

"Jill. Her name was Jill."

And just like that, my head spins, my world tilts, and I pass out on the church pew.

CHAPTER FORTY-FIVE

Father Michael's voice filters through the dull throbbing in my ears, cajoling me back into consciousness. While I was out, he laid me down on the pew and is now patting my hand. A cool wet cloth has been laid across my forehead. I see him breathe a sigh of relief as I come to, and I sit slowly up.

"Are you okay? It seems you were literally stunned," he says.

I pause and take a few deep breaths as I figure out how to explain this unexplainable situation. Fainting was a little too extra, even for me. I'm trying hard to shake off the leftover falling sensation and hold tight to the present moment.

"Jill. You're sure the woman's name was Jill?" I ask.

He nods.

"Okay, this is going to sound insane, but Jill is—was—my mom's name."

Father Michael barely flinches at this reveal, the tattoo already tempering the shock.

"I've been dreaming for months. Dreams of terrifying things happening in the lives of women. Shootings and fights and suicides and drugs. Being taken hostage on a train. These dreams have been ruining my life. I lost months of sleep over them. I can't figure out how to make them fully go away. I'm a new mom. I just had a baby of my own. Everyone who knows me thinks I'm losing my mind or have postpartum something or other. Anxiety, depression, psychosis. My partner was on the verge of taking our daughter away. I've gotten into car accidents and fucked up at work because I don't sleep anymore and couldn't focus on anything besides these dreams."

A door opens and someone walks in from what looks like an office, carrying a stack of papers. I pause and look up while Father Michael waves the person away. We're alone again when the door clicks softly closed.

"Until a few weeks ago. Recently I went to a cabin for a few days and tried to exorcise the dreams out of me. Get them all out. Write about them. Draw them. Scream and cry them out. And it seemed to work. I made some connections. I found some peace."

Father Michael smiles at this, seemingly pleased I found relief from the pain of these dreams, but his brows knit together in confusion as I continue, nowhere near the end of this story.

"Then I started looking into all these details from my dreams and art. And some of the details from the dreams were true. And that led to its own rabbit hole of secrets and emails and revelations, which leads us back to here. I found the address for the building across the street in my dream and recognized the symbol on the church doors as my tattoo, and I walked inside."

I take a deep breath before saying the next words.

"The Jill you met on the train… She was my mom."

Father Michael sits, tense and still, listening intently.

"She—my mom—she had the same tattoo as me. She got it before I was born. All she would ever say about it was that the tattoo felt like it was from a different lifetime and this cross brought her peace during some of her hardest days. I wanted to feel connected to her on my hard days too. I got the same tattoo in the same spot, to remember her, to honor her. And, somehow, my daughter, Jillian, has a small birthmark in the same spot behind her ear. Such a wild coincidence. Like she had met my mom before she was born somehow. As if their souls connected outside of this world."

Father Michael looks stunned. Simply stunned.

"You're... you're her daughter? How could this be?!?" He sits and stares at my face, at my tattoo, and back at my face again. Then, he quietly says, "You said you got your tattoo to remember her. Would you mind telling me what happened to her?"

I sigh, and tears well up in my eyes as I gently tell this man how the woman he spent years praying for has died. "Of heart failure about twenty ago."

I consider leaving it there, letting it be that simple for him. Why tell the whole story when the partial truth is sad enough? He nods and waits. He has witnessed enough suffering and tragedy to know that middle-aged women rarely die suddenly of simple heart failure. His silence holds the space for me to continue.

"She was an alcoholic. She relapsed one night. Alcohol. Drugs. I'm not sure which. I've never known. Never asked. But her heart couldn't handle it, and... and she died. I was sixteen."

Her heart had been broken too many times to continue, if all the dreams were true. Her heart was stronger than most, but it simply quit that night.

Father Michael takes my hand. Tears stream down his cheeks, and he wipes them away with his free hand. My tears fall, silently streaming, but I offer the snotty handkerchief back to him, but he waves it off because, well, gross.

"I'm so sorry for your loss. To lose a mother is always a tragedy. For your mother, Jill, to have her life end while she was still young but had experienced so much, is an even bigger tragedy. I pray she found some of the peace she was searching for before she left this world."

He crosses himself and says a quiet prayer. My heart warms watching him do this, knowing that the last few years of my mom's life left many feeling confusion and pity for her rather than the deep understanding, empathy, and love she deserved. That we all deserve.

We sit together in silence for a few moments, tears on our lashes, breath catching from weeping together for my mom.

"Tell me about your dreams," he says.

So I do.

I tell Father Michael about all three of my dreams. How they came one after another. How I experienced my mom watching my uncle bleed out on the ground after having his head smashed. How her youthful innocence drifted away from her and to a young man with his own problems. Problems that turned into addiction. How I could experience her smile and laugh in the dreams in ways that I rarely did when she was alive. How experiencing her as a happy woman feels like a gift, along with knowing my mom has been by my side these months.

I'm proud of her—in awe of her bravery on that train. This version of her is at odds with the version I remember more and more from my childhood. Lethargic, checked out on the couch, yelling in the car.

Maybe she had already used up all her vitality, all her strength, trying to keep herself alive before I was born.

I stood by my mom's side and witnessed tragedies that would have torn a lesser woman apart, that would have broken someone frailer. Three men died, their lives stolen from them by war, violence, and drugs. The shrapnel from their pain blew back onto her—scarring and shaping her life. And ultimately mine. Her capacity for joy and pleasure and peace was stolen from her at such a young age, making her resilient but taking an unknowable toll on her spirit as payment.

I tell him how she died *and* how she lived. She lived with tenacity and a spirit of never giving up, even—especially—when the world was against her. She lived with a continuous exhaustion we might now call depression, anxiety, or just straight up PTSD. She lived with demons that were not always her own but haunted her daily. She lived full of love and hope for her daughter but had to build a fortress around her nervous system daily to keep from drinking. She lived in a world as a mom who needed and yearned for more but, like so many moms, did not have the support system to help her do much more than try to survive. She lived with too few options and too much pressure from the world around her.

She lived with the need to have fun and to experience calm. All she wanted on most days was to feel normal, like others easily do.

Maybe my mom just needed to smoke a little pot. Maybe that would have helped. But instead, she used legal means to cope and ended up with an addiction to pills before that was ever a headline in the paper. Coupled with booze, the pills became her undoing in a world that she could never quite survive.

I tell Father Michael all of this in a tumble of words, stories, hiccups, tears, and hand motions. He listens intently. When I pause, he asks me to tell him about how I ended up here, in this church.

So I do.

CHAPTER FORTY-SIX

I proudly pull out my folder and notebook, excited to show off the months of work I've put into investigating these dreams, to save my sanity. Father Michael nods and hums appreciatively as I flip through drawings and notes, pointing out details and little clues.

"I just found out the first dream was about my mom recently and then the second here in this church. My working theory was that these dreams were visions of my past lives, maybe a different timeline. Or that I was losing my mind. I haven't been okay in a long time."

Father Michael listens quietly, intently, as I tell him how Gloria shared the long-kept family secret of my Uncle CoCo's head injury. Of my emails with the librarian. Of my hours of Google searches leading me to O'Malley's, the NWI Express, the apartment across the street, and now, this church.

"My mom never told me about her brother's injury. The fight. I was young when she died, probably too young to be told about a suicide or being taken hostage. I was only sixteen. Maybe she would have when I was older."

We sit in silence for a few minutes. I don't know what Father Michael is thinking, but my mind is fluctuating between fresh waves of grief for the life stolen from the young Jill he briefly met and the years my mom did not get to live because of the trauma in her life. And the pressing question of "What now?"

Where do I go from here?

Father Michael takes a deep breath and starts to speak. "I mentioned that I've always felt like it was my duty to witness what happened to Jill, your mother, on the train. I never understood why. For many years, I felt as if I was put in that space, at that time, to calm the shooter down, and I failed. Now I understand what the call to witness was about."

He pauses for a moment and makes eye contact with me. "I was called to witness that moment in your mother's life so we could meet in this moment. So that when you journeyed here, however strange your path may seem, on this day, in this church, I would be here to help you."

I stare at him. "My journey here?! What am I even doing here?" A slight edge of hysteria creeps into my voice. "Everyone I know thinks I've gone crazy. I took time off work to go hide in the woods and try to get rid of these dreams. I took time off work *again* to chase dreams around this city. And it's more terrifying that it *worked* than if it had all been nonsense. I keep stumbling across details and dates and addresses and stories from my dreams that are *true*. And, in the middle of all of this, my baby is at home and I have no fucking idea what I'm doing as a mom. I want my mom here to hold me and tell me I'm going to be okay. And she's *not!*" I finish with a shout of anguish.

We've unlocked a fresh stage in the—God only knows how many—stages of coping with recurring dreams that are also visions from the past journey, coupled with grief. This one feels a lot like rage. I'm not sure if that's better or worse than the hopelessness, confusion, or insanity that came before it.

My breathing is ragged and uneven as I stare at Father Michael. He thoughtfully stares back at me with his hands clasped in front of him, propping up his chin with his knuckles. His calm has the same effect on me, and I intentionally slow my breathing down to match his, the red rage fading from my cheeks.

"I know this will sound crazy, but we can both appreciate that we're in uncharted territory here. Maybe rather than 'crazy,' let's say we're operating in a new realm of possibility. Anything is possible with Spirit, God, and I can only assume His, or St. Brigid's, guiding hand has led you here—with or without the help of your mother's spirit and these dreams."

While not entirely unexpected given we are in a Catholic church, my shoulders tense and rise along with my eyebrows at the mention of God.

Remembering how important this church was to my mom, and how kind Father Michael has been, I fight my reaction to flee and wrap my fingers around the curved edge of the wooden seat tightly, holding myself in place.

"As I mentioned before, St. Brigid had a legacy before the Catholic Church made her a saint. She was a Celtic goddess some say represented three stages of womanhood—the child, the mother, and the crone. Some say she was not one goddess or woman, but a triple goddess comprised of three different women, maybe even sisters."

He pauses as if he wants me to nod in confirmation or understanding, to demonstrate I'm understanding his meaning. The weaponization of religion, of God, has made me mistrust it, fearful of its intentions. But goddess legends and Celtic lore? This is the translation of Source that I need. I just stare, hungrily waiting for him to finish, the Irish lilt of his voice making this all sound like a charming story categorizing the pure chaos of my mind. I didn't know how deeply I needed to be believed, to be heard, until now.

"I noticed the tattoo of the cross of St. Brigid on your mother's neck on the train. You have the same one now. We only made the connection we did because of the cross tattoo. Otherwise I never would have mentioned Jill or the train. St. Brigid seems to have a hand in whatever is happening now."

"Birth, like death, is a liminal space. You're never more connected between the realms of the spirit world and this one, between life and death, than when you're giving birth. You and your mother both have evoked St. Brigid and her protection, maybe not on purpose, with your tattoos. Your birthing of your daughter, Jillian, created the opportunity for you to rest between the realms briefly. You became a mother. You had a daughter. Your mother's spirit may have taken this opportunity to gift you with these dreams, these memories, to take with you back to this current realm, back to your new identity as mother."

I stare at him as if he's the one who is a little bit crazy now, but, after everything that has transpired over the past few months, I believe him.

"Child, Mother, and Crone," I whisper softly. The tattoos... The birthmark. Maybe Jillian had met my mom, her grandma, before she came earth-side.

"If what you're saying is true, could even possibly be true, you think that my mom gave me these memories when I was giving birth? Like she's a ghost or a spirit who haunts me or these are messages from the great beyond?"

He simply nods.

"Let's say we really are playing in the anything-is-possible sandbox. I mean, the odds of this all being one big crazy coincidence are basically zero. I ended up here, talking to you, a witness to the hostage situation who spoke to my mom when... when she still had hope."

I stutter a little on that last part as I realize the truth of it. I remember my mom as a survivor, no matter how her life ultimately ended. What I don't remember is her thriving or feeling hopeful—or even simply happy.

"My mom passes these tragic memories onto me during what is supposed to be the happiest moment of my life—giving birth to my daughter—and now what? What am I supposed to do here, with all of this? These dreams have almost ruined my life."

I pause as I hear myself say these things out loud. Was my birth, my mother's birth to her own daughter, the happiest moment of her life? Or is that what society says it should be? Could this have been possible if I'd had a son? Or did it have to be a daughter all along? The third version of womanhood to complete Brigid's triple goddess lineup? A little girl I named after my own mother, who may or may not be haunting me now. If these dreams—just the dreams—are almost ruining my life, I can only imagine how horrible it was when my mom lived these real life horrors.

"But why would she give me these memories?"

Father Michael has been patiently sitting next to me for long minutes, but now, he stands up to pace a little in front of the altar under the cross of St. Brigid in the shadow of a larger, traditional cross.

Pausing, Father Michael kneels down to pray, to ask for guidance, to give up his thoughts to God, I guess. I sit quietly and watch him. I wonder if my mom's spirit is somewhere here with us —or if she's watching down on us from Heaven. I don't let myself consider she might be watching up from Hell. My relationship with his religion is juvenile, stuck in this binary of Heaven and Hell in the sky and center of the earth.

And then an idea that feels a lot like a truth quietly floats up in my thoughts.

I jump up and start to speak, startling Father Michael out of his prayer.

"Her spirit!" I exclaim. "My mom's spirit gave me these dreams when I was in the liminal space between worlds, between realms, while I was giving birth. These realms aren't between Heaven and Earth, right?"

Father Michael nods slowly and watches me, considering my thought process.

"Father, my mom's spirit couldn't be in Heaven—or free—not if she can pass these dreams to me from one realm to the next. The realm on earth connected to her is the spirit world—here on this earth—not up in the sky looking down from the clouds, capital-H, Heaven," I say as I wave my hands up to the ceiling of the church, motioning to the sky beyond. "Like she's stuck in this physical world and can't rest into the spiritual one."

"Well, that's not what we mean by Heav—" he starts, but I interrupt.

"Okay, not the point, but that's what all the cartoons depict. Anyways, if my mom's spirit could pass these dreams to me, she must be *here* in *this* realm able to reach across the liminal space when the opening is stretched as wide as my bagel-sized cervix to squeeze out Jillian's giant head."

I see him grimace a bit at my visual, but I continue, gesturing with my hands wildly as I'm talking. "My mom's spirit isn't in Heaven. She's stuck here. She needs us, you and me, to release her spirit from this realm so she can live in peace and freedom and joy again. She needs to be released from the holds of her trauma to fully be free."

Out of breath, I let go, and my arms fall to my sides, suddenly still after my outburst in the empty church, pausing as cool wind blows into the church. I'm standing in front of the first row of pews in the center of the church directly under a cross of St. Brigid.

The wind blows hard, and I stumble from shock and fall to my knees. Doors slam shut around us. My hair falls out of my mom bun and around my shoulders, blowing in the unexpected breeze. I sweep it to one side, unintentionally revealing the tattoo again. The breeze swirls around my neck and face, gently moving the sweaty strands of hair, instantly cooling, tenderly calming me down.

Father Michael and I stare at each other in surprise. I wonder if he sees the wind as a sign that I'm correct—an agreement from the spirit world that we're on the right track on this insane and crazy journey.

I continue to make eye contact with Father Michael as I say softly, "Father, you're right. You are supposed to be a witness to my mom's strength and tragedy just as you were meant to be here today on this special saint's day for St. Brigid when I walked into this church. We are both exactly where we need to be in this moment of time whether it is God, my mom, or some other force that has brought us together."

I pause, lick my lips, take a deep breath, and continue.

"Father, you're meant to release, to exorcise, my mother's spirit and dreams from this realm, from this earth, from my body and mind, and into Heaven, or whatever realm is full of peace and rest for her spirit, her soul."

He nods. "Yes, child, I believe you are correct."

CHAPTER FORTY-SEVEN

F
ather Michael and I look at each other as the wind picks up
again.

"This can't be normal, right?"

The wind settles to a strong breeze and circles the room,
releasing the fragrance of the spring flowers decorating the altar in
front of the church, rustling the greenery along the walls. I hear the
pages of flyers and hymns rustle on tables but not fall as air lightly
moves over and around us. A glance around the room reveals that
the doors have slammed closed, leaving no visible source.

I continue to kneel on the ground, hands clenched in fists at my
side, unsure of what to do next. Trusting that this seems like a
natural next step in this wild, unimaginable journey. Father Michael
considers me with a scrutinizing glance but doesn't say anything as
he walks to the altar and reaches under the table. He pulls out a
glass pitcher of wine and a bowl of holy communion wafers.

I watch with a sense of déjà vu and nostalgia from childhood as
he blesses the wine and wafers. He places them, along with a pitcher
of holy water, on a tray and walks toward me where he sets the tray
on a small wooden table that has been used for communion for

many years. I wonder if the church has ever seen anything like this before.

Father Michael pauses, fidgeting with the items on the tray. Then, as if reading my thoughts, he says quietly, "I ask that you don't ever speak these words outside this church."

He waits for me to nod in agreement.

"The church is aware of situations like yours in the past. Spirits passing along messages, dreams, visions, etc. Some of these messages have looked like or been labeled as being possessed or lunacy. Sometimes as miracles. Now we are considering a different possibility. That God has allowed these spirts to stay earth-side to release their pain and suffering. To heal. It is more common to hear of visions being passed when one is on their deathbed and makes a miraculous recovery than in childbirth, but both experiences place the living person in the liminal space between worlds."

"You believe you need to be exorcised, which is quite dramatic by the way. You've got to stop watching so many horror movies. I believe your mother has gifted you with the dreams, her memories, to use your strength to heal the pain of trauma and suffering that are holding her to this earth, to the spirit world on this earth, rather than ascending to the holy one, above us in the clouds as you say."

I didn't realize that I'm holding my breath until I release it from my body in a whoosh. The truth of what he's saying rolls through me, and my body responds and lights up as if champagne has been poured in through my head and is bubbling from the tips of my toes to the crown of my head.

"Okay, wow. I'm not the first." Father Michael's admission is comforting and offers more relief than he may realize. "I can do this."

Should I call Caden and tell him I'm about to be exorcised at a random Catholic church? What if something happens?

I don't think he even knows where I am at this point. The apartment was on the map, but not this church. What if something goes terribly wrong here?

My emotional shitshow must be flying across my face because

Father Michael looks at me kindly and then gestures to the cross of St. Brigid.

"You do not seem to be one who has a strong faith in my God and St. Brigid, but maybe you can consider trusting your Irish roots and put your faith in Brigid, the Celtic goddess. Trust in your female intuition and the matriarchal lineage of your heritage, of your mother's love and her own trust in you, that has brought you to this place, to this moment, in a way that is remarkably otherworldly."

"If you cannot put your faith in God, put your faith in yourself, in your mother, and in your daughter."

"You each share a piece of your heart and, together, your strength can give your mother the gift she never had but always deserved—peace."

Echoing Carmela's word choice—a piece of my heart—Father Michael speaks this truth into the world. Peace. A simple word, but a hard-earned dream for women and mothers everywhere. An impossible reality for a woman, a girl, when Craig was hurt, whose reality was shaped by the decisions of those around her in a world where she lacked many options. She tried to thrive and had to settle for survival. She survived for as long as she could—until she simply had to let go. Her search for peace ended with a few pills and some vodka.

Break it, break another little piece of my heart now darlin'... take it, take another little piece of my heart now baby...

Piece. Peace. This song has been woven through each moment. A red thread connecting me to some of my happiest memories of my mom, to the dreams, to Carmela's words, and now.

In all the years since she died, I've hoped, prayed, my mom found the peace she desperately wanted, needed, deserved. That the pieces of her heart were made whole when she died. Her leaving left us with an open wound and a lifetime of grief—but now I know it was nothing compared to what she experienced before I was born.

Her death forced me to bloom. She let go so I could transform into a new generation unencumbered by the generational trauma she endured. Maybe she thought her dying would be less trauma than her living? I'll never get to know, I guess.

But what I do know is this current reality is quickly becoming more and more believable—and magical. What has been unbelievable for these past months is suddenly reality for me and the man in front of me, Father Michael.

"Okay," I whisper. "Let's do this. How do we start? Are you going to splash holy water on me? Will a spirit appear in smoke and flames? Will I collapse to the ground speaking in tongues? Will there be *snakes*?"

Father Michael simply stares at me, a little stunned. "Child, you really do need to stop watching so much Netflix."

He then asks me to think of my mother, both as I remember her and as I see her at different ages in my dreams. "Now breathe deeply. Turn inward like meditation. Breathe in and picture the dreams, your mother's spirt, flowing through you."

He lights the incense in the lantern and walks to the altar at the front of the church. He speaks as he gently swings the incense back and forth around us.

"Picture your mother's love flowing through you, for she loved you before she birthed you. She survived for you, just as you're surviving this for your daughter. Picture your mother's love pouring through you and then imagine it transforming into your love for yourself and your daughter."

He speaks slowly, melodically, and sounds much like one of the voices on the meditation podcasts I use to fall asleep at night. Between the incense, Father Michael's voice, and my visualizations of motherly love pouring through me, calmness overtakes the champagne fizz flowing through my body.

"Think of each dream, child. Live through each one as if you're the girl, the woman, in the dream. Feel the emotions sweeping through each vision. Channel the grief, sadness, fear, rage, and pain that come with each tragedy. The helplessness. The loss of a future."

I do as he asks and breathe deeply as the fragrance of incense fills my nose, my lungs. I'm holding my hands over my heart as I become aware of tears slowly moving down my face and falling in small drops onto my hands.

Visions and dreams flow through my mind now, spurred on by Father Michael calling them forth. My eyes remain closed as the smoke of the incense burns my nose, as the room starts to spin, as my body slowly starts to move in small circles, as the hairs on the back of my neck rise, and goosebumps run down my arms.

The breeze begins to swirl around the church again. The banners on the walls wave in the wind, lifting off the wall. My hair blows around me as if the wind is circling all around us in tighter and tighter circles.

Father Michael is switching back and forth between Latin, English, and what I swear is Gaelic as he grows louder and more insistent. I only understand the English as he calls Brigid to us to release the crone from her chains on this earth. To release the pain and fear that tie her to this world. He calls upon the crone to let go of her hold on this earth, of the roots of her pain in the past and her roots buried in my soul as my mother, to release her hold on me. He almost sounds like he's wooing her to let go of her grip on this realm and to trust the strength of the woman she has raised, whether she was physically present or my spiritual safety net.

To know that her pain and trauma, but most importantly, her love, created a woman, the mother, who is strong enough to invoke Brigid on her behalf. To know her granddaughter, the child, is the third incarnation of the goddess Brigid and that our matriarchal lineage, our legacy of love, has protected us in ways this world has not. In the ways that she needed to be protected as a joyful teen, as a new wife, and as a hopeful young woman, but was failed time and again.

The wind lifts my hair as if I'm in a wind tunnel—full blown waves and tangles around me. Eyes closed, I feel the air move over my skin like a deep pressure massage. As if the air is pushing and pulling at the visions to move them out of me. To pull my mother's spirit out of me to be released.

"Jill, you have done all you can for your daughter. For your granddaughter. You are the crone. Your responsibility now is to let go. To let go and allow your daughter, the mother, to raise your granddaughter. Your Celtic roots are strong, and your daughters will continue to be born to your lineage to protect, to love, your family. You've done what you can for your daughter, for your granddaughter. Now let go before you enter martyrdom forever. Ascend to peace in the next realm."

Spring is blossoming all around us as flowers miraculously bloom in their bouquets, their ripe scent filling the air as tight buds show off colorful petals. Father Michael lifts the pitcher of wine off the tray and begins to pray in Gaelic as he pours the wine into the flowers and plants around the altar as an offering for Brigid.

As the wine flows, my chest loosens. I can feel my heart taking up more space under my ribs, and my lungs fill more deeply. A release of emotion that has been wound around me since my mom died evaporates. Grief? Fear? Whether hers or mine, I'm not sure, but my eyes fly open as I realize that the dreams leaving me means my mother's presence is leaving me as well. I try to stand, but the wind around me is too strong, pressing me down firmly but tenderly.

I hold my arm out to Father Michael and cry, "Stop, please stop, I don't want to let go. I don't want to lose her. I didn't even know she was here, and now she's already leaving."

CHAPTER FORTY-EIGHT

Father Michael turns to me with grief in his eyes. And I know.

In that instant, I know that to bring peace to my life, to my daughter's life—and my daughter's daughters—I must let go of this tumultuous connection with my mother. I've been holding the dreams close to me without understanding why. Maybe I felt my mom's presence in them all along—recognized her love on a primal level like Jillian recognized my voice after birth.

I start to sob, my hands over my face. Intense grief and loneliness burn in my heart, my eyes, as tears pour out and down my cheeks. I'm not ready to lose her. I'm not ready to let go. I swear her arms are around me with the wind and sounds of springtime around us.

Brigid is waiting. She's here, waiting to walk my mother from this life of pain and trauma to one of peace and joy. She's here to give my mom everything she always deserved and needed but never had enough of in this world. I just need to let go first.

I'm now holding her in this world. She will not walk away from me when I'm in pain. She won't abandon me the way she was

abandoned over and over. She will choose her own suffering if it
means alleviating mine.

Maybe that is why she could not leave until now. She had to wait
until I had someone to love me and someone to love wholeheartedly.
For each representation of the triple Goddess to be complete, to
know I would be held by, and would hold, the sacred love women
have for each other—tenderly and with utter strength, in a way that
allows peace and ease and glory and joy.

I must let go first to show her I'm strong enough to be alone in
this world. To show her I'll always love and cherish her, but I don't
need her anymore. Maybe this is the only gift I can give her that
matters. To love her enough to let her go, so *she* can let go. To allow
myself to fall apart and transform into a woman worthy of
representing the mother, and one day the crone, for the Celtic
goddess Brigid.

Father Michael picks up the tray and walks over to me. He holds
it out to me, and I understand. Once I sip the blessed wine and eat
the communion wafer, the connection will be severed. As fraught
with chaos and panic and fear as it has been, my one connection to
my mother will be released and she will be free, and I'll be... alone,
even if I'm fully embodied in her love. I'll transform into whatever
version of myself is waiting in the wings for me. And I must love her
enough to let go and love myself enough to trust that I'll be able to
handle whatever comes next.

I must be strong for my mother in the way that I needed her to
be strong for me. Her strength was pulled from her with each
trauma, each time she had to choose to survive instead of die, never
given the chance to thrive. While she may not have been strong
enough to be what I needed, she was strong enough to *raise me* to be
who I needed—a mother for myself and Jillian.

Her sadness ripples through me as if she's sharing her emotions
with me, pushing them out between us. I feel how strong her regret
—and her relief—are in this moment. Her trauma, and choices,
defined my childhood. She shows me the sadness and fear and
regret she feels for how her mental health and addiction shaped who
I am today. Of the lack of control she had, and how she was always

striving, struggling to be more than she was for us. And finally, the power that came when she let go of that version of life. To let go and let us transform into who we could be without the weight of her trauma weighing us down into smaller versions of ourselves. To versions that must be small and quiet and invisible to be safe.

Wind swirls around me. Plants and flowers bend to the wind at the edges of the church, rustling leaves and branches. But here, here in the center of the church under the cross of St. Brigid, the wind slows. A gentle breeze blows across my face, arms, and neck—lifting my hair playfully, like a gentle touch, almost like the glide of a hand across my back saying, "You can do this. I'm here. You are strong. Supported. Loved."

As Father Michael lifts the goblet and tray of blessed wafers, the wind gets louder and faster. Air swirls around us, but the center remains calm. We're resting in the heart of the breeze and watching as the church is engulfed in energy and wind currents. My mom's spirit surrounds me, both holding me and wanting to be held. She both needs me to hold on and to let go in this moment. Hold on to her love and let go of our fear.

I accept a wafer and the goblet of blessed wine from Father Michael. "Do you think one wafer should do it? Or should I eat a few?"

He smiles patiently and recognizes this deflection tactic for what it is: a chance to create a pause in this moment. To try and let my mind catch up and comprehend what is happening around me. But I can't catch hold of the moment. Just like trying to hold on to the dreams made them harder and harder to visualize, trying to make this surreal moment make sense is impossible. I get dizzy from trying and know I need to release my need to understand and embrace the unknown.

I close my eyes and lift the wafer to my mouth. As I do, my mother's arms wrap around me. A soft kiss to the top of my head. "Thank you" whispered into my hair. She kneels in front of me. My mom hugs me and tucks her head next to mine, wrapping her arms around me, and we hold each other as we rock back and forth for what feels both like milliseconds and eons.

As we sway, I hear her voice. I'm not sure if she's whispering directly into my ear or in the wind, but I start to hear the song she sang to me, with me, as a baby in her arms, a little girl dancing in the living room, and a teenager in the car with the windows down and radio blasting.

"Come on, come on, come on, and take it. Take another little piece of my heart now baby. Ohhhh, break it. Break another little piece of my heart now darling, yeah, yeah, yeah. You know you've got it, if it makes you feel good."

I hear her again, now in my mind, telling me to release my fear. To own my power. To step into the roles divinely created for me to empower women and mothers who are trying so hard, and still lacking the resources, skills, and community they need to overcome generations of trauma, abuse, misuse, and being pushed into too small lives.

"Own it. Own it. Own it," she whispers to me as she holds me. "The fear kept you safe when you were little and needed to be protected from me, from the lack of safety and tenderness you deserved, but did not receive, from a world that only lifts mothers up on a pedestal of words and empty promises rather than resources, systemic change, and love."

"You, my sweet daughter, embody the triple goddess. You are the mother, the child, and the crone. All three flow in your body and will be there with you as you navigate this wild and precious life of yours. And when you feel a little scared, don't look to others for love and acceptance—that is how you allow fear back in."

"Look inside yourself and feel the gem of love deep in your ribs. Know that I'm always, always here with you—even after you let me go. Even after you free me from this realm. Embody yourself, my sweet girl."

"You, daughter, were all my hopes and dreams. I poured my strength and wisdom and dreams into you, knowing you could carry all of it for the gift and burden they are. You're strong enough to be both a daughter and a mother to me. To be carried by me and to carry me. To set me free even when you want to cling to me for safety and love and comfort."

"I can see you both in this realm and in the generations of women in our matriarchal line before me. All of us have passed along the little bit of strength and hope and faith that we were able to steal from this world and push it, labor it into you. For you need all of us to help you do what you desperately don't want to do, and will need to do soon. Your daughter is waiting for you at home. You created a miracle, just as I created you. And you need to let go of the past, let go of me and be fully present for her, for yourself. To mother her in a way I was never mothered—nor were you. But you will need to let me go, my sweet, sweet girl. My hopes and dreams all came true when you were born, baby cakes, and my love rests inside you here."

She touches the bottom of my ribs between my breasts and then the tattoo on my neck.

I open my eyes and see the painting of St. Brigid. I embody all three elements of Brigid. And in this moment, I must repeat what I did so many years ago—say goodbye to my mom. Only this time, I must let her go too. It won't be the drugs or alcohol or depression this time—it will be me, releasing her spirit and setting her free. Letting her experience peace for the first time in her lifetime.

I pause.

Am I asking the impossible of myself? Is the impossible being asked of me?

To heal my mother. To believe that my mom passed memories of her core traumas to me to release as she never could. To save myself and my daughter, how she never could. And, most impossibly, to let my mother go.

Naturally the thought crosses my mind to be greedy. To reject the wine Father Michael is now offering me. To stand up and walk away and cling tightly to the spirit of my mom that is here with me. To drag her pain and sadness along with me and cling to the safety and familiarity of fear. The little girl inside me simply wants to keep her mama near her. To be held and kissed and loved. Even if it means being broken at the same time.

But the grown-ass woman inside me knows that keeping my mom's spirit here will be what ruins me. And it will ruin Jillian.

I embrace my mom's spirit one last time. "I must be strong

enough for all three of us. I'm strong enough to let you go. I need to go home and be a mama to my sweet daughter. To mother myself."

I sink into my mom's arms, her embrace, once more and breathe her in deeply. I'm not sure if I'm smelling her or the incense, but it doesn't matter—this smell will always be like home. Be her.

Mom squeezes me tight one last time, and then she starts to loosen her hold, to let go, and I know. It's time. It's time for me to let go and be alone in this world. Alone, but loved. And it's time for her to be in peace and joy and love and light in a way she never has been in this world. It's time for Jillian to have the future she deserves —that every woman in our family before us deserved.

I whisper, "I love you" into the wind, and my mother's spirit fades as I bring the wine to my lips and tilt the glass. The bittersweet liquid touches my tongue, rinsing away the dust of the wafer.

Undoing my last connection with my mom.

CHAPTER FORTY-NINE

I sip the wine again. I'm strong enough to do the impossible. Over and over again, I've accomplished goals that statistically seemed impossible. Graduate from high school. From college —twice. Get a PhD. Not become an addict. Have a healthy relationship.

The odds have always been against me, and I have thrived because of the strength gifted to me from my mother. From my mother's mother and the women before each of them. And I know it is this strength she has always counted on. That they were all counting on.

Spirits up and down my matrilineal line let loose a collective breath of relief, and for the first time in their lives, breathe in ease and peace.

So I sip again.

CHAPTER FIFTY

Jillian has been fussing nonstop for the past hour. Whimpers. Cries. Screams. Wails. Thrashing. At times she stops fussing and looks off into the distance, smiling and cooing at something Caden can't see and assumes must be the light on the ceiling or a bird out the window. Then she arches her back and lets out a blood-curdling scream, almost as if a gun suddenly went off in the room.

BANG!

She sucks hungrily at a bottle but pushes it away with her tiny fists when she realizes it is not milk straight from her mama. Jillian's eyes do wild circles around the room, searching.

"Must be searching for her mom. But she's not here. She's gone on whatever this trip to reclaim her sanity might be called," Caden mutters to himself, searching for some way to calm his panicked daughter.

Suddenly Jillian cries out, primal angry wails. Her tiny body stiffens and arches, arms and legs stretching out as if she wants to hold the entire world in her grasp. Then, Jillian goes slack. She lies in his arms lifeless for a second before blinking open her twinkling green eyes. She smiles and coos, playfully looking at and swatting with tiny fingers at something he still can't see.

Ready to sleep after the most epic meltdown of her life, Jillian closes her green eyes and snuggles into her dad's arms. He watches as a breeze gently rolls across her face, fluttering her dark brown hair off her forehead, sweaty from the screaming and crying over the past hour that he couldn't seem to settle.

The breeze moves those sweet, sweaty curls off her face, away from her ears, and he sees her smile and sigh as she falls into a deep sleep, curling her hand behind her ear next to her birthmark. He looks around for the open window that the breeze would have come from but realizes that none are open. No fan is on. He can't figure out the source of the breeze, just as he can't figure out the source of the chaos that has been taking over his small family for months.

And he wouldn't believe it if he weren't already watching his wife lose her mind in these dream vision things, but he swears he sees a brief imprint on Jillian's forehead as if a kiss is being deeply pressed onto his daughter's soul. He watches as she lets out a sigh that sounds like love and peace, then snuggles to his chest.

Jillian sleeps the sleep of a baby blessed in the love and peace that comes from a million sacrifices made on her behalf by generations of women before her. The love that releases the weight of generational trauma before she ever had to carry it herself.

CHAPTER FIFTY-ONE

I tip the last drops of wine out of the goblet and into my mouth, thankful that Father Michael was more generous with the wine than the wafers. Closing my eyes, I take the last sip and feel the faintest breeze flow around me.

When I open my eyes, she will be gone. The wind will have stopped. I'm both heartbroken and at peace with this knowledge. Helping my mother leave this world only minutes after I became aware that she was here with me seems at once cruel and loving.

I take one more shaky breath and open my eyes, smiling as a light breeze ruffles my hair and blows the strands back from my face. A soft kiss is pressed onto my forehead, and I let out a sigh.

Standing up, I hand Father Michael the wine goblet. He takes it in one hand and stretches his other arm out to rest his hand on my shoulder.

"Aye, my child, the love within you is shining for all to see around you. You are a channel of the divine. Of a mother and daughter's true love, for only the truest, purest love could let go of their mother to give her a gift she could not give herself—or to you, my child."

He pulls me in for a tight hug and, when we part, he blesses me in Gaelic. "Can I offer you a traditional Catholic blessing as well?"

I nod my consent.

Father Michael makes the sign of the father, son, and holy spirit across my body. He thanks me for letting him witness a miracle today. I must make a skeptical face because he smiles and tells me to sit with that truth for a little bit and then let him know what I would call this experience.

"Whether you give the credit to God, St. Brigid, or Brigid the Celtic Goddess of Ireland, what happened today was a gift and a miracle, lassie."

Then I look at him and smile, my eyes wide. Where do we even go from here? I'm not totally sure what Father Michael experienced during those minutes—hours?—but we are forever connected by this moment. Love pools in his eyes, hope in his small smile as we clasp hands again.

My journey is over. Wherever this long, possibly miraculous, journey was supposed to lead, it has taken me here. To a special place of healing and magic and strength and wisdom. Both home and not. I touch my tattoo as I look up at St. Brigid's cross once more and thank her. Thank her for her magical ways of crossing universes and creating space and opportunity for generational healing. Brigid blessed our family, blessed me, with the strength and courage to heal the trauma passed down from my generation to the next. I'll stand up to the past. I can endure the pain of healing, but I can no longer endure the weight of fear.

I pick a flower from one of the bouquets decorating the end of a pew and place it in my impossibly, miraculously windswept hair. As I walk toward the door at the front of the church, Father Michael calls out to me.

"Maybe we can meet again next year on St. Brigid's Feast Day on purpose rather than by divine orchestration? I would love to meet the darling daughter of your trifecta and bless the miracle of her existence. It would be a pleasure to know all three generations of the women who incarnated Brigid of Ireland today."

The miracle of Brigid blessing the women in my family with this type of love overwhelms me. How she chooses to live through us, to be worthy of her healing love, to burn down our family's generational trauma so we can *live* and not just survive.

Why did a goddess, a saint, choose me, choose us, to heal?

How did my mom connect with Brigid so deeply that she found us worthy of her help?

What could we have done to be worthy of such love?

A knowing fills my bones, overcomes my soul, as a simple answer floats up in my mind.

"You were born worthy of such love."

Nodding in acceptance of this universal truth, tears stream down my face. A simple answer to a simple truth that I have traveled a long way to learn.

I'll happily bring my daughter, and her daughters, here every year on February 1st. To the site where our lineage was set free, and we found blessings, peace, and the truest mother's love we could in this realm.

I shake my head at the simplicity of requesting a Lyft outside of this church, across the street from my mom's old apartment. The scene of a tragedy at an address that appeared to me in a dream across from a church where my mother's spirit was just released from the chains of generational trauma and pain.

No big deal. I just experienced—quite possibly invoked—a miracle, and now I'm going to just use this little, tiny pocket computer to request a car to take me back to the train station.

As I wait for the car, I look at the windows, wondering which one was hers.

The return trip on the NWI Express is less stressful than my journey into the city earlier that day. I planned to stay in town overnight, but I'm ready to go home. To my own daughter. To Caden. To Alma.

I throw my bags in the car, along with the tote containing my notes. Outlines. Copies of emails. Dry erase markers to scribble my thoughts and ideas all over my windows like a madwoman. The weight of this bag seems lighter, as if the purpose was drained from it when I released my mother from this world.

I'm not sure what to do with it now. I can't recycle it all after the journey that created this tote full of impossible notes, drawings, and dreams. I'll probably put it in a closet when I get home and see if it calls me one day. Maybe I'll write a book, a love story to my daughter and our future generations. It would have to be fiction, though, because who could believe this miraculous story could ever be true?

Who would believe these stories of dreams and ghosts and spiritual realms? Believe in a line of women so strong, bold, audacious, and, most importantly, loving enough to do the impossible to heal their lineage of generational trauma?

I smile as I touch the spot between my breasts where my mom told me her love lives inside me like a gemstone that will never fade and can only grow in time.

We believed. We did it. We forsook parts of ourselves, of our hearts, for our children. For Jillian.

I get in the car, set up my GPS to get me on the turnpike, and pull up the only song that is fitting for this moment. Maybe for this entire drive home.

"Come on, come on, come on and take it. Take another little piece of my heart now, baby... You know you got it if it makes you feel good. Oh, yes indeed."

EPILOGUE

THREE YEARS LATER...

"Happy birthday to you! Happy birthday to you! Happy birthday dear Jillian! Happy birthday to you!"

Jillian claps in delight, eyes bright and looking at her favorite people gathered to celebrate her in our backyard. I take my phone back from Gray and wave goodbye to Father Michael on the phone screen, promising to send pictures of Jillian opening his gift.

Caden rubs my back as we stand behind Jillian for a quick family photo before the three candles are taken off and the cake is cut, adjusting his angle slightly to get the profile of baby Declan, just a few weeks old, snug and asleep in the baby carrier strapped to his chest. The now-faded leopard print baby carrier that makes Alma laugh in delight when Caden wears it.

"Aw, just so fucking sweet. I can't even deal with how adorable of a family you four make."

Alma's voice wavers as she walks over and tries to wrap her arms around all of us for a big family hug. Tears well in her eyes, and she quickly swipes them away with the side of her finger, trying not to smudge her eye makeup, like she has for the past months of pregnancy hormones.

I pull her in and wave Gray over. "Not as adorable as the soon-to-be seven of us make!" I squeal as I embrace Alma awkwardly around her huge baby bump.

"Baby! Baby!" Jillian squeals as the flash goes off for one more family photo.

"I'm going to need that back soon, Caden, even though it looks better on you!" Alma laughs.

"Don't worry, Alm, I already ordered him a replacement and let Jillian pick it out. A rainbow camo print baby carrier will be delivered tomorrow," Gray says with a wink at Caden as they sling their arm around Alma's shoulders and pull her in close.

Gray might not have been who Alma planned on falling in love with, but we are all grateful for their presence in our ever-expanding chosen family circle. After meeting at a work conference, Alma realized that Gray understood and supported her in a way she hadn't experienced before with a partner. Their decision to get married and have a baby last year was the best surprise in our friendship in a long time, especially when Alma pulled me aside during the celebration to whisper, "I already know that you will help me navigate all the pitfalls of motherhood. Who better to have at my side than someone who hit rock bottom as a mom and came back through?"

We had whisper-cried together because I told her I was *also* pregnant and our dream of being big-bellied mamas together would come true.

Laughing, Caden walks Declan to the house. "Let me go put the little guy to sleep, and I'll drop this one off by your bag, Alma."

Following him into the kitchen, I try to scoop Dec out of the baby carrier to nurse but Caden stills my hands.

"He's already out, babe. Why don't you pump, and I'll give him a bottle later when he wakes up?"

I smile at Caden, ever appreciative of his awareness that party prep meant little time for my afternoon nap. I'm going to crash as soon as the last guest leaves.

Or stays because sometimes, Alma ends up staying the night in "her room." The guest room turned Alma's room has been the place of many late-night conversations about birth, nursing, and motherhood as Alma and Gray get ready to welcome their little one earth-side any day now. She and I are both craving our time together and intentionally prioritizing our friendship during these chaotic years to avoid the mistakes of our past. We are creating the village we need.

I selfishly hope the baby comes soon, and our maternity leaves can overlap before I start back at work. While not all things pandemic were lucky, I was able to leverage the success of my maternal health research into more remote work to cut back on my commute time and regain some downtime.

Jillian squeals and laughs as she opens presents and throws tissue paper around the backyard like snowballs, dancing in the golden hour of sunset. I stand back from the group and look out over the chosen family we've created and nurtured. The ones who stood by me while I lost—and found—myself.

Caden returns to scoop Jillian up for bedtime, but I step in and grab her new princess nightgown. "Come on, J. Let's go try this on and read a new bedtime story."

Caden gives me "the look." The one with raised eyebrows that says, "You sure, babe?"

I nod and pick up Jillian. "You know baby girl and I need our snug time."

I turn as I see him eye my butt in my leggings and give me "the other look." The one that means *save some energy for after bedtime if you can*. With a saucy wink over my shoulder, I take Jillian's hand and lead her up the stairs.

Jillian tries to protest every moment of bedtime, but her giant yawns give her away. As we settle in for her nightly snuggle, I turn off her light and lean against her headboard, happily settled in with her warm body tucked close for the next few minutes.

Jillian starts her nightly routine of saying good night to her family in the pictures that line her wall, starting with "Goodnight mama and daddy, good night Gramma Jilly" and ending with Father Michael. That might be my favorite picture of all—the one of me holding Jillian while we danced and sang "Piece of My Heart" on February 1st at his favorite Irish pub in the city.

Probably the first, but not the last time, Janis has been played in that pub.

"Good night, sweet girl. I love you," I murmur as I kiss her hair.

"Good night, baby cakes," Jillian whispers as she squeezes me and settles in.

I stare at her in wonder. I've never used that name with her before.

How could she know?

I take this gift for what it is and smile. Stranger things have happened in the past few years.

I look up at the picture of my mom on her wall, her Gramma.

Good night, Mom, I love you too.

AFTERWORD

I originally dreamed up the idea for this book while taking a nap on a retreat held by Beth Berry after a year in a MotherWorthy mother's circle. I woke up desperate to read the book from my dream and realizing that *I* could write that book. After all, it was inspired by the events in my mom's life before I was born.

The fact that I was even at this retreat was insane and a version of my own before and after. But that's a story for another time, with maybe a watermelon margarita for bravery.

Months later, I sat down at my dining room table every day between dropping off and picking up my two young sons at daycare and preschool, lit a candle, pulled a goddess oracle card, and wrote. No outline. No plan. Just let words flow from the tips of my fingers to the computer for two hours every day.

(There are more strategic and organized ways to write a book. But I am rarely strategic or organized.)

I didn't tell anyone I was writing a book until I was about halfway finished. I figured I was too far in to stop. And, even then, I only told my partner and a few close friends. This book baby, this healing process that I was being pulled through, was too fragile for negative feedback and scoffs that "it would never go anywhere."

After an epiphany over a dirty martini and steak dinner with my partner, I had the ending of my book. Brigid had been popping up in my goddess card pulls but hadn't appeared in the story until that moment. Until then, I wasn't sure how it would all wrap up. How it would all resolve. How do you weave magic into tragic truths?

And then... life lifed. My boys kept growing. We moved onto a farm. I tried to figure out the publishing process and sent my book to over seventy-five different agents and publishing houses with little luck over a few years while doing a million other things.

The book got backburnered hard. I figured it would always be something that I had done, and I would publish it at the printing store one day for my kids to read when they were older. Then, the universe put a brand-new independent publishing house in my path. A few dear soul friends and Paul kept whispering that this book was needed in the world. And the rest is in your hands.

The version of the book you hold in your hands is not the same one I wrote in 2022. It can't be. I'm not the same person. With the help of Jamie and Ashleigh from Renard McGillen Publishing, I broke down my book and rewrote it. This was wildly painful for me as a woman with ADHD and a very full life, but I think you will appreciate the effort. Maggie's story is less scary and anxious and more hopeful. More supported. Just like I am now.

Through Her Eyes is a book I originally wrote for me. For my mom. For my own healing journey. I could not have been less prepared to become a motherless mother. Motherhood broke me down in a million pieces, exposing the gaps in support and the fragility of my sense of self. I desperately needed to be put back together, to be held, by my own mother, but she couldn't. And all of the unprocessed grief and trauma and dysfunction broke through the cracks of the healing I had done over the years.

Everyone wanted me to be "fine," but I couldn't figure out how. I still can't figure out how to be normal, and I'm pretty proud of that.

A note to my boys—you have ALWAYS been my greatest dreams come true. You have never been the problem, the source, or the solution to any of my story.

It's hard to talk about motherhood struggles without sounding like I'm blaming my children. I'm not. Loving my sons was easy. Being a mother in a culture, society, country that doesn't provide adequate community-based supports for parenthood? That's a big part of the problem.

My mental health struggles have destabilized my confidence, my sense of purpose, and more. This book helped me forgive my mom —and also myself.

This book has served as the vessel I needed to bloom where I'm planted.

My life has been full of wonder and magic—and privilege of a million kinds. I can never forget how lucky I have been to have a supportive partner, access to healthcare, transportation, food, and financial steadiness as an adult. My life is a dream come true. Something I could never have imagined as a girl.

And I still struggled once I became a mom. Deeply.

From a young age, I was brought up to believe in the empowerment of women. Of connection. I turned that into a bachelor's degree in Women's Studies and then research into sexual violence for a master's in Public Health, and then a doctoral degree in Health Education. I've worked in, and volunteered at, abortion clinics and bystander training for sexual violence on college campuses.

This story contains a situation where a character chooses to have an abortion. I kept this experience as true to life as possible, rooted in my years holding space with women considering or choosing abortion. Given that one in four women will have an abortion in her lifetime, I felt it important to include this path that women also make choices around motherhood. Having my own children solidified my belief in choice around motherhood because if I was struggling so hard as a woman who had all the resources and privilege and CHOSE to become a mom, I couldn't imagine this difficulty being placed on the shoulders of women and girls.

And all of that brought me here. To be a fierce advocate for community. For "the village." For abundant and well-funded care of mothers.

Maternal mental health is the biggest indicator for children's health.

So, here I am, supporting mothers. Believing in the power of motherhood and community and women.

Believing in you.

And for all of you who believed in me? The little girl who went through so much, who has defied so many odds, who kept on blooming where was planted, is smiling wide and shouting for joy that you hold this book in your hands.

Thank you. A million bajillion thank yous.

ACKNOWLEDGMENTS

First and foremost, I need to thank Paul, my partner of over twenty years, for creating the space, opportunity, time, and support to write (and rewrite… and edit… and edit again) this book. I'm not sure either of us saw publishing a book as one of the millions of chapters of our lives, but I can't thank you enough for believing in me. In this story. This book wouldn't exist in this form without your love. You have always strived to be an amazing partner and father, and I am forever grateful for you. You have created a foundation for our boys and family to thrive. Thank you.

And a million thank yous to my boys. This has been a big doozy to say the least. Paulie, yes I have been writing this book since you were four and it's being published when you're eight. According to you, this took *for-ev-er*, but we do hard things. You two will always be simply the best thing about my life. I hope you always howl at the moon and remember love is the core of it all.

To my own personal Alma(s)… your friendship means the world to me.

Lindsay, you have known at least a dozen versions of me. Thank you for always seeing the best and witnessing my early motherhood. You laid a blueprint for me to follow and I'm forever grateful. From #girlboss to needing my food cut up into small bites while nursing a baby in a restaurant, you loved me as motherhood humbled me. You are the first person who read this book and the reason I kept going. Thank you.

Maya, from our first mom's club playdate until now, you have created magic in my world and bent the universe to show how a multitude of possibilities exist. Thank you for teaching me about mothering in a way I had never heard of before, and that we are limitless.

Sara, thank you for your kind yet direct love and guidance, forever cheering me on, and seeing the beauty in my dreams.

Jamie and Ashleigh, your support, guidance, and coaching helped me write the best book I could… From voice notes full of tears to coaching positivity and love into my book, this has been a journey, and I'm so grateful to have done it with you both at my side!

To my beta readers, Naomi and Abi, thank you for your time, energy, and support! Your words and investment shaped this book into a better version of itself and made me feel like "a real author."

And to the village that raised me up as a girl, woman, and mother… this book wouldn't exist if it wasn't for you.

To the women who walked alongside me, pulled me through, educated me, laughed and/or cried with me (often at the same time), raised me up to be a mother: thank you. Each of you are part of the village who raised me into the woman I am today. Into the mother I am today.

For my own mom who tried so hard and found joy even when it was impossible, thank you. Thank you for trying so, so hard. You did a million hard things I will never have to imagine. You did your best. Especially when you stayed up all night outside my high school to register me for summer swim so I wouldn't have to wear my hair curly to school.

For Pam, who showed up when it was hard and taught me to ask for what I want, thank you.

For Debbie, who taught me to love no matter what, thank you.

For my sisters and brothers, nieces and nephews. I love you all. Look at us writing our own futures.

For Mark who always tells me stories of the best parts of my Mom's life and has loved me like his daughter since day one.

For my sisters-in-law and my nieces—we have the best family.

Isabel, thank you for loving my boys and caring for them with the biggest heart while I wrote in my front porch office all summer.

Katie, Ashleigh, and Tessa, thank you for letting me sit with you at lunch when I moved to Ohio after my mom died.

To Valerie for being the first person to ever use the term "D-MER." Your social media post on it was the ONLY time I've still ever seen it mentioned, and it erased the shame I felt around being broken.

To my girl scout troop and all our adventures and laughter. You all are my core memories of some of the best parts of my youth.

To Sara, Allie, Kavitha, Kari, Hanna, Annie… thank you for your friendship, guidance, support, love, and more in college, motherhood, and more.

To Katie L., thank you for telling me about a different version of motherhood repeatedly until I could hear you. Your laughter is always in my heart. You might be the root of this whole adventure.

Nicole, we will always have Voxer messages sobbing on the kitchen floor together while the PBS Kids aunties took care of our babies.

Tasha, Vero, Lucy, Ashley, Gilly, Judith, Emilie, Lindsay, Marie… may we all continue to grow wild together.

Carmela, fuck. Thank you for believing in me always. And making the dreams that feel insane to me feel so simple to achieve. Your magic has amplified my own over and over again.

Beth Berry, thank you for revolutionizing my motherhood and life. You just might have saved both.

Treacy, thank you for your passion in bringing Brigid's fire forward and believing in *your* dream so I can live mine.

To the AA, Al-Anon, Alateen community, from attending pancake breakfasts to being witnessed with loving kindness when my mom relapsed, this community saved me more than I knew then. You all showed me what it means to "show up" over and over again.

And in no particular order but important to name because these women have woven love over me again and again… Have expanded my world and reality time and again. Maria, Sarah, Natalie, Daphne, Kristy, Annie Warmke, Carie, Mrs. Shamis, and all the other teachers who believed in me.

And last but not least, for my Uncle Craig. Your love and life are ever present in my own.

I could write a short story about everyone here and more for being in my life and community. This book is a tapestry woven together by our experiences and love (or a Brigid's cross where we are each a rush woven together). Thank you.

ABOUT THE AUTHOR

Kate Sorokas has had her nose buried in a book since she learned to read. Her favorite form of escapism and entertainment won her first place in the school read-a-thon in second grade.

Since then, she has gone on to earn a BA in Women's Studies and MA in Public Health with a focus on community health from The Ohio State University. She also holds a PhD in Health Education from Kent State University.

Kate lives on a farm in Ohio with her partner and two sons along with cows, goats, pigs, and more. When she's not wrangling her two wild, loving sons, she's volunteering, holding sound baths, and doing yoga under the moon. Kate is passionate about at least three things—getting kids into nature, traveling the world, and eating amazing food even though she can't cook.

Okay four things—also creating supportive spaces and communities for mothers to connect, reduce isolation, and discover their magic.

This book is part of that magic—and so are you.

 instagram.com/drkatesorokas